I Wish This War Were Over

I Wish This War Were Over

DIANA O'HEHIR

AN AUTHORS GUILD BACKINPRINT.COM EDITION

I Wish This War Were Over

AN AUTHORS GUILD BACKINPRINT.COM EDITION

Published by iUniverse.com, Inc.

For information address:
iUniverse.com, Inc.
5220 S 16th, Ste. 200
Lincoln, NE 68512
www.iuniverse.com

Originally published by Atheneum

ISBN: 0-595-15340-2

Printed in the United States of America

FOR BRENDAN

I Wish This War Were Over

Chapter I

"IF YOU ASK MY OPINION," said my grandmother, "no good can come of it. Helen, you are only nineteen; you should not be crossing the country alone. She is a grown woman; she is forty-three years old. If she is in trouble at the age of forty-three, she will always be in trouble, and her own daughter, practically a child, can do nothing about it."

My sister Clara and I had not asked Grandmother's opinion. Clara, who was able to handle her, calmed her down. She told her that I would be gone only a month and that it would be perfectly safe; she promised that I would stay only in YWCAs and that I would send Clara a postcard every other night.

Clara was younger than I, but at seventeen she was the one with the calm manner and the uninflected, reassuring voice. Now she wrapped herself so successfully in this set of reliable mannerisms that Grandmother actually smiled. She chewed for a while on what appeared to be a mouthful of tacks and finally said dubiously, "Well, I suppose it will do no harm, though if the two of you think there is any chance of reforming your mother at this late date . . ." And then she climbed into her old Packard with the high wheels and bud vases and drove back to Walnut Creek, California.

The year was 1944; travel was going to be difficult. Clara and I went down to the Southern Pacific Station in Oakland and sat in line, Clara on one end of my suitcase and I on the other, for three hours. The station was a high, gray, Spanish-mission construction with stained beams across the ceiling and arched plate-glass windows fronting onto the railroad tracks. The largest and most centrally placed of these windows had been broken and patched with a lattice of planks through which light struggled in heavy dust-moted rays. On the station floor below, people, mostly soldiers in khaki uniform, stood in line, sat on benches, sat or lay on the rust-colored tiling, moved erratically back and forth as if following unspoken commands. Two banners hung from the rafters: *USO—We Care, We Share, We're There*—this one was directly over our heads, belling out in response to air currents. The other banner was a V-Day one, and had the V, in blue on a white ground, followed by three dots and a dash.

I had been given a numbered ticket like the ones for service in the butcher shop; my number was 354. "I hope," I said, "it's a long train. We may be here until tomorrow."

Clara began to cry again. She had been crying off and on ever since we arrived at the station. Her reliable, dependable manner didn't mean that she didn't cry—dependable people often cry a lot; they do this because they aren't ashamed of their emotions.

The loudspeaker blurted incomprehensibly; everyone in our line stood up, grabbing for suitcases and duffel bags. "You'll write? Really?" Clara called as I was pushed away in a stampede that abandoned all pretense of numbered tickets. "Mama will be fine," I yelled. "I'll bring her back with me." My last view of my sister before the crowd closed between us showed her standing stolidly, her single braid, frayed and coming undone, looping over her shoulder, her right hand clutching the hem of her navy blue jacket, her mouth half open, square with misery.

Clara and I were not physically alike. I had long reddish-blond hair and wore a black sweater and skirt and my mother's old leopard-skin jacket, thrown over my shoulders with the sleeves hanging loose.

The crowd pushed me up a series of iron steps and onto the train.

This was the first trip I had ever taken by myself and in a way the first major action I had ever performed alone. I wasn't scared, exactly, but I was apprehensive. I tried to pause at the entrance to the car but the crowd behind me pushed forcefully. The lock on one side of my suitcase popped up. The dusty interior of the railroad car stretched ahead, almost as crowded and confusing as the station had been: green plush, chipped beige walls, ornate ironware light fixtures hanging cockeyed, an aisle full of khaki backs, shoulders, buttocks, duffel bags—every seat taken. I moved slowly, hoping something would happen.

I couldn't see the person who grabbed me and pulled me by the coat sleeve, because my suitcase was between us. A man, I knew that by the khaki knee. He tugged me past him into a window seat which he had been saving with his briefcase. He scooped this out from under me and stood up to put it and my suitcase in the overhead rack.

While he was doing that I looked at him. He was someone I knew. He was an old boyfriend of my mother's.

My sister Clara and I used to lie flat on the floor of the balcony of our house, our noses projected over the floor rim, staring down into the paneled hall below, to watch our mother and the men who came to take her out.

There were a lot of them. There was David, an elderly Jew in a skullcap, who addressed Mama as "beautiful sweetness"; Ronnie the Fag, who wrote for *The People's World*, (*The People's World* was not supposed to hire fags); Fred, who was natty and spoke French and dropped a bottle of bourbon in the hall; Max, from her Spanish Committee, who stuttered. And this one, Mr. O'Connell, who was the president of the local automobile workers' union. He lasted longer than most of them. My drunken mother was a seeker and a searcher; she had been protected by my father, and she wanted people to be sentimental and principled like herself.

Clara and I hated all of Mother's boyfriends. We used to lie in the half-dark and call them names: schmuck, fart, autoerotic pederast. Clara would knit and say names quietly to the rhythm of her knitting needles while I lay flat and bit my nails. Our mother always called out, "Goodbye, darlings," standing under the overhanging balcony, waving up at us, blowing a kiss. She had a stock of evening dresses in jewel colors; emerald and sapphire were her favorites.

Mr. O'Connell was the most attractive of Mother's boyfriends, but that didn't mean that we liked him. He was manly and handsome and purposeful, and Clara and I knew immediately that he was married. Mama probably didn't care. She was insistent that all her friendships were platonic. She used to say she couldn't understand why people made so much of a man being married; he could still be a good friend, couldn't he?

That was four years ago, but you don't ever outgrow the things that have really interested you.

I sat beside Mr. O'Connell reading Louis Untermeyer's *Modern American Poetry* and pretending to be very much absorbed in it.

Around us the soldiers were beginning to settle down. The ones at the ends of the coach put suitcases in the spaces where the seats faced each other and made a bed where three of them could lie side by side. The boy in front of us curled up on the seat and his buddy got up into the luggage rack. The scene had an unreality caused by the fact that people were doing such strange things and being so quiet about it. Mr. O'Connell was reading *Time* magazine. He cleared his throat several times as if he might like to speak to me, but I didn't give him any encouragement.

"How is your sister, Butchie?"

I never found out why Mr. O'Connell called me Butchie. It isn't my nickname. I think it may have been his word of address for all women, the way "hon" is in the South.

"My sister's fine, thank you, Mr. O'Connell."

"It's Lt. O'Connell, dear. And how's Mommy?"

"Who?"

"Your mother."

I had pretended not to hear him just to embarrass him,

but it seemed not to have worked. "My mother's not very well."

"I knew who you were the minute I saw you," Lt. O'Connell said in a self-satisfied voice. He returned to his *Time* magazine.

He didn't pick up on my remark about Mother, which made me feel that he had known her fairly intimately. It was hard to remember with which of her friends she had had episodes.

The conductor came through the car and announced that the lights would be turned off in ten minutes. He said that there was nothing to eat on the train. There would be breakfast, he said, but the servicemen would be served first. He jerked down the blackout curtain in a satisfied way. Lt. O'Connell murmured lousy bahstid in cockney.

While Lt. O'Connell was in the men's room I looked at his copy of *Time*. There was a picture of a Japanese tank with its top blown off, a boy's body like a rag doll hanging out of it, hands down. A picture of eight Waves in bathing suits. An aircraft carrier, canted sideways. President Roosevelt with microphones. French women with their hair clipped. I turned the page and then went back to look at this last one again. The men in the picture were laughing; one of them was still holding the scissors, points down. One woman had her arms crossed over her chest, her cotton dress had been ripped open. She looked like my mother. Slender body, but arms and bust too fleshy; she had been crying.

"Did you get any lunch today, Butch?" Lt. O'Connell had returned from the men's room. I watched him as he walked down the aisle with his legs wide apart. His drill jacket fitted and his tie was neatly tied; above it his face

was square, cheerful, with broad planes and a wide jaw-
bone. He smiled at me as he settled back in his chair.

"No." Clara and I had traveled down to the station on
the streetcar. We hadn't thought about eating. It had been
hard enough to get my suitcase packed in time.

"We'll get you something, dear." He turned around to
slam at his seat back. Perhaps he really is a nice man, I
thought.

Ahead of us the train whistle hooted. It was the kind of
noise that reminded you of something you didn't even
know you had lost.

"'Listen to that, dear," said Lt. O'Connell.

The conductor came into the car and turned off the lights.

I lay back in my seat. The back of the chair tilted neatly,
and with my feet on the bar in front I wasn't uncomfortable. The car smelled of machine oil and dust, with a faint
overlay of smells the soldiers had brought with them: chewing gum, sweat, some kind of liquor. We were moving fast
now and climbing. The engine labored unevenly ahead;
the wheel of one car, forward, squeaked occasionally.

I thought about my mother and the picture of the French
women. That was just the kind of mess she would get into
if she had the chance. No matter that those women were
fascists and my mother was some kind of a sentimental
Red. I had seen my mother look like that picture, with the
same defeated, puzzled air.

"Goodnight, Butch," Lt. O'Connell said.

I wasn't sure I wanted Lt. O'Connell saying goodnight
to me that way; it seemed a little proprietary. But: "Goodnight, Lt. O'Connell," I told him. After all, he had given
me this seat; no doubt he had been saving it for whatever

pretty girl came along. Still, fair's fair. It's the best seat, the one with the window to support your head and shoulder. If you pull up the foot rest and stretch yourself diagonally you can almost lie down.

Fate is peculiar. Who would expect to be half lying beside her mother's old boyfriend all night on a train full of bodies that is slowly climbing a mountain?

Mama had had from her mother a copy of Dante's *Inferno* with steel engravings, the big crowded ones, of the damned in twisting layers, all raised hands and bent knees, squirming across the landscapes of hell. I had loved that book, not because I liked to think about hell (hell wasn't a part of my childhood consciousness at all—not even Grandmother talked about hell), but because I liked the naked people. The soldiers on the train of course were not naked, but they had assumed some of the same postures as Dante's damned: knees up under the chin, knees in pleading postures over the wooden arm of a chair. There was a blue light at either end of the coach, which added to the spectral atmosphere. I fell asleep thinking about that.

Some time during the night I had a nightmare from which I awakened gasping, calling in a choked voice, holding on to Lt. O'Connell. I had twisted in my seat so that my head was on his left shoulder. With one hand I grabbed some warm muscular part of him, with the other I clutched a big hunk of mohair from the seat in front of me.

It was the kind of dream that takes a while to dissipate. At first I had no idea where I was; then I dimly recognized the train, and then I remembered it all, including Lt. O'Connell.

"There, there," he was saying. "Migawd. Are you all right?"

He had taken off his jacket during the night and was in his shirt sleeves. "Hey, now . . . better?"

"Yes . . . yes." Dimly I remembered some part of the dream: my mother, my mother and the scissors from *Time* magazine.

"Jesus H. Christ." O'Connell helped me while I pulled myself loose and settled back in my corner. "You do that often?"

"Yes. Not that bad." This had been one of those dreams where, after your eyes are open, some of it continues to play itself out, transparent against the real scenery—in this case, the interior of the train and the soldiers' contorted bodies.

"Hey, guess what? We're coming into some place."

It was true. In the last few minutes the revolutions of the train wheels had gotten slower and noisier and now the train was braking with what sounded like a rattle of chains trailing along the track. O'Connell pulled the shade part way up. "Reno. By God. How about that?" He seemed pleased, as if he had put Reno there to take my mind off my bad dream.

Reno at first was simply a water tower and some white scrubby ground, but soon a cement outstation floated by the window, and then the conductor came into the car and turned on the lights.

There was no blackout in Reno; the sky was a faint pink, brighter in the direction of the downtown. There were people outside waiting to get on the train and a column of soldiers had formed in our aisle to get off. O'Connell began to pull at his jacket. "You stay here. Just stay put. Maybe I can find us something to eat." I was awake enough now to be interested in Lt. O'Connell's character, and to think

that he was nothing like my boyfriend Will. My boyfriend
Will was infuriated by irrational behavior. He really hated
my mother, but he didn't like me, either, when he thought
I was being irrational; he would have detested being waked
up like this, by me screaming and grabbing. I expected I
would see Will on this trip. He was in Chicago now.

"Okay," Lt. O'Connell said. "Just watch this. You'll
really be impressed." And he was off, dodging around soldiers until he was at the front of the line waiting to get
off. He managed to do this without making anybody mad
at him. I tried to follow his progress through the station,
but almost immediately I lost his khaki shirt in all the
other khaki shirts.

When he came back he had two small round apple-
glucose tarts wrapped in wax paper. The paper stuck to the
bottom of my tart and I had to pull it off carefully. I was
very hungry and ate fast.

"God-awful, aren't they?" O'Connell pulled a piece of
apple cardboard loose from its paper. "There was a stand,
Butchie, a food stand, but it was so damn jammed I more
or less had to steal them, just grabbed and left some dimes.
You ever been in Reno . . . uh, Helen?"

That was the only time O'Connell ever called me by my
true name. I'm not sure why I remember it.

"That's one strange place. Really strange. Why, one
day at the casino, real early in the morning, everybody
really drunk, some of those people been locked to those
bandits all night, hanging on like everything on earth de-
pended on it . . . " He paused and licked his fingers. "Well,
place all gray and funny; the lights had just gone off, a bit
early because it wasn't really day yet; and suddenly *bang*,
we heard it all over the casino, this old girl hits the jackpot,

nickels rolling everyplace, and she was so excited she just stood there and peed in rivers on the rug and the nickels rolled around in the pee." Lt. O'Connell collected my pie-paper and crumpled it in a ball. "Sorry. Coarse details. Not suitable for a lady. Meant something, though, some way."

He started to tell me about his campaign to organize the casino cocktail waitresses, but the soldiers in front of us complained about our talking. We settled down to sleep again.

We had not pulled the blackout curtain back down, and I stared out at the white, sculptured outlines of desert sand hills.

Until I was ten years old my family went to Carmel every summer. We had a house at the far edge of Carmel, in a place called the Point. There weren't many houses there then. Our cottage was near the beach; some parts of that beach looked like this Nevada wilderness. Just a block from the cottage was a wide sloping dune, bare except for a few sprigs of ice plant, where Clara and I used to slide early in the mornings before our parents got up.

The summer weather in Carmel is usually awful, with long days of low cold fog. What I remember, however, is the other days, so clear and blue that the air seemed made of colored drops from a pointillist painting.

My father and mother were very much in love then, I think. It's hard for a child to judge those things, but I remember them coming together to say goodnight to us, holding hands. Clara and I slept in a pine room like the inside of a piano crate. The surf was very loud on that side of the house and seemed to pound all night inside my pillow. I loved Carmel.

My mother wasn't drunk during those summers. She

didn't drink at all, except for the occasional cocktail, until after my father went off to Spain.

One morning all four of us went down to the beach. We had a picnic basket, a large pad of drawing paper, watercolors, several books, some woodcarving tools—knives and routers—for my father. I have a hard time imagining that scene now because we were, by California standards, so normal then. My mother wore a straw hat tied on with a scarf, a knitted woolen one-piece bathing suit, a smock over that. She wasn't tan, because she had the pale red-headed skin that stays blue all summer, unless it gets sunburned.

There is a very bad tide at Carmel. No one swims there, and it's dangerous even to go wading, although everyone does that anyway.

The climax of this memory has me and Clara in the water, upended by a wave. I can still feel my disbelief and surprise—the water up my nose and over my head, sand pulling grittily inside my suit.

My father was at the other end of the beach collecting driftwood, and my mother, who couldn't swim, went into the water after us. Clara was easy to rescue, because she wasn't far from shore and she was better coordinated and more of a swimmer than I. But I had been carried a long way out; my mother had to go in almost to her shoulders. "My God, Selma, only luck, only luck," my father said when he reached us, panting together on the sand.

Mostly, though, what I remember is my mother's face bending over me. I was dazed and dizzy from the buffeting the water had given me. She leaned with her long red hair in a flat sheet, water pouring from it. She was saying something over and over. But it is her face that I especially recall, oval, pale, larger than most faces, perfectly proportioned, like a Dutch madonna's, trails of water beading it, the eyelashes wet and clumped together.

I squeezed the knobs on the blackout curtain and pushed the shade up another inch.

Beside me there was a rasping throat-clearing. "Sun coming up, Butchie?"

The soldiers in front of us asked us to be quiet. This time they were ruder than before.

Lt. O'Connell sat up and put his hand on my wrist. "Come on. Let's get out of here."

I followed him mostly because I was curious. We threaded cautiously down the switching passageway, avoiding the heads, hands, and feet that flopped out into the walkway. There, I thought, is a boy in his stocking feet, with holes in both toes. Dimly I can see his long, grubby, horny toenail. Here's another one, an officer, with his collar undone and his tie across his eyes for a blackout bandage. There's one with his mouth ajar and his eyes rolled back; he looks dead.

In the place between the cars, Lt. O'Connell yelled at me that he was going to get us some breakfast.

The door of the dining car was shut and locked, with rivers of condensed steam running down the inside of the glass.

Lt. O'Connell knocked on the door and then took his shoe off and beat on the glass panel with it. The door opened abruptly and Lt. O'Connell put his foot—not the shoeless one—into the opening.

"Little lady here," he addressed the inside of the dining car, "needs coffee. Passed out."

There was a creak as our host—a black man in a white apron—leaned his full weight against the door.

"Listen, man," said O'Connell, wincing visibly, but not

removing his foot, "listen, this lady, she didn't eat all day yesterday, and, listen, if we could just come in and . . . one cuppa coffee?" There were pushes and stifled grunts from both sides of the door. "Jesus, man," O'Connell said, "if you only knew; it absolutely stinks in there."

Suddenly the door was released from the other side and O'Connell, one shoe off and one shoe on, shot through it, to end up against the outer wall of the galley, where it jutted into the dining car passageway.

The black man stood looking pleased and saying nothing, while O'Connell leaned over and balanced precariously on one foot to get his shoe on. I entered and said thank you, and the black man re-locked the door and went back into the galley.

There were no lights on in the dining room, but things were dimly outlined by the faint glow from the sand hills passing by outside. O'Connell and I sat down at the table nearest to the galley. He lit cigarettes for both of us.

Inside the galley there was the clunk of pot against pot. I had diagnosed it as an angry noise and was not prepared for the appearance of the waiter with a coffeepot and two cups. He poured for us and told us it was really cold out there. Neither he nor O'Connell seemed interested any longer in their contest over the dining car door.

"You know what I do in peacetime?" O'Connell said, as we drank our coffee.

He didn't want me to say, yes, you work for the CIO. Something about the struggle with the waiter had aroused his desire to make a speech. He talked about the General Motors strike and the fight on the overpass. He had a story about another strike where the women lay down on the railroad track. He moved the salt and pepper shakers around.

The waiter brought a plate of doughnuts.

"What's the matter, Butch, you seem sort of turned off about the movement?"

"I've heard a lot about it. All during my childhood." I looked at O'Connell as the morning light turned one side of his face pink. There was a lot of attractive energy in his face, with its straight, black brows. Cocky, I suppose some people would have called him. He played with the salt cellar and I imagined him on the picket line. He would be very good at that, infectious, inventive, funny. In repose, though, O'Connell's face looked different. There was a vulnerable droop to his eyes that reminded me of my sister.

"What do you do in the army, Lt. O'Connell?"

"Well, dear, I fill out forms. I run a truck depot in Chicago and I fill out forms. That's what we do in the army."

"And where is your family? Do they live in Chicago too?"

"Why did you decide I have a family?"

I simply looked at him. It wasn't possible to imagine Lt. O'Connell without a family. If he lost one he would get another.

"Yes," he conceded unenthusiastically. "In a nice housing project. Just a wife. No kiddies." He looked slightly uncomfortable, and seemed relieved when the waiter came out with more cream.

Lt. O'Connell began to talk about his childhood. He sat with his back to the east, the sky behind him gradually getting lighter and brighter, one strange shaped butte persisting as part of the view. "Listen," he said, "I know about your background; it may have been a little screwy, but it was rich . . . "

"We weren't rich," I said.

"That shows how much you know, namely nothing.

Butch, where I grew up the cockroaches were two inches long; you ever seen that kind? And something lots of people don't know: they fly, but only when the lights are off. We kids were scared spitless of them; I used to lie in the dark with my thumbs pushed against my eyelids, to make it hurt, to give me something to think about besides those cockroaches. The greatest treat we kids had was, sometimes if somebody had some money, we'd buy a lot of kerosene and leave the lamps turned on all night. That would keep them away, as long as the lights were on."

"Some people," said O'Connell, "they think it's glamorous or special to be really poor. Well, it isn't glamorous. It stinks.

"I ran away from home when I was fifteen and joined the IWW. Boy was I a redhot. I had hot pants and a hot red card. Boy, I was going to organize the whole damn world."

When we got back to our car it was light and most of the soldiers were awake. I went to the ladies' room. There were no towels. I used the soap kit which Clara had given me. It was some kind of rubberized stuff with a place for the soap and washcloth. It had a handmade Campfire girl look to it. Using it made me lonesome for Clara.

"How would you like it," O'Connell asked after I returned to my seat, "if I taught you to play poker?"

O'Connell said he had learned to play poker in jail. He had been in jail twenty-seven times between 1933 and 1939, all for union activity.

We got my suitcase down off the rack and put it across our knees to use as a table, and O'Connell began his lesson, "Now, you see, Butchie, the smallest combination you can have is a pair . . ." And so on for a while, laying out cards so I would be sure to understand what he was talking about. But finally something in my expression must have caught his eye, and he said, "Oh, for Christ's sake," and made the cards into a mess in the middle of the suitcase. "It's not fair; you shouldn't lead a man on that way."

I was laughing. "Well, you asked for it." I thought of all the times Will and Clara and I had played poker down at the bottom of the garden. Will was an overly analytic player, but Clara was a very good one.

O'Connell called on Christ again and sorted and dealt the cards. After a bit he decided to enliven the game by pretending that additional people were playing and assigning names and personalities to them. Mr. and Mrs. Jones were a meek couple in their forties; Lady Sadie was a stripper; there was also Donald Nelson, the head of the War Production Board; and a fat man named Eustace, who was my son.

The conductor appeared at the far end of the car and banged on the chimes, and all the soldiers lined up for breakfast. I watched them go out and said, "If they marched in step the car would fall apart."

Lt. O'Connell peeked at a card and said he wasn't doing it in his own person, but in that of Lady Sadie.

"What color hair does your wife have?" I asked.

"Christ!" We put the cards away and O'Connell went for a walk. When he came back we played poker again. O'Connell said, "My wife has gray hair, but it used to be brown. Butch, what do you want out of life?"

We were crossing Great Salt Lake, which stretched out on both sides of the raised train track, gray and flat, merging at the horizon with the gray, flat sky. The loneliness of this prospect may have had something to do with O'Connell's abrupt question.

I had a ridiculous desire to write out a list for him:
I want—
to cure my mother absolutely
to grow up
and I want something for my sister
That third wish was hard to phrase, because, except for being young, Clara was a successful person already.

Maybe, I thought, I'll just tell O'Connell about the typing plateaus.

Clara had been delighted when she learned in psychology about plateaus of performance, with the example of the typing class which reached a plateau and didn't improve for a while, and then, all at once, giant step forward, left that plateau to surge into new achievements. "That's the way we'll do it," Clara told me. "One giant step, Helen. No one will expect it." We held hands and promised we would grow up like that, all at once, in a leap from shelf to shelf.

"I don't want anything out of life," I told Mr. O'Connell. "There's no point in asking, anyway."

O'Connell seemed truly shocked. "My God, Butchie, for a girl of . . . how old are you?"

"Nineteen."

"For a girl of nineteen that's a pretty bitter thing to say."

"I'm not bitter at all," I said. "Not in the least. I just don't see any point to it."

After we put the cards away Lt. O'Connell said that he was getting off the train at Ogden, Utah. "That's why I go on the train, you see," he said. "Because I probably could have got a priority for a plane, but this way I get to get off and tend to some union business in Ogden.

"Do you have to go right on to Washington, Butch? Is Mama very bad?"

"She's medium." Mama's boyfriend had said he could hold her together for a few more weeks.

"Why not get off in Ogden with me? It would be really great if you could get off in Ogden."

"And your wife would think it was really great, too."

"Well, son of a bitch, Butchie." Lt. O'Connell had bought a bag of peanuts on his walk and he ate one now and looked moderately pleased with himself.

"Would you like some more coffee?" he asked. "I could go up to the dining car and get you some coffee."

When O'Connell returned with the coffee he repeated his offer. "We really would have a good time. I could show you Ogden."

"No, thank you."

"It's not like any other place."

"No place is like any other place."

O'Connell went back to the dining car with the coffee cups and I got the poetry book out again. It had notes in the margin by me, and also little explosions by Will, like a picture, not a very good one, of a dog throwing up.

When Lt. O'Connell got back he said, "Come on, dear; it will be an adventure.

"The train stops in fifteen minutes," he added, "you've just got time to get your junk together.

"Listen, I'm really a good companion," he went on. "I know lots of things. And nobody ever stops in Ogden. Life is different there. You'll notice it. Nobody you ever knew ever went there."

"Lt. O'Connell," I said, "I am simply not going to sleep with you."

O'Connell screwed up his face. "So tell the whole train, for God's sweet sake. Advertise in the paper."

"Well, I'm not."

"Oh, for Jesus' sake." He got down his suitcase and snapped it shut.

"We'll have separate rooms in the hotel."

"How old did you say you were?"

"Nineteen."

"Well, you act like ninety-nine." This quip evidently cheered him up, because he got my suitcase down briskly, whistling "Avanti, popolo." He put the suitcase in the aisle and held my coat so I could slip into it. "We'll have a great time, Butchie," he said, into the back of my mother's old leopard-skin coat.

My ticket was in sections, one of which ended at Ogden, so I knew that there would be no trouble as far as that was concerned.

Chapter II

O'CONNELL AND I were in a restaurant with blue plastic tables.

O'Connell had really tried, I think, to get us separate rooms in the Hotel Ogden. I had stood in a corner of the dusty hotel lobby while he and the clerk talked. The clerk wrote in his book; money changed hands; the clerk made the top of his head look bored. The hotel smelled of green janitor's cleaning compound. By the time O'Connell came over and said, "Butch, the best I can do is connecting doors," I was tired of the whole business. I walked out of the hotel and across the park and into a restaurant.

It was an ordinary restaurant with the usual calendars and Coca-Cola signs. We waited a long time for a table.

"I imagine you've had a pretty lousy life, Butch," O'Connell said. He poked with his fork at a limp slice of dill pickle.

"Who, me?" It was his sympathy that surprised me more than anything else. Sometimes I thought my life had been lousy, and sometimes I didn't.

"Well, . . . " O'Connell looked embarrassed.

"It was only toward the end," I said firmly, "that Mama was a trial to us."

"The end of what, dear?"

Well, yes, O'Connell, good question. The end of what? Of my childhood, maybe.

Rat a tat, brack, rat a tat, brack. The noise was compounded of the doorbell ringing and someone pounding emphatically with the front door knocker. This was the true middle of the night, and I had gone to sleep in the living room, because Clara had a cold. I woke and saw above me the raftered high ceiling of our fake medieval living room. I realized that the noise had been going on a long time. And Clara was sick, and Will, who was rooming with us, would not wake up if you shot a machine gun off by his ear.

I staggered up, bathrobe clutched around me, and put my groggy head out the door. And there was my mother at her hilarious best, being held up by two cops.

"You this lady's sister?"

Sister. Oh, come *on*.

That is no lady, that's my mother.

"Um," noncommittal noise, may be interpreted either way.

"We really shoulda taken her in, but her escort—guy she was with—"

Yes, yes, I know.

" . . . not willen at all to prefer charges, said she just had a little too much to drink, so we thought give it a go-by this time . . . "

And so my beautiful, drunk mother was pitched into my arms, posing as my sister.

After the cops had departed: "Mama, what on earth did you do?"

"I hit him. Oh, Lord, he deserved it. Helen, he was so funny!"

My mother wore a green Indian brocade dress, tied with the cord from our bell to call nonexistent servants. She was holding a shoe in one hand. She was laughing, flushed, ap-

You must have hit him pretty hard, too.

Laughter. "Lord, did I ever. Oh, Helen" (hugging me), "I hit him with the . . . "

She flung herself backwards on the couch, evening slipper in the air. "Oh, Lord, I nearly died laughing, it served him right, the fresh jerk . . . "

"What did you say you hit him with, Mama?"

"With the *bed leg,* darling, with the bed leg."

Mama, for goodness' sake.

This is a pretty funny story, once you have figured it out, but it was not so funny the next morning when Mama came running out of the house and fell into the reflecting pool, crying out that her hair was full of insects. Clara and I got her back into the house before the neighbors called the police, but she was very noisy all morning, waking up and crying, and wanting to take the curtains off the windows because they got between her and the sky. Will heard her and came in and watched, and that was the start of Will hating her as much as he did.

After we had finished our lunch, O'Connell said, "Well, what about it; let's get a car and go take a look at the countryside."

We rented a car at a garage where O'Connell knew the owner. We got a big black Mercury with gray upholstery. O'Connell drove up Ogden's main street tooting the horn to make the soldiers jump out of the way.

Ogden had just one main street, which seemed to run straight into the side of a navy blue mountain. The buildings, except for the hotel and the station, were white, one-dimensional and impermanent looking. The main street was lined with neon signs and was full of soldiers on foot.

"I got a ball bearing plant here," O'Connell said. "They make bearings for railroad cars. Ogden is a big railroad junction."

The echo of trains and train whistles was the principal sound in Ogden. They seemed louder than usual; perhaps the mountain acted as a sounding board.

O'Connell was a fast, competent driver. We quickly left the town behind us and turned to go around the mountain.

"There's a road here that takes us to the lake. You just wait till we get to that lake. Didn't I tell you I'd show you some good things? You won't believe this."

O'Connell wasn't interested in my objection that I had

just seen Great Salt Lake when we crossed it on the train. He started firing facts at me about salinity and weight; he told a story about a party where a five course dinner was served to people lying on their backs in the middle of the lake. He described Victorian postcards that had a packet of salt attached to them. He drove with one hand and gestured or handed me cigarettes with the other.

Everything he talked about finally brought Lt. O'Connell back to the labor movement. Even his story about the postcards reminded him of one about the chemical workers' union.

"This isn't good union territory out here, though; it looks too much like the Old Testament; people who live here are afraid God is going to come down and zap them one."

We reached a rise in the road and looked down at the water, very still and gray, with a skin across the top of it. The edge of the lake was rough, glittering, and scarred, with some deposits of what looked like pink crust.

"There," O'Connell said. "You see."

He seemed to think that he had made it, but I didn't mind. I moved in and out of liking O'Connell, and I rather liked him just now.

"Come on," he said. "Let's get down there and look at it."

We drove by the margin of the lake for a while, and finally stopped the car and climbed down off the road. There were no other people and no cars, and you could almost believe that none had ever been here. I put my hand in the water; it was only slightly cooler than my skin.

"Mountains of the moon," O'Connell said. He scrambled around and found two or three flattened rocks and a piece of weatherworn bottle.

"You know," he gestured at the pale panorama, "you can

really understand about 'the Lord my God is an awful God,' and all that stuff. It makes you think about how it all started."

"It make you feel lonely."

"It does, Butch. Lonely and small. Come on, dear."

"It makes you think about the first and last things. The beginning and the end."

"It sure does."

"I like to think about the end of the world," I said.

"Do you."

I had the feeling O'Connell would understand if I just persisted. "I tried to write about it once. The end of the world is the final trial; when you imagine it, you're always the last person left alive, one of the . . ."

"Ultimate survivors. Yeah." O'Connell skimmed a flat rock out over the lake and waited for the explosion on the shiny surface and the tiny sound. "Yeah. Lonely, though. Real . . . lonely."

We found a little place to eat, the name of which appeared to be EATS. Nobody was in sight, but there was a sign, "Ring bell for Propritress," and when we rang the bell a pale yellow woman in blue jeans and a man's undershirt appeared.

O'Connell and I each ordered a Coke, and we went out to the blue jeansed lady's back porch to drink them. It was cold and there were bugs, one of which drowned noisily in O'Connell's Coke.

"Drowning in Coca-Cola is not my idea of a good death," O'Connell said. He fished the bug out with his tie clip.

The lady had a sign, in sparkled writing on a dark blue background: "Cooking—Like Mother Used to Do."

"Whose mother do you think she cooks like, O'Connell? Do you think she cooks like your mother?"

"I haven't the faintest notion, Butchie."

"Wasn't your mother a good cook? Mine was. No one ever thought she would be, but she was always surprising people."

"Was she now?" Lt. O'Connell said in an unconvinced voice.

"Well, what about your mother?" I really wanted to know more about Lt. O'Connell. "Couldn't she cook?"

"I don't know whether my mother could cook or she couldn't, Butch, because my mama died when I was eight years old; she died right after the two babies did. And before you're eight years old you're not much of a judge of cooking. And afterwards my sister Kat used to shove beans into my face whenever she remembered it, and somehow we all grew up, the ones that weren't dead already, that is.

"Kat was good to me, really. And I've got a feeling, not so much a memory as a feeling, that it was fairly happy before Ma and those babies died. It's funny, you keep on thinking about it some, no matter how old you get."

O'Connell captured a bug in midair and threw it over the side of the porch.

"I'm sorry," I said.

"All in a day's work. Everyone has something, I guess."

I moved to the rail and looked out. The sun had gotten low, and within the last few minutes the hazy horizon had turned brilliant orange, the luminous gray water reflecting the color in a bright path.

I said, "Do you think life is a mess?"

"It is and it isn't. You say that too much and you end up feeling sorry for yourself, and that gets you no place."

That's what I would have expected you to say, O'Connell.

I was waiting for him to put his arm around me as we both leaned on the porch rail, swatting mosquitoes and watching the brilliant orange sun, slowly growing larger and larger, slip below the rim of the light-tinged gray water. And he didn't put his arm around me. Surprise.

Instead, he leaned down, picked up a worn purple fragment of glass, held it up to the light for a minute, and then tucked it under the edge of the porch rail. "That's just to show we were here," he said.

O'Connell, I wouldn't have thought you'd had your childhood snatched away from you, a childhood that you had liked before they took it away.

You might, if you were so inclined, say that that gives us something in common.

For the first part of the ride back to Ogden, he and I were both silent. The country slipped by, looking whiter and more remote as the light faded.

Finally he began to sing. He sang a song which he said he had learned during his early labor days, but it wasn't a labor song, only a cynical or disillusioned one:

> *" . . . their game would be mud like a chump*
> *playing stud*
> *If it wasn't for that ace in the hole."*

"Look, honey," he said, "I don't mind telling you, having you sitting beside me is doing things to me. When we get back . . . Listen, you can't tell me you're not feeling it, too."

"You promised me you wouldn't do that."

"Didn't promise I wouldn't say I liked you."

"Really, you did."

"It's never one way, that feeling."

"Stop it. Talk to me about the CIO."

"Hell." O'Connell drove for about a mile and said, "I'll

talk to you about the desert; all Irishmen collect little-known facts."

He gave a lecture about the century plant, which does not bloom every hundred years, as its name implies, but every seven. There had been a steel mill owner who gave a party for four hundred people to celebrate the flowering of his century plant. And there was another corporation owner whose wife gave a party when her dog had its kidney stones removed.

"I could make a big speech about the capitalist class, but I won't. Those stories stick in your mind. Why don't you want to sleep with me?"

O'Connell was a good storyteller. He had a true narrative gift, suspenseful touches in the right places. I sat with my head against the car window and thought about my mother, who also had a narrative gift.

My mother told stories which built up gradually. The child she was telling the story to had to collaborate. She would sit in the rocking chair in the bay window, holding me, rocking, looking out at the view. "Once there was a little . . . " I was supposed to supply the missing words.

"Girl!"

"There was a little girl. She had red hair and brown eyes. She was very . . . "

"Good!" I was a predictable child. First the little girl was very *good*. Then I changed that. She was very bad. My mother liked bad better. I could tell.

She squeezed me. We supplied the little girl with friends, enemies, animals, trials. She owned a pet . . . hippopotamus! Something said it would eat her. She . . . sliced it up! We laughed hilariously.

"And then she got a sister." I finished the story in a kind of question.

It's the usual pious thing to say you're not jealous of your sister because the two of you are so different, and with Clara and me it has almost been true. But I always finished those stories with that exploring remark about the sister.

"She had a sister and they liked each other, but she was still the only little girl with red hair and brown eyes," my mother said, loud, right on cue.

My beautiful vague mother was an accurate instinctive psychologist. Sometimes, after I got older, I thought that Mama could have done and been anything, anything in the world, if her luck had been different.

Mama kept the rocking chair going by pressing one foot against the ledge of the bay window, I rested my nose on her armpit. She smelled splendid—healthy, perfumed, sweaty.

"God, Butch," O'Connell was saying, "you can't imagine, life is so awfully peculiar and so short, too. Let's go back to the hotel and climb into bed."

"Stop that. I'll open the door and jump out."

He was still driving with one hand. "Listen. Really. I like you a lot."

What a handsome bastard, I thought. Bright, too. I wonder what happened between him and my mother.

"I want to sleep with you. What's wrong with that?"

"Everything. Quit talking about it."

"Well, you *have* been giving me a come-on, you know."

He moved his hand, perhaps toward the gearshift and perhaps not. I reacted by grabbing his wrist. That last remark had made me panicky. I pushed, and so did he.

It was because we were fighting that O'Connell ran into the dog.

It was fairly far out from town for the dog to be, but still, that was what it was, somebody's pet dog, with a collar and his name, which was Marcus. It was a big dog; a Labrador retriever or something like that.

The car hit with a great impact; I thought at first we had run into another automobile; then we bumped, and swerved, and stopped.

Both of us opened our doors and got out and ran back. It was getting dark, but I could still see clearly. We had run over the dog's hind quarters; there was a hideous mess. I wanted to think that we had broken his spine and that he couldn't feel anything, but the animal looked up into my eyes, and I couldn't any longer think that. It was at this point that I looked at his collar: Marcus.

O'Connell said, "Go on back to the car, Butch."

I didn't go back to the car. I moved to the side of the road and stood watching while O'Connell opened the trunk and got out a wrench and came back and stood behind the dog. O'Connell had to hit him twice.

When we were back in the car I leaned forward and rested my head against the dashboard. O'Connell drove a little way and stopped again.

I said, "If we hadn't been horsing around that wouldn't have happened."

"Accidents happen, Butch."

"If we hadn't been doing that, it wouldn't have happened."

"Okay."

"I hate us."

"Now, look . . . "

The dashboard was cold and I could feel the glove compartment knob making a dent in my forehead. I said, "Damn. Damn. Damn."

O'Connell shifted. "'How about a weed, dear."

"Shove your lousy weed."

"Oh for *Christ's* sake . . . Look, Butch, we can get you a drink."

"Shove that, too."

"*God.*" O'Connell started the car and screeched it off.

After he had driven for a minute or so, I said, "So, okay, let's do it. Let's go back to the hotel and go to bed."

"Huh?"

"That's what it was all about, wasn't it? We've got the name. Let's have the game."

He slammed the car to a halt by the roadside. "'For *God's* blessed shrieking sake."

I pushed my forehead into the dashboard. "We'll go back. And get into bed." For some reason I felt that if we actually did act it out, this seduction scene we had been pretending at, that would give the dog's death some meaning.

"You're out of your fucking mind. No guy wants to go to bed with a girl who has lost her marbles."

"What the hell. Why not?"

"Listen, babe, what you need is a nice hot drink, rum or something like that, and then bed all by yourself."

"You'd better take the chance. It may not come again."

I could feel O'Connell shifting in his seat and turning to look at me.

"Look, dear, it will be the first time in my life I ever turned down . . . "

I swiveled so I was sitting sideways and brought my knee up against his leg. "I mean it."

He started the car again. "Godalmighty, what a screwy situation." He patted me on the knee. "Well, babe, let it never be said . . . Oh, for Christ's sake." And he stepped on the gas and began to drive rapidly toward Ogden, whose lights were visible at the end of the highway.

* * *

O'Connell held my arm while we walked through the lobby, and again I noticed the smell of the janitor's green cleaning stuff; they kept it in a bucket in the mop closet.

Upstairs he went into the bathroom and made a lot of noise running water and brushing his teeth. The door was open between our rooms, so I could hear him clearly. I tossed my cat skin coat on a chair and sat on the edge of my bed, doing my nails. I had all the implements lined up on the edge of the dressing table and was working away at the shape of my fingernails.

O'Connell finally came out with a towel tied around his middle. He said, "Excuse the déshabille, Butch. You can scream and jump out the window if you want to."

He had another towel which he draped over his head like an Arab.

"Look," he said, sitting down beside me, "I've never had a more tempting offer made to me, but something about it . . . Oh, what the hell." And he put his arm around me. He was still wet from his shower and I had on a sleeveless blouse; I could feel the pull where the damp hair on his arm caught against me.

"Oh, God, baby." He put the other arm at my waist and pressed it hard into my belly.

Up until the last minute I had no idea what I was going to do, and when I had done it I wasn't sure that I had done it.

I lifted the nail scissors into the air and brought them down as hard as I could into Lt. O'Connell's back.

He made a smothered noise and leaned against me.

I sat with one hand on the grip of the scissors and the

other on O'Connell's bare, damp arm. Over his shoulder I could see the tan-painted hotel-room wall, part of a sign which had the room rates on it, and a bit of the door, which was brown and had a brass chain, unchained.

I thought, I've killed him. This is the end of my life. The end of his.

I thought, a minute and a half ago this hadn't happened. If I could go back, a minute and a half, to where it hadn't happened, I would know that this is what it would feel like. And then I wouldn't do it.

I slipped from in front of O'Connell. To my surprise he stayed sitting up.

I looked at him and thought, perhaps if he's really and thoroughly dead, so that nothing at all can be done for him, I can just run out of here.

I thought, no, there's nothing for it. And I put my hand out for the phone, which was at the head of the bed.

O'Connell said, "Why in the bloody bitching hell are you reaching for that fucking phone?"

"I've got to get a doctor for you."

"Look, you bitch, get the goddamned scissors out of my goddamned back and get away from that fucking phone."

I came toward him. The tears were running down my face like rain down a windowpane, going into my mouth and making my chin sting. I wasn't sobbing. It was a peculiar kind of crying; I hadn't ever cried that way before.

"I'm afraid to pull them out."

"God, you bitch, they're in my shoulder, not my back, get them out, for Christ's sake."

I knelt on the bed behind him and pushed with the flat of one hand and pulled the scissors with the other. They were lodged in the . . . muscle, I suppose; I couldn't tell what it was. There was a pull and resistance as I got them out, spurt of blood, not as much as I had expected. I got some on my hand.

I leaned forward and kissed him on the open wound, and then I ran into the bathroom and flung myself down in front of the toilet.

When I had stopped vomiting I lay full length on the floor with my forehead pressed against it. Then I pulled myself up and washed my face and held my hands under the tap. The blood which had settled in the creases took a while to be washed free.

I took a dry bath towel off the rack and tried to tear a piece down the side. Finally I pried the top off the used razor-blade tin and started a tear with a razor blade; after that the cloth tore easily. When I came back into the room, O'Connell was sitting up, feeling for his socks. I sat behind him and tied the strip of towel tightly across his back and shoulder and under one arm.

I said, "We've got to get you to the hospital."

"You half-witted bitch, what kind of a story would we tell them? You can't just march into a hospital with a knife wound and then march out again."

"I don't care. They can put me in jail if they want to."

For the first time since I had stabbed him, Lt. O'Connell turned and looked right at me. He said, "You stupid dopey little bitch, you can go to jail if you like. God knows, it might be good for you. But do you think I want to be telling this half-assed stupid story to a bunch of cops?" He sounded just a shade less angry than he had sounded earlier.

"We'll make up a story. You fell. You fell on something. We don't know what it was."

"Yeah, absolutely. Somebody stuck the scissors in the

ground with the points up. Even in Ogden, Utah, Butch
. . . " He stopped, both of us, I think, realizing that he had
called me Butch again.

We were sitting facing each other on the bed. I got up
and went around him to look at his back. "It's beginning
to soak through. You need stitches."

O'Connell rose and began to walk toward the bathroom.
I stared at the sturdy broad shoulders with the padded
backbone, blood dark down the middle of it. He was still
wearing his towel.

I said, "The hell with it. Either we go to the hospital or
I call up and get an ambulance here, and that would be
worse."

I drove O'Connell's rented car, and O'Connell leaned
back against the gray padded upholstery and looked
thoughtful. I said, if you get blood all over that plush
they'll send you a bill, and he said, Screw it, Butch, and I
said, honestly, I'm really sorry, and he didn't answer.

O'Connell finally came out of the emergency room looking cross and sturdy, with his arm in a sling. He went right
by me and out the door without looking at me. But I caught
up with him on the sidewalk and said, "You can't drive
that car, so you've got to have me with you."

He fetched up a sigh and said, "How do I know you're
not going to murder me again?"

"Honest, I won't. And anyway, you can't . . . "

"Aaah."

We climbed into the car. I looked up the street through
the windshield. This was the same street that the hotel and
everything else was on; up ahead I could see the "Hotel"
sign and two "Eat" signs flickering on and off, very badly
synchronized, so that it made you itch to look at them.

O'Connell said, "Come to think of it, what's so absolutely fatal about going to bed with me anyhow? Others have enjoyed it."

I'll bet they have. I said, "I swear by everything holy I'll never do it again. I swear by the war effort, I swear by the CIO . . . "

"You're feeling pretty good, chum. Cheers a girl up, apparently."

"Does it hurt?"

"Of course it hurts, stupid."

"I mean, a lot."

He relented. "Oh, Christ, no, not a lot. In fact I can hardly feel it at all. I told them I did it on a can opener," he said after a minute.

"A *what*?"

"Can opener. The kind that sticks out of the wall."

We both began to laugh, until some jeeps came down the road in high gear and drowned us out. When they had gone by O'Connell said, "Quit sitting so close to me, you goddamned cheat."

"Chit," I said. "Spit. Shit."

"I don't like to hear a lady use words like that." Said with a great deal of disapproval.

"You wouldn't." I got the car into gear and thought, so now I'm a lady again. I said, "We haven't had any dinner.

"We could buy some and have it sent up," I added.

O'Connell came to the station with me at eleven-thirty that night, carrying my suitcase in his good hand, to see me off on the midnight train.

"Good-bye," I said. "I'm sorry I stuck you." This seemed inadequate.

I think he said, "Not to worry." The train let off a big gust of steam at that moment and I couldn't really hear him, but I think he also said, "My fault, anyhow." I climbed the train steps and turned around to wave, but he had already started back across the station waiting room toward the hotel. I watched the back of his khaki jacket, with the white sling bisecting it and a large pin glinting under his ear. He was listing slightly toward his hurt shoulder; he looked as if he had been wounded in the war.

Chapter III

WHILE MY TRAIN CARRIED ME toward Chicago, down from the high plateau which contained Ogden and into the great central basin of America, I thought about my golden girlhood.

Maybe the principal fact about my girlhood was that it was sharply divided into *before* and *after*. *After* occurred in two stages; the first stage was the Christmas Day when my father announced to us, with presents spread across the living-room floor, that he had something he wanted to explain. He wanted (he had trouble with this, mumbled, played with the discarded wrappings, stared at his feet) . . . of course we, young as we were, could still understand and agree with him . . . it would be difficult, but we would understand . . . In short, he had sold a half interest in the storage company that supported his family, we would not exactly starve, there would be a regular dividend check, and he was going to Spain to fight for freedom. He was proud of his daughters; they too, would be soldiers for democracy. He was leaving in five days. He put his arms around us; my mother sobbed into the gift wrappings. Clara and I sat stoically staring at our just-opened creative, instructive presents: chemistry beakers, wax for batiking.

Stage two of *after* was the moment when we heard, one afternoon in August, with a mockingbird singing his overheated heart out in the eucalyptus tree in front of the house, via a yellow Western Union telegram, that my father had been killed in Spain. Both Clara and I had been in bed with measles. We moved from our own bed to our mother's bed and lay together, all three of us, in a quivering, heated mass.

After that our girlhoods were less golden, but in California there were always some bright, astonishing moments. In spite of the fog there was a great deal of sunshine in Berkeley. There was sunshine in the winter; it was sunny and warm on Christmas day. On the first of February you could make a picnic and go lie in the yellow grass in your shirtsleeves and eat tomatoes off your stomach.

Our house was one of the minor sights of Berkeley. On the outside it looked like a combination between a small apartment house and a medieval castle. The inside decor was depression moviehouse, walls stippled in orange and cream, brass light fixtures arcing out from the walls on stems and capped by heavy, pierced shades which made them resemble lanterns.

The architecture of the façade was Mediterranean or Arabic. There were arches and there were four twisted columns somewhat irregularly placed across the front. And also

across the front of the house, much too close, so close that
if you were not careful you stumbled and fell in, was a
large reflecting pool. The mailman had fallen into it twice
when he stepped back hastily after talking to someone at
the door. And several of mother's boyfriends, on nights
when it was dark and the pool was not reflecting, had done
so, too. The pool was less than a foot deep, so that all any
of these people got was a shoe full of water; nevertheless
we had special accident insurance because of the reflecting pool.

It was my father who had gotten the accident insurance.
He had been proud of his strange romantic house.

The house had a name: Tir n'a Nog, the land of youth
of the Irish fairy stories. Mother's mother, who had been
a dancer, had used this idea in one of her performances, and
we had a photograph of her posing in the dance on the
balcony of the house.

Clara and I grew up knowing that we were different.

"It would be a lot better if they would turn off those
lights," I said.

This was an imitation mahogany rather than a tan railroad car. It had a group of poker players down at its far
end. But the big difference between it and the one O'Connell
and I had been on was that on this one nobody had come
by to dim the lights.

"Sure would," my seat mate, a small, thin soldier, remarked neutrally. He tipped himself down into the middle of his backbone and pulled his cap over his eyes.

I wadded up my jacket to make a pillow and thought
some more about Berkeley, timing my thoughts to the slap
of cards from the other end of the carriage.

SCENE: a Thursday morning in October. Clara and I are walking down the hill to Hillside School. We are aged twelve and ten, respectively. Clara has our books in a leather satchel with a brass lock on it, and I am carrying our lunch in a straw basket exactly like the one Little Red Riding Hood fetched across the forest to Grandmother's house. The day is bright blue. Berkeley is spread out below us in an aquamarine and white panorama. Clara's braids are tied with green yarn on one and blue on the other. I wear a paisley dress, formerly my mother's, which I myself have cut down and stuck back together again; Clara's dress is from Swan's Cut-Rate Department Store and was probably intended to be a waitress's uniform, although it fits Clara's small straight body perfectly. (Swan's has a lot of small-boned Chinese customers.) Both of us are pleased, in a modest way, with ourselves and our appearances.

"Good morrow," I say to Eleanor, my best friend. I have been reading about Mary, Queen of Scots, and think this is the way the doomed queen might have greeted someone.

Eleanor surveys me speculatively for a minute and says, "Hi." Then she puts her arm around my waist. We walk together into the classroom, Eleanor leaning her head against mine.

Eleanor probably had a crush on me; if so it was composed of repulsion and attraction in equal measure. Her father was an orthodontist. Eleanor was my one normal friend. Clara and I each had one such: one normal friend, Eleanor for me, Marjory for her. Perhaps we consciously limited ourselves to one normal friend apiece, so as to cut down on the number of people coming into our unpredictable household.

"I love your pond in the front yard," Eleanor once said.

"It's a reflecting pool. It's a copy of the one at the Taj

Mahal," I answered. I was incorrect in this. The Taj Mahal pool is end-on, while ours ran the width of the house. Eleanor thought my family was romantic.

Perhaps I have given the incorrect impression that we were rich. Grandfather had had some money, but he spent a lot of it on the house, which in spite of being odd and interesting looking, was not very big. And my father's warehouse company had consisted of only one warehouse.

We kept fish in the reflecting pool, but, possibly because of the people so often stepping into it, there was a high mortality among the fish. Sometimes we forgot to replace the dead fish, and then after a little while we would have mosquitoes instead of fish.

Grandmother had come to see us during one of these mosquito periods, and said that we all needed keepers. Clara and I had perfected a way of making our eyes perfectly blank, as if we understood no English, when we looked at her; and we looked at her that way then.

"Keepers!" she said. "You're all of you perfectly hopeless. You've got as much responsibility as a bunch of six-year-old children."

Mama seemed surprised. "Why Mama Reynolds. Just because of a few mosquitoes? Everyone in Berkeley has mosquitoes." She swatted one and went out to pull the plug in the pool. "I hope the pollywogs don't all go down. We have the most beautiful frogs and I really like the noise they make."

"Mama," said Clara. "Aunt Chloe and I did an experiment with rats. You have one rat that you give a balanced diet to. And one that doesn't get enough protein and one that gets hardly any at all."

"And the one that got the balanced diet bit Clara," I interjected.

"Shut up, Helen," said Clara calmly. "Anyway, it shows that you don't have the right energy to defend yourself if you don't have the right food."

Mama had a great many interests and enthusiasms, but the principal one, the one that really made her tick, was her social conscience.

It is hard for me to go back and recapture what Mama may have been like before Daddy went away, because when people change they do so very gradually and if you are a child living with them, it is all part of the same person, who now sometimes drinks too much, and who has a succession of men coming to take her out.

Once a long time ago, when Mama and my father were planning to go to a party, I complained bitterly and Mama said, "Helen, Mama has to go out, but Mama will think of Helen every hour," and she drew me a series of pictures of the way the clock would look at the times when she would be thinking of me. I was very little, about four.

It was a pretty funny childhood, and I didn't really know what to think of it. I sat on the train and stared across the aisle at a WAC's sturdy elastic-clad knee, and thought about that, what to think of it. We had been different and strange, exotic and cut off, and none of it had prepared us for anything at all.

"God*damn* it to bloody Hell." Someone in the poker game had apparently just lost a lot of money. "Son uvva *bitch.*" This awakened my seat mate, who sat up, adjusted his chin, and blinked. He had a narrow face and close-set eyes. "Jew like this seat?" he asked.

I tried to bring him into focus. "Huh?"

"Would jew like this seat." He gestured at the thin,

green plush under his hip. "By the window. More room."
He politely blocked a yawn. "I been. Asleep."

I was appalled at this evidence of human decency.
"Thank you," I said. "Thanks a lot." I muttered something
about the ladies' room. While I was feeling around for my
purse he fell back to sleep, his skinny head angled against
the window.

There was grit in the worn figured aisle carpet; it
crunched under my shoes like sand.

Chicago was as far as this train went. In Chicago I had
to get off and get on to another train. And in between
trains I would have a whole day in Chicago; I was going to
spend part of that day journeying into the suburbs looking
for Will. I hadn't been writing to Will. I think I blamed him
for Mother's exile to Washington, and that really was my
fault, not his; I was her child, for Heaven's sake, and Will
was just the lodger, her daughter's boyfriend. But it was
Will who had gotten me to talk to her, that last month
when the drinking was so bad. Will had suggested an institution. If Clara and I wouldn't go for that, he suggested
a job. In Washington. Will would find her the job. Will
really wanted her out of there.

The first night we talked to her about this she had stood,
very drunk, on the upstairs landing, leaning her arms on
the carved imitation medieval railing, with the tears wetting
the whole bottom part of her face. She was so drunk she
couldn't stand straight, but instinct made her know that if
she leaned forward like Juliet on the balcony rail she would
look graceful, and she did.

I thought about my possible reunion with Will, and then
decided to stop thinking about it; it made me too uncomfortable.

In the ladies' room I tried to console myself by staring

at my greenish, wavering face in the flecked mirror and repeating whatever comforting rhymes I could remember. "Helen, thy beauty is to me . . . ?"

For some reason, the all-time favorite quotation for me and Clara had been a passage from a story, a love story I had read aloud to Clara, a story about the loss of love and the endurance of love: the woman's husband is being taken off to jail (this is happening in the South someplace), and she calls out to him as he is being led away: "If I don't see you again in this life, Michael John, I'll see you in glory." Oh, how we had cried; I suppose it was connected with our absent father. I rested my elbows on the glass vanity shelf and thought about the word *glory*; when I said that word to myself I saw a dry yellow hill, and, yes, it probably was the hill in Spain that I had imagined my father dying on, a California type of hill, covered in blond, crisp grass.

After I was finished in the ladies' room I went out into the space between the cars and had a cigarette. It was very cold and gritty there. I stood with my back against the wire rail, not holding on but shifting when the train shifted. I blew out a column of smoke which was snatched instantly from my lips.

> *"Passengers will please refrain*
> *From flushing toilets while the train*
> *Is standing in the station; I love you . . . "*

That was Mama on the train from Berkeley to Portland. We had decided that Portland was to be the New Far West; Mama was very excited about going there. She danced around the train compartment wearing a green dress. She couldn't always have been wearing a green dress, could she? We stayed in Portland only three months.

Clara learned to knit in Portland; Clara became a very good knitter.

Twenty-six hours later, outside of Chicago, the train was halted for an hour and a half on a siding. I stared at the grim building backs, paint flaking, wet mops stiffly angled from back porches, and thought about O'Connell. This was the world that O'Connell came from. The train lights and the peeling paint made artistic, wavering shadows on O'Connell's kingdom. I sat for a while and thought about O'Connell to see if I was feeling anything, and I wasn't. I had been a little bit worried that I might.

The train said fight, fight, fight, fight, etc., echoing back and forth under the roof of the station, the last noise being the one that a steam engine makes at the end of a long series of puffs. I stood in line with the soldiers to go up the stairs. My seat mate wanted to go up with me and carry my suitcase, but he had to catch another train and so I made him leave and run for it.

I thought about Will, and felt better about getting off the train and going out into Chicago and looking for Will than I had been feeling.

Will had rented a room from us his first year in college. Then he got drafted, and someone in his family had managed to get him into a camp outside of Chicago, where he could be home part of the time. I had to take a chance on finding him there now, since I had not been writing to him.

I came upstairs, quickstepping to keep my place, and got in line to get some breakfast. Toast, coffee, oatmeal. Well, oatmeal is good. They put the sugar in your coffee behind the counter in order to save sugar and you couldn't get them not to put it in.

After breakfast I went into the ladies' room and discovered that in Chicago it is possible to rent a cubicle with a real tub in it, and so I did. Then I came out and sat and wondered whether to do my nails again. It was nine-thirty; still too early to make an unannounced visit to your boyfriend's mother.

I got the manicure set out. Beside me sat a thin strongsmelling lady wearing a tight, black dress, shiny blackmarket nylons, and thousands and thousands of little pincurls, each held in place by a black-market bobby pin. She was swinging one spike-heeled foot and reading what appeared to be a Bible.

In the toilet part of the restroom someone was enthusiastically throwing up. Gasp—aaawk. Pant, pant. Probably she had just knifed somebody. A fat lady across the aisle was eating an apple.

I gave up manicuring as a profession and got Louis Untermeyer out again.

Ladies who sit in ladies rooms
Have fallen arches and prolapsed wombs.

Chapter IV

WILL LIVED AT THE END of a four and one-half dollar taxi ride, in a tended and uncrowded suburb with wide lawns, big white or red houses, cast iron deer, and swinging driveway gates made of twisted metal with curved embellishments on their tops.

This neighborhood is only slightly better, I thought, as the taxi meter clicked and the driver called out bits of information—that's the Armour house, meat packing; there's the Zeppelin house; he manufactured Zeppelins—this neighborhood is only slightly better than the one where Mama, Clara, and I have our ramshackle castle. But that slight bit of difference is like other crucial margins in life, the one between in and out, the one between there and almost there. Will's father used to be a Federal judge; he died secure in his own bed, like a sensible man. Will's mother never, never came home drunk. As the taxi moved down the tree-lined streets I began to have conversations with an imaginary Mrs. Jessup:

Me: Hello, Mrs. Jessup. I'm Helen.

Mrs. Jessup: Why, my *dear*. (She is tall and slim, dark, with a silver streak in her hair from forehead to nape. She is marvelously dressed in a clinging black blouse and a petal-shaped black skirt. Her movements are very precise. She makes me feel like a clod.)

Version 2: This Mrs. Jessup is cordial, motherly, deep-bosomed. She takes my coat. Her house smells of apple pie. Her living room is enormous, slightly messy, magazines here and there, bright colored slipcovers, oriental rugs. She too makes me feel inadequate.

All in all it was a relief to be greeted at the door of Will's handsome, wide, white house by Will himself.

"Hello, Will," I said. "How are you?" I dropped my pocketbook on the doorstep and held out my arms.

Pause.

A leaf rustled as it detached itself from a nearby tree and spiraled into an adjacent flowerbed.

Will looked the same as I remembered him except that he was wearing a private's uniform. Trim waisted, straight nosed, with a curly cap of hair and a mouth almost too pretty for a man's mouth, he was the same, immediately part of my past. And angry with me. And who could blame him. I hadn't written for two months.

I bent over to pick up the pocketbook. When I stood up Will reached out, and there was another pause. Then we came together, he put his arms around me; he kissed me.

I had been thinking only about Will, hoping that he

wasn't too angry, and so I was surprised completely. Because as his hands came around my back and cupped my spine in a neat arrangement, one above the other, I remembered O'Connell. I had a perfect tactile recall of the way O'Connell's hands had felt when he touched me, wet from his shower, his damp fingers pulling on the thin material of my blouse.

"Listen," Will said. "I'm really glad to see you."

Another leaf rustled home.

"Come on in. We're having lunch."

Will's mother sat with another woman at a small table in a bay window framing a garden. She didn't look like my imaginary picture of her—she looked a little like Aunt Chloe, whom Clara and I had loved, and who had died. Mrs. Jessup was small, fuzzy haired, with an active contorted face. "Helen," she said. "My dear." She got up and ran around the table. She wore a dark blue smock with sunflowers embroidered on the pockets. "How wonderful!" She stood on her toes to kiss me. Up close I saw that her face was marked by fine lines, most of them horizontal, a few crosshatched ones on the upper lip. She stared with anxious monkey's eyes. "All the way from California! So . . . far!"

"Mama, dear," said Will.

"What? Oh, yes, of course. This is Aunt Blonde."

That was what I thought she said. It seemed suitable. The other lady was indeed blond; handsome, pop-eyed, a bit buck-toothed.

"Bon," Will's mother amended. "Bonnie. Mrs. Bonnie Clavering."

Oh.

A maid named Edna produced a placemat and some cutlery, and I sat down at the table in the place where Will had been sitting. A kitchen stool was brought for Will. They seemed to have arrived at the dessert part of lunch; dessert, I said, was all I wanted.

"Canned peaches." Aunt Blonde stirred hers. "Obnoxious, rilly." Blonde was young to be an aunt, about thirty-five; she had a raucous, well-bred, eastern voice. "Poor Helen."

"They have Vitamin C in them," Will's mother ventured. "At least, I think they do. Don't they?"

"Some, Mama." "None." Will and Aunt Blonde said this in chorus. The look they exchanged was level and combative. They were old enemies, you could tell that.

"You will loathe Chicago," Aunt Blonde promised.

"She won't," Will said.

"Don't interrupt, dear." (Will's mother.)

"Chicago is *grisly* meat packers and their grisly lantern-jawed daughters."

"Now, Bon." (Will's mother.)

"Of course, so many awful things have happened to me here."

"They have, Bon, dear, they certainly have. When did your train get in, Helen?"

Aunt Blonde was not going to be sidetracked thus. "My husband went mad in Chicago. Absolutely stone staring mad. That is enough to ruin anyplace for anybody."

Will sat on his stool beside his mother, eating canned peaches from a dish on his knee. "Peaches have a lot of *A*, Mother," he said. "They're good for you, really."

Mrs. Jessup looked reassured. "*Do* describe your trip for us. I think of it . . . something like crossing Tibet in a yak caravan."

"Tibet is camels," Blonde objected.

"Tibet," Will corrected, "is ponies. But you *could* do it on a yak, Mama."

"Heavens." Blonde turned to me. "Welcome to Chicago."

"Mama," Will said, "is interested in travel."

Mrs. Jessup nodded. "I read about it all the time. And when Will's father was alive . . . "

"He dragged you everywhere," Blonde finished for her. "It was ab'slutely amazing."

"I loved it. He was so much like Will. So interested. So interesting."

Blonde put both hands above her head and stretched. "Edna," she called out to the kitchen, "how about some of that marv'less coffee?"

"Helen and I are going out to look at things." Will set his empty dish decisively on the table and leaned over to kiss his mother. He and Blonde ignored each other.

"Don't let him take you to the university," she said. "It's abs'lutely ghastly."

Once out of Will's house, driving down the wide treed streets in Will's father's old, smooth-running, handsome car, I felt myself looking at Will anew. A new Will.

Will's father's car had leather upholstery. I moved my hand along its channeled, padded seat back. Will looked new to me, not because of his car and house, which were what I had deduced about him from knowing him in Berkeley, but because of his mother, who was different from the lady I had imagined. Most of all, because of the way Will had behaved with her, entirely different from any Will I had seen up to now.

"I liked your mother."

He looked at me bleakly. He was a good driver and could

do this without making the car wobble. "People take advantage of her. She thinks everybody is good."

Yes, there had been that hopeful question in Mrs. Jessup's brown eyes, the kind of look that gets disappointed.

"*I* dissapoint her," he said, picking up my unspoken thought.

"Don't be silly. She's crazy about you."

He had started to drive too fast, rocking the coffee-colored car around curves. "Why didn't you write?"

Why didn't you write is the hardest of all questions to answer. You can't just come out and say: because I didn't feel like it. Because I was angry with you about my mother. Because I thought you maneuvered me into sending her East, when, really, it was me, all by myself (not with any help from Clara) who did that. Because, Will, you have things I covet, that solid nice house, those solid nice childhood years, and I don't want to want them too much.

He pulled the car over to the curb and parked it with a thud. "Helen, my God." Leaning forward, one hand on each of my shoulders. Oh, Christ.

Will was a good kisser. He always had been good at kissing. Young, with hard firm surfaces, smooth, creased, thumping, starched, he felt good. He pulled me close; the two of us made an energetic, effective creature.

A little flame of sexual desire popped up, like a pilot light, somewhere below my belt line. I repeated to myself that I felt awful. The town whore, I said to myself. Town hoor (pronunciation borrowed from John Steinbeck).

"Honey." Will bent his head and burrowed his nose in my shoulder. "Stay in Chicago."

"I can't."

"Why not?"

"I have to go. Help my mother."

"Oh, God."

I started to say, don't call on God, then didn't say it.

Will lifted his head, kissed the side of my chin, fished around in his pocket. "Cigarette?"

"Yes."

He lit our cigarettes with one match, with one hand. Will was good at things like that. "Thanks." The car smelled of leather. The heavy, clean windows framed a curving street, twin tan brick pillars on either side of the road with the name of the cross street on them, more of those wide comfortable houses set back at the tops of their tended lawns. You want what you haven't got. Somebody stuck in the Arctic for six months will kill for a handful of raw liver. I have been exploiting Will. Hoor.

"So what's wrong with your mother now?"

That's more like it. Now we can fight.

"She's been drinking again. And she hasn't any job."

"She *had* a job."

"Not any more, she doesn't."

Will was right to be irritated at this. The job that Mama used to have was the one he had found for her. "I don't know what happened," I said.

"It doesn't matter what happened. It'll happen again."

"Maybe not." Even I couldn't get much conviction into that one.

"Helen, every time you go to see her . . . "

Here it comes. Good. Let's fight.

"You pick it up. You get like her. It's as if she has some infectious disease."

"That's not an infectious disease. They've got a name for that. Heredity."

"Oh, balls. Helen." He put his hand against the windshield, stared at it as if it were an art object. "This is hard for me to say. I have trouble figuring out what I'm thinking."

I touched the extended arm. Hard and smooth and crisp. Then I pulled my hand away.

"If you go to her," he went on after a minute, "you'll be eaten alive."

"No."

"Goddamn it, *she* is *your mother*. She's supposed to take care of *you*.

"Besides, I . . . " Will's troubled, neat face telegraphed what might be coming next. He was going to say something like, Helen, I really care for you. Maybe: Helen I love you.

"No," I said.

"Huh?"

"We sent her East, Will. Made her feel guilty, kicked her out of her own house. Let her know her own children couldn't stand her."

Will started the car. Thud. Scenery went by. Streets became narrower, houses closer together. There was more traffic. "Tell me about the army," I said.

"No."

Mrs. Jessup had explained that Will was home on a four-day pass.

We drove by a large post office, stopped for a traffic light. Will gunned the motor with a satisfying roar. A crowd of gray people crossed the street. "Why didn't you write?" He grazed a pedestrian.

"I did. I just never mailed it."

"Really. Hey." Will brightened. Almost anybody feels better if he knows he has been on your mind, either pro or con.

"Clara got a B plus in history," I told him, after another couple of blocks. "She says *you* did it for her."

Will had coached Clara in history all last semester. Every evening under the bare, swinging light bulb in the kitchen, Will drawing maps, Clara chewing on the raw end of a braid, Mama upstairs thumping and dropping things, getting drunker and noisier as the evening progressed. Happy memories we have, Will. Oh, good Lord.

Chicago unrolling on either side of us got denser, tighter, grayer. The last suburban tree receded in the middle distance. I watched it in the rearview mirror. I pointed it out to Will.

"How can you tell it's the *last* tree," he asked, in irritation. I had known he would ask that. It had looked like the last tree, so pale, scrawny, oxygen-starved, minimal; it seemed the edge of a timberline. I tried to explain this to Will, who grunted. "Do you still chew gum?" I asked. We had just passed a movie theater whose sidewalk was shiny with round squashed coins of chewing gum.

"Sure." Gum was Will's big vice. He knew that the chewing of gum was out of character for him, and he liked that. He fished a package out of his pocket, took a piece, offered me one. We chewed; scenery passed.

"I don't know what to ask you," I said. "If I say, 'tell me about the army,' you're going to say: 'What's to tell?' "

"I never treated you that way."

He was right. He hadn't. When I asked Will a question beginning, "tell me about" he characteristically thought for a while, got his ideas in a row, scowled, and then gave a short lecture. "Tell me *one* story," I suggested, "from the army. One thing that happened."

"Je-*sus*, Helen."

I persisted, pretending not to understand his irritation. "What do they think of you? Tell me one thing somebody said to you."

Will popped his gum. I watched his face out of the corner of my eye. He looked irritated (crease between the eyebrows), but he also looked interested (slight movement of lips as if talking to self). Another terminally final timberline tree, withering in a dirt well full of gum wrappers and broken glass, passed us; Will was too busy to react to it. "The best thing that happened was that the guy in the bunk next to me wanted me to help him design the city of the future.

"He was designing the city of the future," Will went on, "because everybody in the barrack has a hobby: some of them carve wooden pixies and mushrooms, some collect pornographic stories, there are a couple who make ships in bottles, and there is this middle-aged farmer who is designing the city of the future. He wants it to have antimagnetic streets, and the people should wear antimagnetic shoes so they can skim along just above the surface of the streets. And he had two questions for me: what should the streets be made of? and what should the shoes be made of?

"They all think I'm mysterious and brilliant. A rumor went around that I was the youngest Ph.D. ever to come out of Chicago."

Will wasn't bragging; he was stating a sociological fact. He must be lonely in the army.

"That was a *good* story about the antimagnetic city," I said encouragingly.

"Don't be patronizing."

Right. Wrong. Oh, hell. "I hope you told him chewing

gum." Wrong, again. A pause. Very dense traffic now. Buses, taxis, suicidal pedestrians. Will drove crisply in and out of small apertures, sliding the big car. One hand steered, the other tapped fingers on the buffered end of the leather armrest.

"Clara is knitting you a sweater."

"Hey. What kind?"

"Heather mixture. She says mistakes show up less in heather mixture."

"I miss Clara."

I had felt, before I started sleeping with Will, that he and Clara should get married. I had said this to each of them; each one stared at me as if I were speaking in Basque. Clara muttered, "Don't be soppy." Will said, "She's much too young."

"Remembering things makes them seem sad," I said.

Will steered around a truck. Horns sounded. "Helen. I don't talk about it much. In my letters, I mean. But I remember. A lot. Some nights, in the barracks, I sit up, I put my hands around my knees, I listen to all the snoring and groaning and farting. And I think about you."

"I think about you too." I started to reach for his hand, and then reached only halfway, a tentative, placating gesture.

Will sighed, the noise you make when you've been holding your breath. "Would you like to go to the Art Institute?"

"Sure."

"It's really good. One of the most complete collections in the country. It has . . . " We exchanged glances in the rearview mirror. He had been about to fire a lot of statistics at me. He stopped in mid-sentence. "It has the most beautiful Renoir in the world. That's why I want you to see it. Because of the Renoir."

This was a strange attachment of Will's to Renoir. One might have expected Will to like intellectual painters, the ones who worked just in black and white, or those who drew only straight lines, but Will liked Renoir instead; the lush color, the rosy haze over the vision released something in him. "This picture is gorgeous." He drove confidently into a parking space to a chorus of automobile horns. He seemed not to hear them. "I like your coat."

I didn't tell him that it was my mother's coat, for which she had gotten too fat, that she had given it to me and settled it about my shoulders and said, "Now, darling, you're going to be almost as beautiful as your Mama."

Chapter V

THE ART INSTITUTE was a white, American marble and granite building with a short flight of steps up to the arched entryway. Will let go of my waist and said, "Race you to the top," and was all the way up before I had understood and gotten up three steps. I said, "That was a dirty trick." He looked pleased with himself.

Inside, the Institute was official and solid, with guards squeaking ponderously across the galleries. There was a pedestaled sign in a metal frame which said that while many other museums have put their most valuable and beautiful pictures in Fort Knox for the duration, we are leaving ours out, because we think beauty is just as important to the American public as Mom's apple pie.

"Win the War with medieval art," said Will. "What would you like to see?"

"Medieval art will be fine." I sat down on a bench and

Will walked up and chewed gum in front of a gold and blue three-paneled painting. "I don't know what to think of that."

"It's there, but it doesn't *feel* anything," he announced after a minute.

I stared at the triptych and had the distinct impression that it felt a lot. This not-feeling-anything was an old question with Will; he was always asking himself if he or something he was examining had felt anything, as if it were a state that could be determined by some test like taking its temperature.

"Not feel anything," Clara had said. "What does he mean he doesn't feel anything? Everybody feels something."

Clara was baking a cake. This was very nice of Clara, for cake baking was not her specialty; she was more skilled at fixing mechanical objects. She went at the cake as if it were a chemistry experiment, and the results for some reason which I hadn't figured out were never just what they should have been. Mama still did most of the cooking, even if she did get cigarette ashes in the stew.

Clara scowled and measured out the baking powder. Her braid fell forward across her neck and had a little flour on it. "How can he not feel things? It sounds stupid to me."

"Anyway," I said, sitting down on the kitchen stepladder, "I'm the one that doesn't feel things."

"You feel much too much," said Clara. "It's peculiar because he's such a sensible boy. Maybe it's Grandmother," she gestured with the baking powder spoon (our grandmother was staying with us again), "the monster life in death is she/that drives men's hearts to perfidy."

"Barratry," I said.

"Calumny."

"Oy, Jesus, I've forgotten how much baking powder I put into this stupid cake. Helen, will you shut up? What happens if I put in twice as much baking powder?"

"It tastes like insect spray. You put baking powder in there; I saw you."

"Well, we have to eat it anyway; it has all the eggs. We can't get any more until next week." Clara sat down on a chair and put the bowl in her lap and began to stir.

"Anyway," I said, "Will is beginning to think that maybe we shouldn't get married because he isn't sure if he feels anything."

"What on earth does he *mean?*"

"I think he thinks a bell will ring and a little man will pop up out of the top of a machine holding a sign that says 'jealousy,' or 'hatred.' "

"I think what he simply means is that he's scared," said Clara. "You're both pretty young, you know."

"Why don't you marry him, Clara?"

"I?" said Clara in astonishment. She stopped stirring her cake and looked out across our large messy kitchen. Directly in her line of vision was a cupboard with a speckled enamel top and a container for flour with a grinder on the bottom of it. Mother in a burst of something or other had painted half of it red, and the other half of it wasn't. Clara said, "I don't want to get married. I don't mind if Mama drinks. I like it here." Then she said, "Listen, I'd like to take another year or so and get Mama straightened out . . . "

"That's easier said than done, Claire,"

"Just the same it's our *job*. We *have* to. And then," she waved the spoon and splattered cake batter on the floor, "then I would like to volunteer and become a WAC Hygienic Technician."

I said, "My God." A WAC Hygienic Technician. What a marvelously practical dream. Clara, my darling, my sweetheart, I'll bet almost nobody on earth ever had one like it. Well, you go right ahead, even though they will make you cut your braid, you become a WAC Hygienic Technician, and we will get Mama all spruced up and I will go marry nice Will and we will live an orderly life in which nobody feels too damn much. And if you ask me there is entirely too much feeling around anyway.

Clara began to stir again, and finally worked up a good, fast momentum. "You know," she yelled at me over the noise, "in a way I can understand what he's talking about, can't you?"

"No." The subject of all this came in at that point and leaned against the half red cabinet with his hands in his pockets. He had on tan pants and a turtleneck college boy sweater and those shoes that are part dark tan and part light tan. They were fashionable then, and they are the hardest shoe in the world to keep clean. Most people gave up after a couple of tries, but Will's still looked neat.

I said to him, "Will, I think I fell in love with you because you clean your saddle shoes," and he gave me a furious look. One of the troubles with Will was that he was really very bright, and understood everything.

"I read a book," I said, examining the triptych with neutral interest, "that claimed they weren't interested in perspective and proportion; they could have put them in if they wanted to. Do you think that's true?"

"No. I don't." Will scowled at the altarpiece. It had the usual mother and baby in the middle, with saints on the side, and a small kneeling family—the people who had commissioned the picture, probably—off to one corner.

Everyone in the painting looked stiff; that's the style of medieval painting, but this family off to the side looked especially so, and I wondered if Will disliked them because they held their shoulders in the same tense way he held his.

He moved back and forth in front of the picture a couple of times and then returned to stand beside my bench and reached down for my hand. "I've been thinking about us," he said in a muffled tone. "You mightn't believe . . . " His voice lost a little of its self-consciousness. Will liked to enunciate principles; he found them reassuring. One was coming now. "The things that pull us apart are the things that draw us together."

That sounds (I thought this, didn't say it) like one of the vaguer Greek philosophers.

I looked up at Will. He was very serious. One lock of his dark brown hair had strayed across his forehead. He had stopped staring at the Madonna, and concentrating on the institutional floor, scowling, his eyelashes brushing his cheeks. He looked sad. "We're so different, Helen," he said. "I've got the logic. You've got the life."

Maybe it was because I was moved that I was flip. "Well, you certainly *do* need life."

He let go of my hand and walked off and stood in front of something small and gold.

"What you like about me is what you can't stand about me," I offered helpfully.

He jerked his head at the picture. "I'm sick of aphorisms. I'm sick of talking about it." Then he came back and settled beside me; in a moment he was tickling me under my coat.

Will was full of surprises.

We scuffled and the guard arrived. He stood behind us: "Nalook, kids, if ya wanta do this kinda thing, finda park bench, the museum is for people that wantta look at the pictures."

"Have a stick of gum," said Will, sitting up, Sunday-school Will with his fresh, frank, and good face.

"I wish this war were over," he announced to the guard. Surprise on guard's face.

I realized shortly after the event that it was the fed-up-with-figuring Will who had seduced me in the bottom of the back garden.

We had walked down there one evening in late June, an evening cool and pale, fog lying in patches below us and in patches up against the house, Will quiet, one hand in pocket. I was full of a project. I said, "It would be midway between a play and a novel, Will; there would be parts that would be acted out and then the parts that could only be read silently, the ushers would pass them out . . . "

Will was supporting me with his free hand. "Helen, for God's sake, it's like everything you do: it's full of vim and vigor and for a moment it sounds great." The path down to the bottom of the garden was very steep; we went sideways part of the way because the last rain had washed the ground so clean it was hard to get a foothold. When you reached the bottom you fetched up sharply against a picket fence; there the earth met the supports of the fence in a vee and you, when you sat down, were forced to lean against them in a pleasantly dizzying way. Below us was a sharp drop into the neighbor's patio where there were two striped deck chairs and a redwood table.

"You're so damn practical, Will; nothing would ever get done in the whole world if people didn't act silly and plunge."

"Yes and no. The trouble with you is you have too much intelligence to believe something like that when you say it."

"I've got too much intelligence," I said, "I've got too little intelligence. I am too enthusiastic, like Mother. I'm not enthusiastic about anything. I'm too vague. I'm too purposeful. My hair is too red . . . "

"Oh, God," said Will. "Oh, hell. Oh, shite and onions." He sprang at me and the fence creaked; it was quite an acrobatic feat. For a minute it was just a grand free-for-all scuffle, fence going squeak, squawk; and then we wound up with my bottom against the pickets and Will on top of me; and without any warning at all I had a wave of passion sweep over me from my breast to the pit of my stomach. A wisp of fog went by like smoke behind Will's head. I thought of the mess there would be if the fence gave way and we were dumped stuck together onto the neighbor's redwood table.

Being flip about it was part of my defense, as Will pointed out afterwards when I complained about the difficulty of taking off an all-rubber girdle while lying wedged into the vee made by the fence and the ground.

I said Darling Will, Dear Will, Sweet Will, Honey Will. Will said nothing at all that I can remember. The fence squeaked; and, far away, a sign of a quiet foggy night, I heard the fog horns.

It was funny afterwards; I had wondered for a minute whether Will would act self-conscious or embarrassed, but he was perfectly practical and gentle, helping me to swivel around so my feet were against the fence and my head uphill. We lay on our backs and looked at the sky. A hole formed in the cloud, a watery star blinked. Will had a cigarette and gave me one.

"Do you want to get married?" he asked finally, in a level voice.

I began to laugh. I blew cigarette smoke straight up into the sky and felt around until I found his hand and squeezed it, and blew more smoke out. Without realizing it, I had been influenced by all the stories of men leaving girls after they have gotten the all-rubber girdle off. Then I turned over and kissed him. I suppose he thought that was an answer. He said gloomily, "We are both a little young, of course."

We finally sat up and I felt around on the ground until I found the girdle and Will zipped up his pants, a sound which seemed awfully loud in the still, foggy night, and then we started up the path, Will first and me holding on to his belt and singing "Deep Purple." It was a highly inappropriate song for Berkeley, where most of our summer evenings were like this one, white and spooky.

When we arrived in the high-ceilinged, dark, badly lit living room Clara was there, working away on the mouse's cage. The mouse was in her pocket. She had bought the mouse for a scientific purpose, but now it was a pet and it was not allowed to breed or to be the subject of experiments.

She was doing something with pliers to the wheel on which the mouse used to race. Clara said that the mouse had a high metabolism and wouldn't live long.

I have no idea what made me say it. "Guess what, Claire, Will asked me to marry him."

I knew as the words came out and bumped against the baronial ceiling that it wasn't even true; Will had said only, "Do *you* want to get married," an inquiry based on embarrassment, with no personal commitment behind it. Clara said, "Wow!" and scooped the mouse from her pocket into the cage and slammed the door on her. Then she stood up, with her face ready for kissing. Clara liked to go to movies; that must have been where she got the idea of the kiss. She read only the books that I read aloud to her, and we had never known anybody who had gotten engaged.

I had felt Will's arm go stiff and saw him turn his face, with all the lines etched, to Clara to be kissed. I quickly said, "You mustn't take me seriously, Claire; it was only a joke."

"A joke!" said Clara, appalled. She had grown up in Bohemia, but she loved order and arrangement.

"We were just talking. It was silly. I'm sorry I said it; I was teasing."

Clara said seriously, "I think you should," and picked up the mouse cage. She and I and mouse went up the stairs, bump, clatter; halfway up I turned and saw Will standing below us with the muscles of his face still looking as if they had been chopped out of ice. I said, "Will, turn off the lights, will you," and then I said, "Good night, Will."

He said, "Good night, Helen," very quietly. I knew he hated that feeling that the ground had begun to move out from under him.

Will and I were in the restaurant of the Art Institute.

It was a most attractive restaurant, with a pool in the center of it which reminded me of the pool in front of our house, except that this one was clean and made of white marble and had large orange carp in it and well-cultivated lilies.

Will said, "It's too cold to talk here," but after we had gotten seated we both found that it wasn't. The place was a courtyard, which was protected. I had a dish of ice cream, and hunched over it.

I could tell from the way he stirred his coffee that Will was planning another attack. "I don't think you should go to Washington and see your mother," he said finally.

"She needs me. I can help her."

"She doesn't really want you there."

Will had said that during the hassle before Mother left. "She doesn't really want you hanging on to her. She wants to go off by herself." Now I said, "It seems funny to say it, when she lets herself go to pieces so, but she really does have pride, and she has delicacy, too; she's too proud to appeal to us. Just the same the idea gets across in her letters."

"What are you going to do?"

"Feel my way along. See her and see how she is."

He made a noise in the back of his throat. I said, "Sometimes I don't understand you. Anybody can see why you think Mama's a trial. But you're nice to your own mother."

"My mother may be simple, but she's a responsible person."

After that we both ate in silence for a while. He said, "I don't know why I put up with you; sometimes I want to wring your neck."

It would have been too damned hideously mean to say, Will, Clara and I both felt crummy after we sent Mama off into the night and across the country, and we blamed you.

It had been more my idea than Will's. Not really any of it had been Clara's.

Will and I had moved through the museum and were now sitting in front of the most gorgeous Renoir in the universe; it had everything one wants from a Renoir. Pink

light, heat, bees, fragrant grass, languor, heat-flushed woman flesh, soft red hair coming down. A different world of
love and threatlessness.

"You see," said Will. "You do see, don't you? You see
why I left it to the last."

I see, Will. "It's beautiful."

"It reminds me of you," he said, squeezing under the
leopard coat. "That's the way I feel about you."

Oh nice, Will. Thank you so much.

But the woman in that picture is my mother. No, not
really, but there's something there, the red hair, the droopy-
eyedness. She's fatter than my mother; she's more sure of
herself than my mother. She doesn't drink. She sits there,
exuding life from under her armpits. That part is like
Mother. I look something like my mother, that's why Will
thinks I'm there. I'm sorry, Will.

"What?"

"It's perfectly lovely."

Will and I could love each other better if we were not
always on different stages of the wheel. It's not exactly that
we're traveling on different tracks; maybe we are, but, more
important, we're out of synch. Here is Will feeling young
and wild; here am I feeling old and tired. Each of us has
borrowed the other one's personality, like an old married
couple. Maybe that's what we are.

Will sat behind me on the marble bench, squeezed me
under my coat, murmured into my ear, blew down the back
of my neck. "Oh, God. Oh, God, how beautiful. Oh, God, is
that gorgeous. Darling, do I want to make love to you."

Will's hands were warm, they touched my breasts under
my coat. He smelled good. His starched shoulder was crisp.
His cheek brushed my hair.

He said, "Darling, let's go to a hotel."

It's possible, I said to myself, but it seems stinking, to postpone this decision by saying I have the curse. I'd rather die than postpone this by telling Will I have the curse.

Will. Dear. Don't.

In point of fact, Will, I simply don't know how I feel. When people say that, they don't usually mean it. But when I say it now, I do, honestly, truly not know how I feel. My mind is a big pale room; all my emotions and opinions are being sucked into it. Think of it as a roomful of steam. Think of it as the roof of a train station, full of smoke, clouds, pigeons, soot. Think of it as chaos. Think of me as an idiot. Think of me as a bitch.

Let's wait until we're forty-five. When we're forty-five, Will, relations between us will be as soothing as an old sock; we'll never fight; we won't worry about life because we'll understand it all. Who wants life the antimagnetic force at the age of forty-five? Will, I promise you, when we are forty-five we'll always feel the same thing at the same moment; I'll go to a hotel with you then.

I stood up and lied, "The guard is going to throw us out."

We got off our bench and turned to go, Will with his arm still around me. He didn't yet realize that he had been snubbed, and made a big silly thing out of each occasion when a piece of sculpture loomed up and we had to separate to go around it. When we got outside and on the steps we paused and looked down them and I said, "I really ought to go on the train which leaves at five-thirty; Mother's boyfriend says she's in pretty bad shape." This was as much of a lie as the curse would have been, only not as nasty. Mother's boyfriend had said that he could hold her together until I got there.

Will let go of my waist, which he had clasped again after we got through the museum door. "God. Christ. My aching ass. Your mother."

"Shit," I said. "You forgot shit." There was no getting around it; I wanted to fight with Will. I put my hand into my pocket. I said, "Listen, I know you hate my mother, and I can understand why. But you make her worse; you make her vaguer and more enthusiastic. I've seen it happen."

Will said, "Nuts. I suppose I made her try to do herself in too. How about her pride and her delicate feelings then? That was a pretty delicate scene, that delicate scene." He's made his point, but he carries on, "Pretty proud, too. Pretty proud and delicate, that scene."

SCENE: The upstairs hall of our house, complete with balcony for looking down on mother's boyfriends.

Clara and I emerge from our room, I in a blue and white flannel bathrobe, Clara in an old chemistry smock which she wears instead of a bathrobe. Morning. Light struggles dustily through imitation Gothic windows. Quite a while since anybody has washed them.

Clara: (sniffs, bends, rises, sniffs) What in the name of suffering Caesar is that ghastly, awful, horrible smell?

Clara is a schoolgirl and swears a schoolgirl oath. Both she and I sniff around for a while. Finally Will emerges from his room, left. He wears khaki pants and a blue and white striped shirt, since he doesn't own a bathrobe, because he has given his bathrobe to me and I am wearing it now.

Clara: Something smells here.

Oh, well, And on and on. Finally we open (we do not have to break down) the door to Mother's room. The horrible smell, I should say right here, is not the smell of gas, but that of human waste products. Shit, if you prefer. And vomit.

The windows of Mother's room are shut tight and the casement fasteners fastened. One window shade three quarters of the way down, one a third. Bed a heaped mess of clothes—no, not clothes; blankets, white terry-cloth spread, sheet with a great rip in it, with my mother arched catty-corner across the whole of it, her arms up and wide, like the crucified Jesus. Her face looks peaceful except for the lips drawn up at the corners, exposing the little eyeteeth.

There is an empty bottle of sleeping pills and a note on the dressing table. Mother took sleeping pills because they are reputed to be painless. Maybe they are. I wouldn't care to try them.

The note says: "Dear Helen and Clara: I am sorry that we don't get on. It is my fault. Lovingly, your mother."

Later I found, but did not show to Will, the rough drafts of the note.

Some of the versions went, I am sorry that I have been a bad mother; I am sorry that I have not given satisfaction; I am sorry that I did not come to your graduation. Across the bottom of this last one was written, in the kind of scribble that you might do with your eyes closed, "I hate myself."

Clara and I burned the bedding. Mother never asked what had happened to it.

"You can't judge her by what you see now, Will. She's had a bad time."

"Not as bad as you."

"No, it was worse for her."

We were sitting on the steps of the museum, looking down into the windy street. Will said, "Helen, she's bad news; she's headed off the cliff; you've got to scrap her."

"You talk as if she were an old car; for God's sake, she's my mother."

He said, "Her whole world and everything in it failed; it's not part of your story at all." He fished around in his pants pocket and found the package of chewing gum: he offered me a stick and took one himself. "And now it's all fallen apart and she drinks to keep up the old warm thrill. It's not your affair; let her drink herself into a quaking mass and shovel it into an urn and send it to Novky-novgorod or some place."

He chewed ferociously. I said, "The more rational you are the less I am. It's no good, I have to see if I can get her straightened out."

We sat and chewed gum and stared down into the street. The sun was getting low and the shadows were long and cold; they moved in front of the cars that came windily by, churning up chewing gum wrappers.

"So you won't stay in Chicago."

"I don't think I should."

"How about just a little while?"

"If I'm going to go, Will, I'd better do it."

He stood up and gave me his elbow, as if he were going to escort me into the black and white ball. As we went down the steps he said, "The next girl I get is going to have a completely different kind of insanity." We got into the car without speaking and he started it with a venomous jab.

"Get your bags," he said. "I'll drive you to the other station."

Suddenly I couldn't stand any more. "No." I tried to

soften it. "I want to take a bath. You can get a bath there for a quarter." That sounded so peculiar that I just let it lie. If Will knew anything about train schedules he knew that I didn't have *time* for a bath.

When we got to the station he pulled into a bus stop and said, "Well, Helen, good-bye."

I said, "Well, Will, good-bye." He had his hand out, resting on the steering wheel and I looked at it, a capable hand, small and clenched.

I said, "It's silly for us to fight about my mother. That's just one of the things about me you have to take, like if I were cross-eyed."

He was silent, staring out of the windshield of the car, and made me feel he knew that my mother wasn't really the issue between us.

He said, "I wish I'd never met you." Oh, God, poor Will. There are lots of things I wish had never happened to me. The traffic screeched by us and people ran, clunking their suitcases and cartons hopelessly along with them. There was a cloud of pigeons that came messily down every time the traffic was stopped by a light somewhere out on the street. I reached out to touch Will's hand and he jerked it away. A bus pulled up behind us and began to honk for its parking place. I kissed him on the cheek and said, "I'll write to you." He didn't respond at all. Then I opened the door of the car and got out, with the bus blatting and squawking behind me, and I shut the car door and ran up the approach to the station. The pigeons all rose as I came dashing up, and one of them got me on the sleeve of Mama's old leopard-skin coat.

Chapter VI

I SAT in Chicago's Western Pacific station waiting room on a large, hard, uncomfortable bench.

What I was supposed to do now was fairly complicated. I had to change train stations as well as trains; trains going east from Chicago left from another, completely different, station. I sat on my bench and thought about this, and, without much warning, it seemed unmanageable.

My suitcase was in a locker; I must go collect it, then run up or down a lot of stairs, then out to find a cab, after that . . .

How on earth, as Grandmother would be delighted to ask me, had I ever managed anything, *any*thing at all? If my head were not attached to my shoulders . . . Fortunately, God doesn't make people with detachable heads; Helen, you're safe.

I had been in Chicago only part of a day. I'd arrived here at eight o'clock this morning; it was four-thirty now. It felt like a week.

There were an awful lot of people in this station who looked just as dislocated as I felt. Perhaps we had all ended up here by a process of mutual attraction; all of us who couldn't manage life's details had come to sit, or lie, or camp in this station together, whole families of us, babies in strollers, barricaded by suitcases . . .

Helen, you absolutely must get up and get cracking.

I reached into my purse, in the mirror compartment, where I had put the locker key; new kind of panic: no locker key.

I am going to miss that train.

At a time like this, all you can do is have a cigarette.

Finally I found my locker key and pushed myself and my suitcase up some stairs, out to the cab stand, and, by a combination of pleading and shoving, into a cab, an old, tired, green-and-yellow Plymouth, which was driven by an exceptionally careful cab driver who just managed to miss every green light.

I leaned in a corner of his cab smoking hard.

I'd had six cigarettes in the last half hour.

Ever since Daddy died, I'd had a recurrent dream about missing a train. There must be a connection between death and trains; I didn't know what it was.

"In Davenport, Iowa," the soldier who was sharing a cab with me said, "we have a four-city interstate bus system."

At the new station I presented the cab driver with three dollars, staggered through people greeting and being greeted, down miles of echoing vault, past dress models revolving on pedestals, ads for razor blades projected on walls, finally to a gate labeled *The Shenandoan—Washington, Baltimore, New York.* The gate was closed, however, and a man on a stepladder was taking the letters out of the board where the sleeping car locations had been posted.

I put my suitcase down and sat on it.

That dream about missing trains is supposed to be very common. I read an article about it once. In the most frequent form you're stuck, you can't move, you're expecting something.

It's supposed, really, to be a sex dream, so the something that you're expecting isn't necessarily bad.

The Davenport, Iowa, soldier had also missed his train, and was casting admiring looks at me.

"Go away," I said to him, not out loud, of course, as he still hadn't moved. He got out his pack of cigarettes; he was going to come over and offer me one. "Stay away."

Something hit me a clap between the shoulder blades. "Well, Butchie," said a familiar voice, "you seem to have missed your train."

O'Connell was wearing a tan raincoat, his sling, and a forage cap. He looked sweet. "Came down to see you off," he said. "But you didn't go."

"How did you know what train?"

"There are only two trains a day to Washington, Butch; I took a chance." He extended a package wrapped in tissue paper. "I even bought you a present."

I was standing up now, trying to remind myself what he looked like. I had a curious conviction that I couldn't remember what color his eyes were. I felt lightheaded; the station seemed to be swaying slightly. "You shouldn't have. Bought me anything."

"Don't worry. It's not the Hope Diamond."

When I didn't move he unwrapped the package himself and put it in my hand. It was a souvenir glass ashtray with a gold picture on its bottom of the Merchandise Mart. Over this, in florid script, was my name, or somebody's name: *Butchie.* Well, I thought, I really don't care whether you call them all Butchie or not.

"God-awful, isn't it?" O'Connell said, hopefully.

"I like it."

"Honest? Yeah, well . . . it shows I was thinking about you."

"When did you get in?"

"An hour and a half ago . . . just wanted you to know, before you went to Washington . . . But you didn't go."

Don't pretend you didn't know I wouldn't. I bet you arranged it.

He and I stood and looked at each other. There was a certain amount of embarrassment around, oddly.

"Look, all I really intended was to come see you off. And now we've seen each other, why, you go slope off to the Salvation Army or wherever; I'll understand. I'd like it if you would have dinner with me, but, Butch, you go slope off if you want to."

Well, thank you so excessively much. Oh, for God's sweet sake.

I said, "Let's have dinner."

He transformed himself into the old, upbeat O'Connell. He gave me a big squeeze with his good arm and then winced, because the shock apparently translated itself to his bad one. He said, "What do you want, dear. Do you want a big vulgar restaurant or do you want a squeaky arty restaurant? How about a charming expensive one?" He squeezed again, and winced again; when I looked doubtful he said, "Come on, let's spend money. What else is money for?'"

"You could save it for your old age."

"The hell with my old age, you got to live now; old age may find you after the lid has gone off everything."

We had arrived at the taxi stand; I said, "O'Connell, there aren't any taxis anywhere in Chicago."

"The hell with that too." He pushed his way past the wide hips of the suitcase sitters.

A taxi came up and he got the door open before any of the fat ladies waiting for cabs had dismounted. "Excuse me, madam," he said to the nearest one, "this lady has got to see her obstetrician right way." And he shoved me into the cab with his knee, which was excusable since he could use only one arm.

"You'll love this place," he said, having mispronounced a French name for the cabdriver. "This is not a place for Mom's apple pie and the greater American values. It's for whores and their business managers."

"Thanks loads."

The restaurant had a striped awning and a doorman. I objected that I wasn't dressed for such a place, but O'Connell said my fur coat would see me through. "That and money. What they really like in these joints is money."

After we had ordered, he sat back, holding the ostentatious gold menu. He was a little old to be a lieutenant; otherwise he didn't look out of place in these surroundings. His dark quick Irish face could have been that of almost anybody, any rising American.

"Well, how about it, Butch?" he asked enthusiastically, "Did I do all right? Did I get you a cab?"

"You did all right."

He put his hand, square and with square freckles across the back, next to mine on the table. He looked down at our aligned hands and said, "Ah, Christ, Butch, I don't know," and took his away.

"Lissen, at the Fairfield plant there was this feeble-minded black guy that use to hang around outside the gate. His wife had died in a car accident. Nothing to do about unions or the race question or anything, but he wanted to tell people about it. He used to start out, 'Parmme sir, I know that you white and I colored . . . ' and then he would tell his story."

I waited, to see what point O'Connell was going to make. "Well," he said, "I feel like saying, 'Parmme, Miss; I know that you young and I old . . . ' "

"Don't be silly." I am cross with you, O'Connell.

He scowled at the three piece orchestra, which had appeared at the other end of the restaurant. "At that Fairfield plant we had this girls' union singing combo."

"What's a girls' union singing combo?"

"They were supposed to sing union songs. At meetings and stuff. Christ, were they awful. They used to lean on each other and imitate Bonnie Baker and sing 'Oh, Johnny, how you can love.' "

"Does your wife sing?"

"Christ!"

"It would be great. You could sing socialist songs together."

O'Connell sat back, looking despondent. After a while he said, "Anyway, this bunch of stupid singing babes, they wrecked a whole organizing campaign for me. You know that song that goes 'Oh you can't scare me, I'm stickin to the union'; well they changed the words to 'Oh you can't scare me I'm screwin to the union.' No reason that I could figure out. The girls said none of them ever heard of anything dirty like that."

Both of us had ordered pressed duck, which arrived with two waiters and a great deal of paraphernalia. O'Connell watched gloomily. "Bunch of gold-plated shit." He moved around in his seat, and I got the idea that his shoulder was hurting him again. That's right, feel guilty.

"Is something the matter dear?"

No, what could possibly be the matter.

"I've thought of you, of course. It's funny, because I've had dozens of girls."

Well, thanks.

"I wondered afterward, if you'll excuse me raising it, why you did it. And I thought it was as much my fault, though can't explain why. Couldn't ever explain it to another guy, anyway.

"And then, anyway, I felt responsible, or something. And also there's special kinds of attraction. And then extra special kinds, if you know what I mean."

Oh, yes, I know what you mean.

"And so I found I ended up feeling guilty about it somehow, Butch. And also . . . don't know . . . kind of a feeling that that's something . . . sounds screwy, but an event like that binds people together."

Yes. Yes.

"But I don't know dear. Then there's the fact that I'm old and you're young."

Now you are barking up the wrong tree, O'Connell.

Oh, for the love of God. O'Connell, for Christ's sake. You haven't any right to exist. There you sit, clogging up my life, with your wife that you do not care about and

and your CIO that I do not care about and your age that I do not care about. Anybody could tell me, and anybody would be glad to, free, that it will be nothing but trouble.

"Lets talk about the CIO."

"What's the matter with you dear? You're so sour on the movement?"

"You can't reform me."

"I'm not reforming you. I like you the way you are."

Don't do that. Talk about the CIO.

"You got something. Don't know what it is." He examined the piece of duck which was on the end of his fork. "Cardboard with brandy sauce. Do you like it?"

"It's all right."

"High hearted youth comes not again," he said very glumly. I could feel him watching me out of the corner of his eye, but I refused to react to the quotation. "Look, Butch," he said more cheerfully after a minute, "after this war there's going to be the hell of the most awful uprising; do you know it?"

For the first time in my life I could imagine it, the socialist upheaval that my mother's pamphlets talked about. When O'Connell described it, it seemed real; I could see him in an old battered automobile, drinking Cokes and giving orders. Marshalling his boys, and his girls' union combo.

O'Connell said, "Listen, babe, I don't know how it will happen. All I know is that it's got to.

"Some things," he said, "are real and you can't get away from them, and when you try they follow around after you saying look at me, I'm real, you can't get away from me. Here I am, real, and there's not a damn thing in the world you can do about it.

"What the hell, Butch," O'Connell said, "you're with me."

I tried hard not to give in. "Maybe."

"Hell on wheels, maybe. You can't dismiss life with maybe. That's life; you can't say maybe to life."

No, you can't.

I looked down at O'Connell's hand and said, "You have square freckles on the backs of your hands."

O'Connell said, "You're with me, Butch," and put his hand on top of mine. And I knew then that was it.

I said, "Yes. I am." I didn't have to add: I'll stay with you tonight. We both knew what I meant.

Chapter VII

O'CONNELL AND I found a room at the Hotel Roseleen. It was the fifth hotel we had tried and O'Connell said, squinting at the turquoise paint applied so thickly that it had bubbles in it, at the skinny turquoise-painted radiator with iron roses in relief on the legs and on the top of the finials, at the window shade frayed across the bottom and slightly askew, at the chenille spread with most of the tufts rubbed off, "Butch, that old Roseleen has been having a hard time lately. My Gawd." He threw his suitcase on the foot of the bed. "Well, baby, come give us a kiss."

O'Connell stripped me of my clothes quickly. He was very good with buttons.

I did not either love him or not love him when we were both naked in the middle of the room. The rug was gritty and threadbare. I thought about how dirty my feet were getting. "Ah, baby, darling," O'Connell said, and put his arms around me. His belly stuck out a little and was warm. I said to myself oh, well, what the hell. I had never slept with anybody except Will and that had had a proper and sacramental quality to it, even in the fog at the bottom of the garden. O'Connell steered me toward the limp chenille bed, kicking my shoes out of the way. On his path there he reached out a hand and twitched the window shade down another notch.

O'Connell and I stayed in the Hotel Roseleen for two and a half weeks. We stayed there more or less together. He went home for varying periods of time—sometimes at night, sometimes in the daytime. He also went to work, which he did in days grouped in threes—Monday, Tuesday, Wednesday, then off two days, and so forth. It was all very confusing, involving as it did juggling the army, his wife, whose name was Mary Frances, and me. I lost track of day and night. All hours and occasions looked much the same, with the room painted that ridiculous dark bubbly color that drank up all the daylight, with the window opening out onto an air shaft where people threw paper cups and condoms. Sometimes I slept in the daytime and sometimes I slept at night. It occurred to me that I had been very tired for a long time.

But I didn't just stare at the blue room in a state of suspended animation waiting for O'Connell to materialize in the bed next to me. I walked around Chicago, sometimes in the daytime, sometimes at night. I went and looked at monuments. I sat on the beach wearing my prostitute's fur coat and watched the water come slapping in. It was nothing like the Pacific Ocean. I drifted for hours around department stores, taking in the smells, which were so different from those of the Roseleen, the self-indulgent, padded, department-store atmosphere, which still flourished in spite of the war and which seemed to be the opposite of the war or of any kind of real life; it was the most total fantasy in the world, that small enclosure of department store in which everything smelled new.

"What have you been thinking about, Butchie?" O'Connell asked.

"I've been thinking about the end of the world," I said, which was mean of me, because of course that wasn't an answer. O'Connell was much better than Will about picking up clues like that. He had a natural curiosity and he was interested in how people's minds worked. "All those things in the china department at Marshall Field will come sliding off the shelf," I said. There had been a row of blue pots with tight-fitting lids at the edge of a display. I had imagined the catastrophe clearly: the wall bulging, glass shelf tilting, all those perfume pots ending in a heap of bright shards, one of them just the right size and shape to put in a brooch. I could pick it up, mount it, and wear it. Perhaps I could train myself in actions like that: *How to Profit From Disaster*: you can come out on top, no matter what life hands you, learn to crack the nut and suck the meat. I moved my head so that I lay with the crown of my head under O'Connell's chin.

"Listen, Butch," he said, "you've been spending too much time by yourself. The end of the world, you can't fool me. The end of the world *is* a light in the sky."

"Horizon to horizon," I said. "Cracking it open like an eggshell."

"And then the dead pushing aside the gravestones and standing up."

"That's a Catholic version," I objected. "All I've got is

the California one. What we know about are earthquakes.
The crack appears under the house and drinks it."

O'Connell shifted his arm. "You're worried about your
dear old mama, aren't you, dear?"

O'Connell, of course I am worried about my old mama,
since the legend for this year is that I'm out here on the
edge of America's heartland riding trains and screwing
old men so that I can get my mother, my beautiful, feeble-
minded, insubstantial and unsatisfactory, unreliable and
loving mother back. Move over on the bed, O'Connell, my
darling, till I tell you about my mother and the earthquake.

She wasn't ever frightened of things like that, things
that were really frightening. I think she figured: why waste
your energies on that, what everyone agrees is worth getting upset about. She thought it was maybe a little vulgar
to care about such a thing. She sat in her chair looking
thoughtful while the house creaked and the clock bonged
and she said, "Each of us must remember what she is thinking now, girls; it is a kind of game, it is a way of getting at
the very heart of what you feel about things." And as soon
as the tremor had passed she made Clara and me get paper
and pencil and write down all the thoughts we'd had while
the earthquake was shaking.

O'Connell lay on his back staring at the ceiling. The
light fixture was frosted glass with clear glass lilies on it.
There was only one light bulb although there were sockets
for four, and there was a colony of dead flies in the cone
of the glass shade. "Catholics know about the end of the
world from being poor," said O'Connell. "That's what the
end of the world will be. The most crowded-ever slum. No
place to sit down. Butchie, of course I knew your mama
pretty well. I guess you knew that."

That day, in addition to looking at the dishes in Marshall Field, I had been to the library and had read four issues of *Time* magazine and a bunch of Chicago papers. I had eaten lunch on a small noisy traffic island across from the museum and had asked myself what I was doing in Chicago.

When O'Connell said this about my mother I thought: oh, that's one thing that I'm doing here. That remark of O'Connell's had a strange effect. It tightened something under my diaphragm, a center where string or wire gathered in a knot. It felt as if six pieces of something coincided at that one point; as if O'Connell had reached his hand in there, taken the knot, given it a twist.

The population of the Hotel Roseleen was 70 percent servicemen and their dates, 20 percent prostitutes, and 10 percent old people who had no other place to live. The prostitutes and old people were a permanent population among whom I began to recognize some faces. There was the bosomy old prostitute with the hat made of black-and-white-checked silk, there was the old man in the tan spotted raincoat, there was the blond prostitute who looked like me, all except for the fur jacket. There was the retarded old man with the simple idiot's face and the aimless, well-meaning, blue pig-eyes who always asked the same question: "Hello lady. Howsa *lady* tonight?" The servicemen were different every night and their girls did not fit any pattern. Some of them were quiet and looked at the floor and some were drunk and giggled and some held on to the serviceman's arm. Any servicemen who arrived with the local prostitutes I counted as prostitutes' dates, not as servicemen. There were always some servicemen in the bathroom about two in the morning throwing up.

We did not have a private bathroom in the Hotel Rose-leen. There was a men's bathroom in which I could hear the servicemen throwing up at 2 a.m. ("Jesus, Butchie," O'Connell said, "you'd better not stand in that shortest route between the door and the can in there; you're liable to get knocked down.") And there was a women's bath-room in which I sometimes found people crying and where once somebody fainted. I dragged her out in the hall by her shoulders and her boyfriend came and picked her up and carried her into their room.

That night I cried and told O'Connell I had to leave Chicago and go on to Washington.

"I know you do, Butchie." He was smoking a cigarette, looking up at the ceiling and gulping smoke rings up at the frosted glass fixture with the lilies on it. "I am not only the only human male in captivity with three balls; I am *ab*solutely the only one who can do that lying on my back. What, babe, you mean you never noticed?" O'Connell made a motion as if he were going to push down the sheet. I had noticed that O'Connell made dirty or raucous remarks when I raised serious questions. "The only thing is—may-be three days longer? Four? Oh, hell, babe, of course I shouldn't . . . beautiful babe like you . . . "

I didn't try to figure out what O'Connell really thought about me. My father had died when I was thirteen. Thir-teen was certainly old enough for me to have been watch-ing him and absorbing information on what men were like. But my father had been away for two years before that, and maybe I had been too busy watching and wondering about my mother to pay attention to my father. I didn't know much about men.

O'Connell looked sad; but, I thought, he looked puzzled

as well. He moved his eyebrows around and opened and closed his mouth like a fish, sending the smoke rings up lazily. He did it by a sudden contraction of the diaphragm.

> *"I've got no pence to lend*
> *And no pence to spend*
> *And no pence to send home to my wife . . . "*

The whore upstairs had her radio turned on loud again. I think she did this when she was alone, but maybe she had a customer who needed the rhythm to make him feel less self-conscious.

I took O'Connell's hard, freckled, square-fingernailed hand in mine. I really liked O'Connell's hands. There were several things I could do when I wanted to make myself feel that I couldn't live without O'Connell, and holding hands with him was one of the simpler ones.

The next night was the night we had the fire in the Hotel Roseleen. It was three-thirty in the morning; I had been asleep. O'Connell was asleep too. He was a good sleeper and snored when he lay on his back.

I was still not used to sleeping in the same bed with someone. It seemed both romantic and awkward. O'Connell was big and heavy and took up lots of room. The bed sagged noisily on his side; sometimes I woke up and thought that it was like lying on the roof of a house. But other times this sleeping together in the same bed seemed important because it was part of Chicago, part of the way I had decided to do things when I broke my journey there.

I was only lightly asleep, and I woke up when a voice yelled "Fire!" and feet pounded along the hall upstairs and something scraped like furniture being moved.

I put on my flannel bathrobe with red piping and O'Connell put on his checked bathrobe with the woven cord. I had to go to the bathroom. We were groggy, and bumped into each other. We didn't turn on the light. Perhaps we both had a confused idea about electricity and fires.

O'Connell opened the door into the hall, and let in an enormous gulp of smoke like a bank of San Francisco fog, but stinging, tight, dark blue, making haloes around the hall lights, traveling across our room in a greasy coil the same height as the airshaft window, which it was heading for in its effort to get out.

"Jesus H. Christ," said O'Connell. He shut the door quickly. The trail of smoke flattened and hung in the air at eye level. In just that moment all the air in the room had gotten blue and cottony. I looked down at my feet and saw that what I remembered from girl scouts was true: the smoke is less dense toward the floor.

"O'Connell," I said.

I am not afraid at all of boats and the ocean and not much so of earthquakes or cars, but I discovered I was very much afraid of fire. I moved my fingers; they had gone numb at the tips. My throat hurt. I listened for the crackling sound fire makes or for screams; I heard neither. The bumping continued. There were more feet in the hall. A window rasped in the room above us, another one sounded across the hall, a door slammed. Somebody said: "Oh shit." O'Connell went to the window and opened it all the way. I followed him so I could lean against him while we looked out, first down and then up. I had had that light-well scene pretty well fixed in my mind, and it was just as I had remembered it: three stories below us, the bottom of the light well. There was no exit from it and that was not the ground floor of the hotel. Five stories above us, the sky. The bottom of the well was made of glass and metal and was very dirty.

"Out the door, then, Butchie," said O'Connell. He soaked two washclothes in the washbasin and wrung them out and we tied face masks for ourselves. Just before we went out the door O'Connell kissed me behind the ear.

The smoke in the hall was heavy and sticky. I remembered pictures in *Time* magazine of commando training, the soldiers inching along on their stomachs. I thought: I suppose they had bullets going by overhead. I looked at the floor. It was made of hexagonal tiles and was dirty. I tried not to breathe. We bumped into someone. The noises upstairs got worse; someone was yelling, Oh, my God. Oh Jesus. Oh, dear lord. Oh Jesus. O'Connell found the handle of the door to the fire stairs.

We went down the stairs very fast. There were people above us and people below us, but not a lot of people, not the whole population of the Hotel Roseleen, going down those metal stairs. The stairs made a hollow metallic sound that reminded me of recess at school.

The Hotel Roseleen's lobby had a desk, a framed picture of an Indian and a horse, an oilcloth couch. We reached the lobby at the same moment as the fire department. O'Connell maneuvered me around the hoses and running firemen and out into the street.

There we leaned against a brick wall. We pulled off the washcloths. I wrung mine out and put it in my pocket. It was cold and there were a lot of people standing in a silent huddle.

A broad finger of light grew up the front of the hotel, outlining the angles of the Hotel Roseleen's blacked-out sign. The bricks that we were leaning against were wet and had a condensation mark along a seam; I could feel this through my bathrobe. I put my hand inside O'Connell's and pushed both of our hands into his bathrobe pocket. The fire engine grew a ladder, which teetered its way up toward the hotel's top floor. Another siren sounded in the distance. A lot of people came out of the Roseleen's front door. Some of them were crying.

We stood by the wall for two hours and talked to various people: a soldier and his girl, an old lady with stained white hair, the feeble-minded man, whose scaly blue feet were completely bare.

"Aren't your feet cold?" I asked him.

"You are a nice *lady,*" he said.

Finally the firemen brought out a stretcher with a rolled up package on it. The old lady told us that it was the prostitute who had worn the checked silk hat. No one asked how she knew this. The firemen curled their hoses through the front door. A fireman with a badge over his heart told us that we could go back in unless we lived on the tenth floor, and O'Connell and I did not.

I had been standing inside O'Connell's bathrobe because we were both cold. I untangled myself and we went into the hotel, stepping over the puddles in the lobby.

Our room was damp and smoky and the bed very cold. "Were you scared, Butch?" O'Connell asked.

"At first," I said. "At first I was really scared." Daylight was outlining itself against the light-well window.

I went to sleep with one hand under the small of O'Connell's back, and dreamed about my mother. I was chasing her down a long Chicago street under a streetlight that moved with us as we ran.

When I thrashed around trying to get away from the dream I partly awakened O'Connell, who rolled over with his back to me and said: "Don't ever leave me, Butch." I thought: what a really dumb thing to say. Then I put my hand under him again and went back to sleep.

"What do you think you can do for her, Butch? Why exactly are you going back there?" O'Connell and I were at breakfast. Somehow the fire and the excitement of the night before had opened up the question of my mother between us.

"She's scared. She's upset. She needs me." I stared at the chrome napkin holder and made faces at myself. I had big purple circles under my eyes. I had a sore throat.

O'Connell didn't say anything, for which I was grateful. Will would have told me that that was a good line, and would have accused my mother of emotional blackmail. "We sort of made her go East," I said. "You see, I had this boyfriend . . ." And I told O'Connell about the long interview, late at night, in the high-ceilinged Berkeley living room. Only one light on, in the standing lamp on the staircase landing, my mother leaning back in the decaying old Morris chair, her hair all over the place, wearing her orange kimono with the green circles on it. She had a glass of whisky in one hand and the bottle on the table beside that. The light from the landing shone on her face from one side and lit up the regular messy waves in her red hair. She kept taking deep drinks of her rye—not her usual drink but all we'd been able to get at the liquor store that night— and saying: "Yes, of course. I see. Of course I understand. I would have a *much* better chance of starting a new life somewhere else. Washington is a *fine* idea. I have friends in Washington. Washington will be a new start. I always believe in new starts, don't you?" She refilled her glass and said, "Will, I thought you didn't understand me, but of course I see that I was wrong. This job you have arranged in Washington sounds *perfect*. You *do* think about me. I am very ungrateful. It is exactly what I needed, and the farther away from the scene of my past defeats, as the poet says . . . " She turned toward Will whom she hadn't really been addressing until now and said, "Do you really think I will be good at selling dresses? I never thought of myself that way. But if you think so . . . "

"You'll be good, Selma," Will said, sounding not too convinced. Will's second cousin owned a specialty shop in one of the Washington hotels. Will had applied pressure. But he was a little sheepish about it. He admitted that he wanted primarily to get my mother out of the way. He said that it would be better for her and better for me and Clara. He said that the ideal thing would have been to send her off for a cure. But, he said, if Clara and I wouldn't hear of it . . . Will had become very concerned with our affairs since he started sleeping with me. He checked up on lots of things. He kept a chart of when my menstrual periods were due and asked me about them each month.

Clara was sitting on the steps with her back to the lamp. I couldn't see her face. The light caught her blond hair, which was done in one braid over her left shoulder.

"Darling Mama," said Clara, "don't go if you don't want to."

"But I do." Mama took a big gulp of whisky and splashed some down the front of her kimono. "Really. It will be new. A new start. A new *me*. How good of you all to . . . "

"Jesus, poor Sel," said O'Connell. "Poor everybody." The waitress arrived with our eggs. O'Connell put on lots of salt and pepper and messed his egg around. "So when did the boozing start up again?"

"Oh, right away, I guess. Will's cousin was furious." I

remembered Will getting that letter, ripping it open with one finger so that the envelope was topped with angry shredded scallops, throwing the letter at me as if it were a hot ingot. "So what the hell did you expect?" I had said to him. Knowing all the while that I was the one who had done it to my mother. Not really Will at all. Will wasn't her child and I was. I had pushed her out of her own house because she was ashamed and guilty and wanted to please.

"Were you in love with my mother?" I asked O'Connell.

He ate a big mouthful of egg and buttered some toast. "Butchie. That is one hell of a question."

It was, and I knew it. If O'Connell said no, he was a heel who took advantage of hopeful drunken ladies, and if he said yes, I was sleeping with the man who had been in love with my mother. For some reason this made me start to giggle. O'Connell stared at me speculatively for thirty seconds or so and then handed me a piece of lavishly buttered toast.

"Christ, baby, you are the absolute pits and end. Eat some breakfast. That kind of stuff needs nourishment. Death to the fascist aggressor." He put cream in my coffee.

"I have a sore throat," I said.

"Me too. Were you ever in a fire before?"

O'Connell took the afternoon off from his job and we went on a picnic to the beach. He wore his army greatcoat and I wore my fur and we went to a place where you could light a fire. We toasted Spam over the fire and I sat half inside O'Connell's greatcoat and watched the fire and ate Spam with my fingers and listened to O'Connell talk about the General Motors strike.

Chapter VIII

THE NEXT DAY in Marshall Field, under a display of plaster models in fall clothes, I ran into Aunt Blonde, aggressive, expressive as ever. She descended on me making cries of triumph in the back of her throat. "My *dear*! My word! What on *earth* are you doing still in Chicago?" She was wearing a tan herringbone suit and a round straw hat with a striped bow on the back; she looked fine, including the white even teeth which stuck out in a projecting bow.

"Will's heart is broken, absolutely broken." She seized me by the arm. "You haven't written to him at all. Come now, you must have lunch with me . . . Why, what on earth" (she didn't wait, but pushed me in the direction of the elevator) "are you in Chicago for? Have you come to see Will? He'll be utterly thrilled. You must call him. Immediately."

As the elevator door thudded shut behind us I said, "I'm here because I'm living in a cheap hotel with a married Army Transport Corps lieutenant."

"Good heavens." Blonde pulled her glasses out of her purse and looked at me, for the first time, as if I were a real person. "Why, my dear child, I think you *mean* it. Oh, good grief. You stupid child. You *do* mean it; you're serious. I can hardly believe it. Now come and have a *good* lunch."

"You can tell Will if you want to," I said, as we were led to a glass-topped table in a window over the dress department. "Will ought to know."

"I wouldn't dream of telling Will." Blonde unfurled her napkin. "You *are* an idiot. Have a soufflé. The soufflé is what they do best here."

I had hated Blonde in Will's house, and now, curiously, I didn't hate her. She managed to get it across somehow that the loud voice was to show that she was deeply interested.

"How's your husband?" I asked.

"My husband is as mad as a hatter." Her brows contracted slightly.

"I go and see him and he won't talk to me." I saw, to my astonishment, that the clear, bright blue eye was alight with a glycerine tear. It detached itself and came artistically down her Max-Factored cheek.

"Tell me," she said, "where do you live in sin?"

Blonde wasn't a good listener, but she exclaimed *heavens* very loud. She wanted to know what O'Connell looked like, and more or less how he was in bed, although she didn't put it that way.

"It can't last. You must put a stop to it. Before *he* leaves *you*."

I realized then that I really had made a decision before I met her that morning. "I'm going to Washington tonight."

For once she was quiet.

"Why don't you come back with me and help me pack?" I asked her not because I suddenly loved her so much, but because I knew how easy it would be to change my mind if O'Connell returned early. She would be insurance against that.

"Well, I must say," she exclaimed, "I have never been to a sordid, dirty hotel where a friend of mine was living in sin." She took an enthusiastic puff on her cigarette and applied lipstick. "Does the clerk look at you funny?"

Aunt Blonde drifted around our room in the Hotel Roseleen picking things up and looking under them, and sniffing in the corners at the dust. "How very strange," she said. "Are you just going to pack and leave, like that? And leave him a note?"

"I guess so."

"But how do you feel about it?"

"Oh, I like him. But anybody can tell it's no good."

"Easy come, easy go," she said. She began to sing this song, which I had been thinking about on the night O'Connell and I first were together, and which I vaguely remembered as one that had been popular when I had been too little to care about such things. Probably incorrectly, I always imagined any such song to have been sung by Mama, dancing around in her green dress.

Blonde opened the drawer, singing, and began to throw underwear at me to put in the suitcase. A bra had just sailed through the air and gotten entangled in the chandelier when the door opened and O'Connell came in.

Blonde walked over to untangle the bra.

"Hello," she said finally.

O'Connell stood in the doorway. For a minute I thought he was going to leave without speaking to me.

It was Aunt Blonde who saved the situation for us. "I'm such an intrusion," she kept saying, in what seemed real distress. "I am *so* sorry." Her cheeks got pink. She looked pretty.

Finally O'Connell and I had to persuade her to sit down and have a cigarette and a drink. O'Connell produced a bottle of bourbon and some tooth glasses.

Blonde and I sat on the bed and O'Connell sat in the chair, which was upholstered in oilcloth.

There was a moment's pause after we were all seated. Then, finally, "My God," O'Connell said, "it looks like a Sunday-school gathering. Maybe we should all sing *Mother Dear.*"

"How does it go?" I asked.

He had not really spoken to me yet. He had been addressing Aunt Blonde. "You," he said to me now, "are the limit."

"I was going to write to you."

"It wasn't fair, Butch, and you know it."

I did know, of course, that it hadn't been fair. I forced myself to look at him. "I didn't think I could leave, otherwise, Connie. I'm sorry. Tell us how the song goes?"

"Jesus Christ." He said to Aunt Blonde, "She really wants to know. She thinks I'll sing her a Sunday-school song."

"I like your songs."

"Good God."

Mother, Dear had a catchy tune. In a moment we were all singing.

"Well," said O'Connell, "I suppose we need another drink."

"I certainly do," Blonde told him. "Then I have to go."

Aunt Blonde stayed for almost an hour. We killed half the bottle of bourbon and O'Connell told a story about John L. Lewis and another one about the Ford organizing campaign. O'Connell had one characteristic that I especially liked—he never repeated one of his many stories, and they were usually funny.

Aunt Blonde kissed me on both cheeks when she left. "Write to me," she said, as if she meant it.

"Oh, God, baby," said O'Connell after Blonde had gone. He pushed me against the door jamb and held me there long enough for me to be sure what it was he wanted. Then he closed the door and lifted my skirt. "Oh, baby darling, dear." And he pulled down my pants and touched me with his hand. We didn't even wait to get into bed, but did it right there, leaning against the door.

It is very hard for a girl to come in that position.

"God, baby," O'Connell said, after he had carried me to the bed and taken off most of my clothes.

"You take your things off too, Connie." A man with all his clothes on and his fly open, and a girl with nothing on but a bra and garter belt and stockings is just too prostitutional a combination.

"Ah, I'm getting old and fat." He ran his hand the length of my arm. "We'll have to wait a minute."

He kissed me between the breasts, and rested his chin on my solar plexus. "I don't see what you want with me, really, when you come right down to it."

"*Omne animal* and so on."

"Huh?"

"That thing about being sad after you make love."

"It is sad to be sad on a Sunday," droned O'Connell into my diaphragm. He applied his mouth and made a noise like a harmonica.

We fought for a second and kissed, and then we rolled over so that I was on top. "Christ, what a perverted witch."

"I can't make it," he said after a minute. "I'm sorry, dear."

"It's all right."

"It's not all right. I'm old and you're young."

"But I love you *because* you're old."

"Well, thanks a lot, Butch."

"I mean, there's something special that wouldn't be there if you were just a young boy that I knew."

"Or even a young girl. Or even an old girl." He rolled me over onto my back.

"Stop it and let's get dressed."

"I don't know it's as hopeless as all that. Maybe it's not hopeless." He began to work on the hollow under my chin with his tongue.

Afterwards he said, "I just can't tell you."

I put my arm around him and stared at the ceiling. "It doesn't change anything. I'm going. I'm leaving today."

"So all right; have a neon sign made."

"It wouldn't last, anyway."

"Why not?"

"How could it?" I wanted to add an endearment: *dear.* But I didn't. "What are we going to do, live here in a crummy hotel room till we hate each other?"

"Ah, baby," he stroked my shoulder. "How can you be so cynical?"

"Someone better be."

"You're a funny baby. Darling."

"O'Connell, for God's sake, stop it . . . Anyway," I added,

because it had rankled a little, "you could be comforted soon enough if you felt like it."

"Mrs. Clavering?" He made a razzberry.

"She's attractive."

"Sure she is. So are a lot of people . . . I don't know though," he added, reflectively, "I didn't think I'd get you."

"If things were right, you wouldn't have." I hadn't intended to tell him that. It just slipped out.

"Hey, what does that mean?"

"You know perfectly well things are bad for me right now. If they weren't I wouldn't be here in bed with you."

"Well, that tells me, doesn't it?"

"No, because maybe it's better. Maybe I know things that are better than the usual ones."

"And maybe not." O'Connell kissed me. "Ah, Christ, dear."

We were gloomily silent for a minute. "Anyway," I said, "I have to go."

"I suppose so. And look up your bloody old mother." He sat up on the edge of the bed and reached for his underpants.

"Butch," said O'Connell at the train station, "you will write to me, now, won't you?"

I didn't say, what about, though that was what I was thinking. "Why don't *you* write to me."

"If you have such a thing as an address, I'll do that." He pulled his book out of his pocket. "You mightn't think it; I'm a very good letter writer."

I told him the YWCA in Washington, which he wrote down. Then we stood and stared at the page in his address book for a minute, and then we both began to laugh.

Chapter IX

IT IS HARD TO EXPLAIN to people about our life in Berkeley. For one thing, we tend to sound more eccentric than we actually were, at least until the very end, when Mama became so unreliable. We were strange and unusual all right, but there were other people like that in Berkeley, and even more of them in Carmel. They were all people who had come West because they thought life would be freer there, and then had made some money and invested it in what they considered the good life.

By the time Clara and I came along it usually was the grandparents who had first felt this way, and there was a whole generation of children who were my mother's age, and then grandchildren like us who had grown up on the top of the mountain or in a fake castle with the waves breaking at its foundation, taking dancing lessons, writing poetry, and trying to paint in oils. My mother was not very good at painting in oils.

Our friend Aunt Chloe wore handmade fabrics only. Even the plant or animal that the material came from had been hand-cared-for. She had a scarf woven from the hairs of her dog, a Maryland retriever with a curly red coat. Aunt Chloe was the one who taught us art and the sciences. She bought a pair of rabbits to demonstrate the facts of life to us, but for some reason that no one ever figured out, they refused to breed.

Mrs. Voss—I don't know why we called her by her full name—was a small talkative woman with one shoulder higher than the other. Her interest was the conservation of sea birds; she went for long walks wearing boots that laced up to her knees and a Norwegian seaman's hat pulled down over her ears.

Maud was a vegetarian. She grew soybeans and marijuana in her garden, and smoked dried marijuana in a pipe.

And so on. There was a great industry among the women of teaching each other's children. Sometimes, when she felt like it, my mother ran a class in current affairs, and she took a group of us to San Francisco to march in the general strike.

I was nine at the time of the general strike, and I remember it well. Mother took turns with me and Clara, holding hands with one of us and letting the other one carry the picket sign. I can remember looking up into her face, and seeing her upper lip slightly dewed with perspiration. She laughed and squeezed my hand and said, "Oh, Helen, honeydarling, God, I'm so excited."

Mama was the only active socialist among her friends,

although they all felt the same way about strikes and the working class.

You have to think of both sides, as Will used to say, scowling and balancing; when he did that you could easily imagine him in a grocery store with a nice fat melon in each hand. So against that day when Mama walked with her head up, getting across even to me that she felt proud and fulfilled, I will now balance the evening she came home and finally told us that she had been asked to resign from her Spanish Committee.

It was called the New Committee for Spanish Freedom. When my father died I had been too angry at the world to notice or care about other things, but I think now that there had been competition among several organizations for Mama's name. I remember long consultations in the living room, and Mama alternating crying and saying oh, but then, something will come of it, by which she meant my father's death.

For a while there had been several committees, and then there was just the New Committee, which was run by a trim, well-dressed, blue-eyed woman named Betty May. Betty May came to the house often. She was nothing like our dancing and nature-study friends; she was very crisp, and made lists which she checked off, and tapped her pencil against her teeth, narrowing her blue eyes and looking at Mama.

"Mama for goodness sake, Mama what is it? Look, Mama, come on and tell me, probably, it will be better, really it will, if you tell me . . . "

Mama had come home and had gone directly up the stairs. I don't know what it was, not the unevenness of her steps, because Mama had reached the point some time ago of being drunk often, so the uneven step wouldn't have told me anything. Somehow I knew that she was upset and I had gone upstairs to her.

She was thrown across the bed with the pillow over her head. "Go away, Helen, go away. There's nothing you can do.

"Go away, please Helen, leave me alone.

"Your grandmother always said they couldn't be trusted; I guess for once she knew what she was talking about.

"I didn't cry until I got home. I'm glad for that; they didn't know what I felt. I just sat and looked at them.

" . . . said that I was drunk all the time and couldn't be trusted. Oh, godalmighty Helen . . . "

I thought of Betty May and the fact that she looked like our grandmother. This was the second year of the war and the things that Mother could do to take her mind off herself were becoming fewer and fewer. Aunt Chloe was dead and Mrs. Voss had moved to Inverness and Maud had gone up the Oregon coast. They weren't the kind that adjusted well to the gung ho wartime atmosphere of Berkeley.

"Mama," I said, "maybe we should go somewhere. Maybe to some different place where the people would be new. Rent the house and go and do something different."

"Helen, honey, you're good to try; it's not worth it."

"Maybe Seattle, Mama, or Portland. Those places are smaller."

Clara came up from the basement and sat down on the foot of the bed; I suppose she'd heard us talking. She had a line of grease across her face from the heater. She sat and thought for a minute and then began to undo her braid; it was coming apart.

"Let's go away, Mama," I said.

Mama sat up. "Claire, your hands are dirty."

Mama worked on Clara's braid while crying and gulping. Clara said, "I like that idea about Portland, Mama; it's not very big and Reed College is there. Reed College is a progressive school."

I got out the dominoes and the card table without any legs and spread the game out on the bed. We played a complicated form of dominoes, with two sets of counters. Mama was good at it because she was daring, not because she was any good at all at arithmetic.

She continued to cry during the game, but she sat up and played with us. Her red hair hung forward over one shoulder and she stopped occasionally to brush away the tears with the back of her hand. She didn't have a drink all that evening.

Well, another day, another train.

This one was Chesapeake and Ohio, the line of the slumbering pussycat, and it was in somewhat better shape than the others I had been on. But it was still crowded and smelly and full of soldiers, one of whom was trying to sit, with his blanket roll, under the water cooler.

> *Oh the train goes choo choo choo*
> *And my heart goes you you you*
> *And I feel so*

No I won't do that, I won't, I won't.

What puffickly awful drivvle.

"Shit," Clara and I used to chorus, "hell, ass, damn."

"Dried-up old bat," we would sing about our grandmother, to the tune of "Hallelujah, I'm a bum."—"Dried-up old bat/Whose bosom is flat . . . "

We didn't know any really outrageous words, the way girls that age do now. But we did our little pioneering best.

I talked to Clara on the phone, one night while O'Connell and I were living in sin. She wasn't very encouraging. She told me that O'Connell was going to leave me; men always left girls. She had seen a movie; but I did not let her tell me over long distance phone the plot of the movie in which the man leaves the girl.

She had also sent me a letter, and that was even less encouraging than her phone conversation had been:

Dear Helen:

My goodness, why did you want to get mixed up with O'Connell, don't we have enough trouble without borrowing it, as a famous expert on the subject, namely grandmother, would say.

Frankly I simply do not understand what in hell is the matter with you. You were anxious enough to go see about Mama and I let you because you were so anxious, and now you're stopping off every single place along the way you get the chance. What gives anyway? You act as if you're in one of those movies about looking for something, well, you're not going to find it on the train between here and Washington, I can tell you that much, and the girl in the movie never does either.

The people down the hill from us, the Brunells, have had me babysit three nights this week, I don't much like the children but the money is okay. You gave me too much of the dividend check last time and I haven't spent it all, so here is some of it for you. I don't want you living off of O'Connell, altho I guess an occasional dinner is okay.

Marjory and I are going to Playland at the Beach this

weekend. Marjory says we should go even if it rains because she, Marjory, is going to be a sociologist and part of it is seeing what happens when it rains. So I hope I don't catch a cold.

I really miss you Helen and I wish you would get finished and find out about Mama and get back. On thinking about O'Connell I think that he is more attractive than Will except for being married.

All my love, dearest Helen. Please write soon and tell me everything, you've been stopping everywhere and not describing at all and you promised you would.

Love,

Clara

On this train ride I had managed to sit beside a woman, or at least a WAC. She was a firm stout hockey-playing type of WAC, with nice fat legs and a good round no-nonsense bosom. I wondered what WACs thought about. Parmme, Miss, I know you a WAC and I a delinquent. But tell me what you think about my mother. Can she be rehabilitated? What about my lover. Maybe he can be rehabilitated? What about me.

WACs do typing, not rehabilitation.

Now came the usual business of turning off all the lights and nailing us in with the blackout curtains. WAC shifted around and sighed and disposed her fat hockey-playing hams. You take up a lot of room, lady.

We got into Washington at eight twenty-five. My introduction to Washington was a football banner, inscribed LOOSE LIPS SINK SHIPS, hung from rafter to rafter of the Washington station, below it about four hundred people, half in service dress and half in unservice dress. Dash, crash, migawd, help. And through the entranceway, framed by the opening, one could see the Capitol. I found myself cab-waiting with the WAC, and it developed that she was, thank God, not going to the YWCA. I shared a cab with three people going to, or near, the YWCA. Off we slammed through wide, fairly clean streets. My mother was some-where in this city.

The dragon who guarded the YWCA was as horrified by my walking up to the desk and asking for a room as she would have been if I had demanded the keys to the building.

I was made to understand that one wrote beforehand, and that it was a matter of pride that no one came into the Y and simply asked for a room and got it. I thought of saying, all right, you dried up old bat, and then abandoned the idea, and instead told a long story involving a sick mother and a home far away. I am not usually very good at this sort of thing. But this time I tried sincerely; the Y lady munched her lips in and chewed on them, sprung and unsprung a yellowish-gray curl between skinny fingers, and finally got down on hands and knees under the desk and came up with a key. I suppose one room had to be kept free for girls whose mothers had tried to commit suicide, and so on.

As a result of all this trouble I got a small gray broom closet with a small gray bed in it. I unpacked one dress and hung it up and sat down and read a page of Louis Unter-meyer and then went downstairs to the cafeteria, where I bought a plate of scrambled eggs. After that I bought a map of Washington and went into the Y lobby.

All YWCAs have the same smell. It's the smell of wax

and linoleum, disinfectant, stale powder, and girls' sweat. There is a noticeboard of things you can sign up for and there is a lot of wet loneliness which has been mopped into the corners of the rooms but will come seeping out and get your shoes mildewed if you let it.

Mother's present boyfriend had written a letter to me and Clara. He was a genteel sounding, old, I suspected, lush, I suspected, named Ford, as in motor cars. He had said in his letter that he would stay with Mother until one of us got there. She was such an interesting person, with so many possibilities. But his own problems were going to force him to leave Washington soon, and she did not seem able to accept this. He, Ford, didn't know whether we had gathered from her letters to us that she was having difficulty with the reality principle. He finished by saying that perhaps Mother would have to move, because the landlady was being most uncooperative.

I called the number Ford had given for Mother in his letter, and the woman who answered hung up on me.

"Excuse me," (you old bat), "do you have my mother here?"

The old bat was thrilled spitless to learn that I was the drunk lady's daughter. In an effort to keep me there and find out more about me she became positively cordial. She was a greasy gray-haired old bat and she had a long skinny house on P street that had seen better days, long long ago. Now it had a flowered carpet punctuated by ribs of nap, oatmeal wallpaper rubbed smooth at shoulder height, a curving staircase with a loose bannister rail, a table, and a row of room keys on hooks. The bat wore a shiny black dress and had varicose veins. She wanted to know all about me.

You mean my poor drunken mother wasn't good enough to live here?

"Well, dear, she was just a teensy bit on the noisy side. But of course one could instantly see she was a lady." (So nice to see ladies acting worse than the old professionals.)

"Why of course I can give you her new address, dearie. My, you do look like her. A very pretty lady. We just thought that after that little trouble she would be happier and I would be happier . . . "

The address was produced and I wrote it down. I thought it best to thank the old bat; you never know.

The sun was out in Washington, D.C., and although it was now November it wasn't cold. This street, P Street, sounded like a joke. I looked on the map for M Street where Mother was now, and, as one would suppose, it wasn't very far away. I decided to walk to M street, new address kindly supplied by Bat.

Wide streets, trees. Fallen houses, still not too bad. The bare outlines of trees visible, with a few leaves still clinging. Houses of stone, heavy, with a pinkish cast, built in rows, iron gingerbread fences, deep, high windows. History, for the love of God. Lincoln rode by here and lifted his hat. I wished I felt better.

I reconnoitered around outside of Mother's new M Street dwelling before I rang the bell.

The outside of the building was in slightly better repair than the P Street one. Next door to it, though, was an all-night garage, whose precipitous, greasy driveway led bowel-ward, casting its pall over things.

The woman who answered the door was incredulous. "Daughter?" compressing her mouth and letting her gray eyes get pointy. "It's outside and down the steps."

She watched me as I made the circuit, down the front
steps and around a little wall made of tan stone and then
down some basement steps, and I could hear her thinking
to herself, daughter, daughter indeed. It wasn't so much
that Mama looked young, although she certainly did look
younger than she was. But she gave an impression of not
having any past at all, and she seemed like a child herself.

There was just one bell, which I rang; it made a loud
noise. I stood there pressing my hands together and praying
in poetry.

Footsteps. I wished I believed in God.

The door opened inward to reveal my mother, her red
hair in big, deep, evenly spaced, messy waves down her
back, holding together with one hand a green silk, tar-
nished, gold-dragoned bathrobe, and clutching a cigarette
in the other. There was a moment's hiatus; I couldn't be
sure whether she was drunk or not. Probably not very if at
all. It was bright outside and dark in her hall. While she
leaned toward me I looked at her: her eyes slanted down,
almost green eyes, dark circles under them of course; the
vulnerable chin had a little sag under it, but the curve of
the throat going down into the green bathrobe was still
all gentleness and vulnerability and soft luminosity;
Renoir's skin tones but the flesh not as fat, no, not nearly.
She threw down the cigarette and the bathrobe came open:
she was absolutely stark staring bare underneath. Mama,
for goodness' sake.

Grab for the bathrobe. "Helen. Honey. Darling. Oh,
my baby." The bathrobe came open again. Dear Mama, do
stop to tie it.

Her arms were around me. I realized with a jolt that I

was now a little taller than Mama. Her breasts and shoulders were heavy, not the rest of her. Soft scratchy feel of Mama's hair; the bathrobe recaptured, she held me by the hand. "Darling Helen. I can't believe it. Darling, darling. I just can't believe it." We passed through a cement hall and a dark brown painted door with an institutional letter on it: B.

Inside, Mama turned toward me and put a hand on each of my shoulders. She was crying and saying, "Oh, my little Helen, I can't, I just can't . . . " *Believe it*, I suppose she meant. Around us was Mama's room, badly lit, with brown and gray rumpsprung furniture pressing in from all sides.

She finally took me by the hand and led me to a lumpy chair. There was a persistent smell, surprising in this setting: Mama was baking a coffeecake, or some kind of cake with cinnamon on it. I searched around for the stove, and finally found it, a two burner hotplate with dependent oven, the whole not hid by a ragged, greasy curtain.

Mama was still crying and began a search, tugging at drawers. There was a dresser, which squeaked when a drawer was pulled. She finally returned, blowing her nose, to sit opposite me.

"Oh, honey, I wasn't expecting it. I'm not in such good shape." The hand holding the handkerchief was shaky. She leaned against the back of the chair, quite graceful and quivering, handkerchief to eyes.

"You know, Helen," after a minute, "this place is so fantastically ugly; I was planning to get it fixed up, paint it or something."

My poor Mama, where on earth would you start? The room was square and had a bed, which was unmade, an Indian bedspread wadded up across the foot of it; three chairs with the stuffing coming out, one red, one brown, one dark brown; a rug made out of dust and doghairs; a window, high up near the ceiling, which afforded a view of the feet of passersby on the sidewalk and their urinating dogs. The present paint, if that was what it was, could be described as gray.

"I thought I'd paint it yellow," she answered my unasked question, "yellow is so bright and pretty; it would bring the sunshine, don't you think?"

My dear sacred heart of Jesus. Dear Mama, you are the end. Shakingly laugh, snuffle, and chuck the wet handkerchief under the bed. "The maid will come and get it in the morning" (funny joke), "oh, Helen, darling, I can't believe it, can't believe it, can't believe it." Hand on either of my shoulders, new kiss, not quite so shaky.

"Dearest, I haven't looked at you—you really look wonderful. I'm so glad I gave you that coat. Oh, my dearie Helen, darling, how is Clara? Do you know, I dreamt about both of you last night, I really did; oh, honey, I can still hardly believe it, but I should have known." And she sat back down in her chair, laughing better.

Mama had always been inclined towards spiritualism or metaphysics even though these were frowned on in socialist circles.

"Clara's just fine, Mama, she loves school, she sends you her love."

"Good heavens above, my *cake*!" She grabbed the nearest object, a limp flat gray pillow wedged into the private parts of a chair, and used it as a holder to pull open the oven door. The coffeecake wasn't burning; she had decorated the top of it with berries and two had rolled off and were glued blackly to the floor of the tin oven. "I must say, Helen," shutting the oven door and putting her finger in her mouth, "no one would ever dream to look at it, but this place is really expensive. It takes all my money and it's such a horrible place; rents are incredible in Washington. After Will's dress-shop job I had another job for a while but I don't seem to have any luck any more; I've got a good chance for a new one, though, a really nice job it would be, doing research."

I felt a lift and then a sag. Research. I put it away to return to later, and we relapsed into the silence of burning coffeecake berries, with me staring at my mother. "I didn't know you had another job, Mama; what kind was it?"

"Oh, sweetheart, it was filing things in a bank, if you can imagine, me! I truly am not made to file things in a bank."

I am more of a free and untrammeled spirit was implied. She pulled at a dragon; the one at her knee was coming unstitched and had a long tail of gold thread dependent from it. "I have a friend, dear; I don't know whether or not you knew, quite a nice friend, actually."

She didn't know that Ford had written to us; I nodded noncommittally.

"He's not a politically conscious friend, but then, politics seem a little . . . harsh to me now. I met him in a bookstore," she added shyly, pulling off a piece of thread.

Poor Mama still had the idea apparent in old novels that every chance encounter might be an important one. It can be a little embarrassing to have your own mother looking soulfully at the refrigerator repairman.

"Then at least he can read."

"Oh, well, yes, dear; he's most literate." Sigh. "He's very . . . gentle." She scowled at something in the direction of the gray window, and another piece of dragon was unzipped.

"Let's have your cake, Mama."

The plates weren't exactly clean, but the cake steamed gently, with bubbled berries and cinnamon. There was a large, wheezing refrigerator out in the hall from which Mama got a stick of butter; she gave me a fork and herself used a spoon. "The silver's mostly dirty and you have to go down the hall to wash it." She cut me a slice of cake and patted my hand. Hers was shaking again. In order to eat, we pulled two of the rumpsprung chairs up to a table blanched with the intersecting rings of many glasses, and sat with our chins almost resting on the table. Mama's cake was delicious. She didn't seem to be hungry. Yes, I do know the signs. I've been trying to pretend that I don't, but I recognize them fully; she had been drunk last night and now had the father and mother of a hangover. I suppose it was good of her to be making coffeecake under the circumstances.

"Mama, you don't look at all bad." That wasn't what I'd meant to say.

"Thank you, dear." A little catch from Mama, the pale blue and white luminous hand shaking again, spooning up tiny bits of coffeecake.

Her hair hung forward, and those waves were like the ones the Dutch painters used to put in their madonna's hair.

She made tea to go with the coffeecake, and I had a willow cup while she had one with a futuristic pattern of orange and brown squares.

"His name is Ford," she said. "It's a funny name. I suppose it suits him somehow."

I sensed that there was a question about Ford, which I assumed to be the question of what was to happen between them.

"Is Mama Reynolds still with you?" my mother asked
in a bright voice.

"You know Clara and I can't stand Grandmother,
Mama." Grandmother liked Clara; it was Clara who finally
convinced her it would destroy our initiative for her to
come live with us.

I thought of things to tell my mother. The winter storm
blew one of the stained glass panels out of the hall window.
We have a tame bluejay who lives in the back garden and
will take bread out of Clara's hand. Clara's doing a science
project on methods of discouraging oxalis; she said it was
hard to get lab animals but you could always find enough
oxalis. The pool had duckweed in it, and overflowed into
the front hall of the house, and Clara and I spent a morning digging into the drainhole where the weed had its
roots down in the pipe.

Mama sighed and smiled. But when she picked up her
futuristic cup, it clanked against the saucer.

"How about getting dressed, Mama? I'd like to see what
new clothes you have."

While Mama was down the hall in the bathroom I poked
around in her stuff.

I started out by trying to tidy up, beginning with putting
all the dishes together in a neat pile in the corner of the
table. Then I got some clothes—a gray bra and a girdle
with its guts coming out—off the floor and put them on
the back of a chair. Then, down on my hands and knees,
I looked under the bed, and besides the usual hair, fingernails, Kleenex, and bobby pins I found a stocking with a
runner in it and a three-quarters-empty bottle of bourbon
lying on it side.

The bottle was near the overhang of the mattress, where

it would be handy for someone lying in bed to reach over and grab it.

After that I started to snoop. There was a lot of under-wear in Mama's drawers, intimately married in a mess of hooks, lace, and straps. Imitation coral earrings. Imitation jade beads. A Chinese brooch made out of red lacquer. A pamphlet by V. I. Lenin. Receipts from stores. The begin-ning of a letter to me and Clara, which I didn't read. The bottom drawer had several boxes, all empty except for the tissue paper, in which things had been brought home from shops.

Her suitcase was standing in a corner. It had in it shoes, a douche bag, and a bottle of mineral oil.

In the cupboard to the right of the stove where Mama had stacked groceries (canned peaches, flour, and a tin of lard) I found a bottle of green pills labeled "Take one for sleeplessness." And in the bottom of the bed, when I was no longer looking, but was simply trying to be helpful by making the bed, I found a gun.

I left the pills where they were. Maybe Mama was sleep-less now. Anyway, there were only three of them.

Because I could hear her coming back down the hall, I stuck the gun in the very back of the grocery cupboard. The shelves were built at an angle, and it was hard to reach that far back. Mama was shorter than I now; maybe she wouldn't be able to find it.

I finished making the bed while Mama was getting dressed. She came and put her arm around me then and her hair fell across my face. She was wearing a yellow knitted dress, one from Berkeley; it had bands of artsy-craftsy blue embroidery at the cuffs and around the neck.

When I turned her around to look at her I saw that she was smiling.

God, I thought, she looks beautiful, in spite of sag under the chin and bags under the eyes, those greenish-blue eyes that turn down; there's a little broken vein in the right one, but no one would ever notice it.

She looks as good as new. Better, almost.

I don't think she's been drinking this morning. She doesn't smell of it. Smells of perfume (too much). She really is a beautiful bag.

"What shall we do, Mother? Shall we go out to lunch?"

Another sigh. The fact finally emerged that what she wanted to do was to take a rest. "Yes, darling, with my dress on. I don't want any lunch."

She went to the door with me, looking sad and beautiful, lost, forsaken. She kissed me, and I felt the tremor go along her arm. She could hardly wait to get to her baby, her bottle, hidden under the bed. Another kiss. "My darling; my sweet, pretty Helen." Now she thought of me, her other baby, and said, frightened, "You'll come back, darling? You'll come back, right after lunch?"

Chapter X

I WALKED SLOWLY BACK toward the YWCA, thinking about my mother.

Washington, D.C., was clean and bright; the sun was shining through a slight cold haze, and there were almost no chewing gum wrappers on the sidewalks. The windows of the shops had been recently washed and they shone quietly. There was a feeling in the air that seemed to say it was going to get really cold.

Instead of going directly to the Y, I turned up Connecticut Avenue. This was a wide street: good shops. The first one I passed was a florist's, with bowls of African violets, the back of the store lined with colored glass mirrors and refrigerators where mourned tiers of red roses.

When Aunt Chloe was dead I went to the florist and asked him to put on the card, "With love from Helen and

Clara," but he wouldn't do it. One apparently does not send love to the dead.

Ahead of me on Connecticut Avenue walked a woman in a coat like mine—leopard. I wondered how old my coat was. Hers was new. You could see the difference; the fur all went in the same direction and it had a glossy shimmer. When my coat was new and Mama was new perhaps they were pretty together.

I finally went into a bookstore and poked questioningly about, even bending over to pull things out from under the tables. The books felt small and listless in their imitation cloth bindings, each with a message in the front about conforming to the wartime production code. There wasn't much poetry; nobody, but nobody, could pretend poetry was a help to the war effort. Finally I bought a children's book: *Abraham Lincoln.* It had been pre-war, and had bright pictures that looked, even machine reproduced, as if just made with wet chalk to rub off on your hands.

Back at the Y, I discovered I wasn't hungry really, but I went to the cafeteria anyway and wandered abstractedly, collecting salad, rolls, custard, and a hardboiled egg. It helped to observe the people around me and I made mental notes for Clara:

SCENE: *the cafeteria of the YWCA*

The cafeteria is painted hospital green, and has small-paned Tudor windows on the street side. Many round tables are arranged symmetrically, each one with four chairs. The cast of the play consists of 102 women who are eating lunch.

There is no dialogue in this play, only a subterranean muttering which may be, please pass the salt, but is too blurred to identify, and the sounds of people eating. Chew. Glug. Munch. Gulp.

Clara would be good at that; Clara is good at sound effects. So is O'Connell. He can make a noise like water going out of a bathtub.

After lunch I went back to Connecticut Avenue and walked until I found a little, very fancy grocery store, its front casement window painted black and gold and filled with cans of pheasant. I sacrificed a page of ration stamps and bought Mama a bagful of impractical groceries, like South American coffee and Brazilian nuts.

She had been out of sugar that morning, and the man found me a box of pink sugar crystals. I said, I think she would like green better, and he took this seriously but there were no green.

I walked back slowly, holding the groceries on my hip and looking at the sights of Washington. It seemed an unusually orderly, pale, well-organized city, with its wide streets and wide sidewalks and green streetcars so well engineered that you hardly heard them at all.

There were servicemen in foreign uniforms; the English uniform of rough-dung-colored wool (pants stuck into the tops of boots) the most prevalent. I passed an Australian airman, in blue and with a beret, and an Indian gentleman in a turban.

I tried to feel, for Clara's sake, that I was in an exciting place where people who were deciding the fate of the world had congregated. I couldn't feel this because it was all too neat and polite; no one was jostling or shoving or dropping Coke bottles and chewing gum. There was no loudspeaker, no O'Connell in a car.

Nothing important was happening, except perhaps in Mama's room, and that was an inward thing, important to Mama and me and Clara only.

* * *

"Dear Honey, what beautiful groceries."

Mama was stretching in front of the grocery cupboard with the groceries in a bag on the table. The signs of trouble were all there: she leaned back on her heels and started to lose her balance; she held a can of mushrooms close to her nose, scowling at it. "Such . . . beautiful groceries. *Mush*rooms. I never would have dreamed, Helen. You are much too good." She put her hand out behind her. The can of mushrooms fell off the shelf, never having really been on it; it narrowly missed Mama's unshod toe.

Coming up behind her to help, I thought, I wish you would drink gin or something, Mama. Bourbon smells like the green and purple wrath of God.

"Some of these groceries are pretty funny, Mama; do you like smoked oysters?" The smoked oysters came from Chile. Who ever heard of a Chilean oyster?

"Of course I do, dear, I adore them. And I think Ford likes them too."

She thought for a minute and added emphatically, "Ford lives around the corner. He lives on Fifteenth Street. On the third floor." As if the third floor made it even more proper. Poor Mama had always been worried about this question. "Things are entirely platonic between us, Helen, dear, you understand?"

"Yes, Mama. Move your foot, for goodness' sake."

"Ford is an absolutely perfect gentleman." She shoved into place a can of plum pudding. "I absolutely adore plum pudding, Helen. He's so gentle and so sweet."

"How nice, Mama. Where do you keep the paper bags?"

"Put it on the floor by the stove and we'll put garbage in it." She sat down on the table with her arms supporting her stiffly on either side. "Darling, I must say, darling, you look so well and you are so pretty."

"How would you like it, Mama, if I made some coffee?"
The coffee is Colombian; nothing but the absolute best
for the working class.

Mama laughed a little falsely; I suppose she got the im-
plications of the coffee. "Why darling, lovely." Very carefully she moved, resting her weight on her fingertips, then,
very carefully easing herself off the table and over to the
bed, where she sat down on the edge with her knees together and her hands resting on them.

The bathroom was down the hall, a long, gray, cement
hall with an uneven floor. When this building used to be
a house, inhabited by Scarlett O'Hara—no, no, by Henry
James's sister—when it was a house, this was the basement,
and it had in it the kitchen and the black servants and the
black beetles and the cockroaches. In the bathroom, you
filled the coffeepot at the bathtub spigot. The tub had a
sticky gray ring around it.

There seemed to be no basket for the coffee grounds,
so I made camping coffee from the recipe in Clara's Campfire Girl handbook—boil the water and throw in the
grounds. Mama came over to help me, just a shade unsteadily, precisely watching her feet. She had washed the
cups since breakfast—good Mama—and she put them
at the circle-bleached table, with the pink sugar in a bowl.

That pink sugar was super. Win the way with super pink
sugar.

While I was waiting for the coffee to settle I faced up
to the problem of what I was going to say next.

"Mama, Clara and I have been worried about you."

"Dear Helen, darling, me too."

"We've thought about ourselves. About you. About all
of us." That certainly wasn't going to get us anywhere.

Mama sighed and sucked in a breath reflectively.

"What do you think is going to happen to you here, Mama? In Washington?"

"Well, dear, I told you, I think . . . "

"About a job. Yes you told me about that."

"Oh, no, no, dear. I mean, yes, but that's not what I meant. Then I haven't told you. About Ford."

"About Ford. Yes, Mama, you told me about Ford."

"No, no, dear, I didn't because . . . " She reached out and touched my hand. "I know that it's hard for a child to understand. I've been reading lots of books on psychology lately . . . It began with an effort to understand myself, you see, because things hadn't gone well for me lately, so . . . where was I?"

"Ford."

"Oh, *yes*, darling. Well, you see, Ford and I are getting married."

It is a good thing, Clara, that you and I are hard as nails and smart as pussycats; we must get it from our father, because Mama really does not have the sense to come in out of the rain. If her head were not attached to her shoulders she would lose it, just as Grandmother says. The first thing she would do, if she went to New York, would be to buy the Brooklyn Bridge, and the second thing would be to go home with a nice man who wanted to put her in the movies.

Mama had been engaged five times that I knew of. She was engaged to David, the Jew in the skullcap. She was going to convert to Judaism for that engagement. She was engaged to Ronnie the Fag. She was engaged to Fred, and I think that it was Fred who really got her drinking.

She was always sure that it was going to be perfect. I

don't know that they all had even asked her; perhaps she just thought that it seemed like a good idea, and was certain to happen.

Fred did ask her, and Clara and I heard him. He said, "Say, Sel, what about it, maybe you and I should commit merger." He drank a toast to her and said, "You're a classy looking gal and you've got a nice house here." Fred worked for the National Labor Relations Board and wore bow ties. Clara and I listened to him one night until Clara began to cry. Clara didn't cry quietly like a lady, she bawled as if she were four years old and had shut her finger in the car door. When Mama came upstairs to see what on earth was the matter, that was what Clara said, that she had gotten her finger caught in the door. Mama said, "Why, poor baby, why poor honey, it must be this one, yes I can see it very clearly. Listen, some ice; is there any ice, Helen?" There usually wasn't any ice, or else the ice trays were so firmly frozen that it wasn't possible to get them loose. In the resulting melee Fred left, and Clara always said that the crying had been an act, but I don't think it was.

After Mama had fallen asleep I left her and went out onto the street.

I was surprised to find that it was still light outside— I had the same feeling that you get when you've spent the afternoon in the movies. The sidewalk shimmered with a sunny invitation to liberation, and I wanted to throw my arms up and go dashing through all the unencumbered space that did not contain Mama and her meanderings and the question of what should be done with her.

There was a little park surrounded by streetcars across the road from the Y. I walked over there and sat on a bench with my hands in the pockets of the cat skin. A man came by and asked me for some money, which I gave him. A squirrel came and dug up a nut. I had never seen one do that before and I watched him with great interest. He looked very industrious and intent and cute, bent over, with his ears laid back and his elbows turned out.

Mama had suggested that I go to see Ford. Ford had a seat in the Library of Congress where he sat and did research. It was always the same seat; it wasn't like looking through the whole library for him.

"Research? Research on what, Mama?"

Mama looked startled. "Why, darling. Just research."

I lighted a cigarette and put my hands back in my pockets, because the warning of cold was there. Mrs. Voss used to smoke without using her hands, the cigarette jutting out like Roosevelt's and dropping ash on her front.

When I had finished my cigarette I stepped on it and the squirrel left, bounding and thrusting out his tail for balance.

I went across the street to wait for a streetcar. The sun was still out and Washington was bright and clean and official looking, and all the good clean healthy well-adjusted Americans who did not have drunken mothers were scampering around with their tails out to balance them. I leaned against the window of the streetcar and looked at the well-kept buildings and the streets almost free of chewing gum wrappers. The girls in Washington were neatly dressed, but they did not have much dash. There was a hairstyle at that time where part of the hair was up in the front and part of it was down in the back, everything nailed very firmly to the head with about a million bobby pins. Well, they all looked like that.

I started to say to myself that they looked like the wrath of God and then I had to retract it, because it was not true at all, really. They looked pretty and sweet and charming.

At the Library of Congress I got off and watched the streetcar wheel silently away. Those streetcars were amazing. I don't suppose they exist anymore. They used not to make any noise at all.

The library was a white marble or granite building. It had columns and some steps, not as many as some of the other buildings in Washington. There was a group of youths, four boys and five girls, on the steps taking pictures of each other. They had a banner which said "The Sioux City Sues."

When I went by them I thought that they were only about a year younger than I and that the world was pretty peculiar. One of the boys whistled as I passed him and I thought that it was like having a pass made at you by the youngster you were baby-sitting with.

There was a youth chewing gum on a three-legged stool who guarded the main part of the library, but he finally let me by when I told him I had to deliver a message.

Inside, the library was mahogany, which creaked, and there was a great circle of desks genteelly shaded by high-quality sturdy lights. I stood behind Ford's desk-number for a while, studying the possible Ford, his neat shoulders and white hair; and then I leaned over him and whispered in his ear.

"Why my dear. Why my dear. So glad." Whisper. Whisper. "Let's go outside." He shoved his books into a brown leather briefcase.

"You *must* be Selma's daughter," he said, when we were out on the white granite steps. "I *knew* immediately. I am *so* glad." He took my hand in his soft one and looked cloudily down at me.

He was a little taller than I, small-boned and narrow-shouldered, rather sweet looking, with a hopeful smile and neat, almost handsome features. His white hair fell forward into his face. His face looked a little crumpled and pinkish around the eyes, but he wasn't drunk and hadn't been drinking recently. It wasn't until he spoke, in a high, fluty, inflected voice, with a movement of the shoulders to accompany it, and a weary fall at the end of most phrases, that I thought: Oh.

Oh, so that's it. Oh, for the love of Heaven. Oh, God, when Mama kept saying what a perfect gentleman he was of course I should have known. He clasped my hand and we moved toward a bench.

"Well," he said, "how *nice* to have you here."

"Thank you for writing to us."

His eyes clouded slightly. "Not at all, my dear. Not at all."

Poor Mama. Poor Ford. "Ford, let's go walk on Capitol Hill. It's getting dark, but we could still see the view or whatnot. You could point things out to me."

"Oh, certainly, my dear. What a *good* idea." He shifted his briefcase to the other hand and took my arm.

"I have the greatest *respect* for your mother. That marvelous vitality." We entered the Capitol grounds and started to circle around toward the front of the building. There were plantings and bushes with labels on them.

Ford told me that he worked for the outfit that advertises in the backs of magazines and offers to find your ancestors for you. He sat every day in the library and looked up ancestors and wrote up a family tree. He got paid by the job.

We arrived at the front of the Capitol. We were on a hill looking down Constitution Avenue; at the other end of the avenue was the Washington monument. As we stood there, the lights went on, and the buildings lining the street were silhouetted in faint brown shadow, like an old-fashioned photograph. Ford coughed politely. "I never *tire* of this scene."

I said, "Mother has a gun in her bed."

"Oh, my dear. I looked for it, you know, but I couldn't . . . What did you do with it?"

"Hid it behind the groceries. The bottom of the bed seemed a bad place."

"I don't *think* it was loaded, my dear. I don't even *think* she has bullets."

Still and all, a gun in the bed. Messy, sloppy housekeeping, if nothing else.

We turned and started to walk around the Capitol to the back, which was the entrance that, Ford told me, the senators used. There was an archway and steps for taking pictures of delegations.

"I wanted to help your mother. She looks . . . you know, with that warmth, that vitality . . . "

She looks like one of Renoir's women.

"One always has ideas about reforming people. And I, myself . . . Well, frankly, I've had a drinking problem, too . . .

"Perhaps I've helped a little. One has the idea of re-claiming something . . . like a work of art perhaps. But now I have to move on. She seems not to believe it."

We walked to the delegation steps and sat down on them. "I've *told* her, but she simply doesn't listen. You see, I have *other* friends. You understand what I mean."

Ford and I got on the streetcar. He was silent now and I thought that he might be embarrassed. Then on inspection I decided not. He was one of those cloudy people who get wrapped in their own cotton. He sighed and shifted his high-quality, saddle-leather briefcase. He was a respectable looking man; his shoes shone and his cuffs were white and stiff.

The sign on the marble plaza in front of the Supreme Court said "No roller skating." The building was lighted from below to look more monumental.

Ford's apartment was tiny and respectable, painted dark green, so that being in it felt like being in a growing plant. I sat on the bed, covered dark green to match the walls. Ford, in the kitchen, which was simply one wall of the closet, made me a scotch and soda. "It doesn't do to drink in front of your mother, you know. And of course I don't drink; I'm a reformed alcoholic."

"How is she, Ford? Really? Does she ever stop now?"

"Oh, yes, my dear." He produced a bowl of peanuts. "She stops for days at a time." Bowl extended, Ford stared down into it. "I do wish I could give her more."

"What happened in the other place where she was living?"

"Well, my dear." He sighed and sat down. "She got very angry at me. I had been telling her I had to move on . . . New York, you see. And she couldn't believe it.

"She got angry. Abusive." Ford examined a nut. "Strange, really."

Mama had said some pretty surprising things about Betty May, who pushed her off the Spanish Committee. Not the night it happened, but later.

And Grandmother too. Not very long after Daddy died, when Grandmother was on one of her Clean Up the House campaigns.

You dried up old sexless witch. With your prim little man-chewing mouth and your flat saggy little desexed breasts and your sterilized hair. Sterilized hair, sterilized body hair. Clara and I had stared at each other in amazement. I wrote it into a poem, sterilized body hair; a poem for me and Clara.

"She simply will not listen when I say I'm going. But now that you're here . . .

"I met her in a bookstore, you know." He was gobbling up the peanuts at a great rate. "She has a strange quality, an appeal."

I walked around Ford's apartment. Its one window looked down into Fifteenth Street where there was an office building and another apartment house and a row of trees. The street light shone on the tops of the trees, making their almost bare branches look artificial.

There was very little in the apartment to show what Ford was like. There was a shelf full of books, but in spite of Mama's remark about his literacy they seemed to me to be book-club books: a novel about shipwreck, a true-life story about having a blind daughter. There was a stack of *Time* magazines and a photograph of Ford about ten years younger.

He told me that in New York he was going to work at Brentano's bookstore. He had a friend who worked there. "Actually it's funny because I wouldn't have thought I was aggressive enough, but I'm good at selling things; the right things that is."

Ford would live with his friend in New York. His friend had an apartment, a much nicer apartment than this one. His friend had very good taste. Ford got an anxious look in his eye as he heard himself say this.

There was only one peanut left in his outstretched hand, and I decided that this meant it was time for me to leave.

He walked most of the way down the stairs with me and we made a date for tomorrow night. It would be quite a social event; he and I and Mother would go out to dinner and then to the movies.

Ford and Mama and I had a good time at the movies. I had walked over to Mama's with considerable trepidation, but Mama was perfectly all right, sober and dressed up, wearing a cloth coat with a shaggy, tan fur collar, her hair neatly combed and braided and glued to her head. The only indication of her perhaps condition was that she said she didn't want to eat dinner before the movie, but that was fine with me; the evening seemed more of an occasion with dinner later. We took a cab downtown and Mama was nice while we stood in line; she teased Ford who, she said, looked away during the battle scenes, and she told about the time I had tried to climb up on the stage to rescue the dog from Wendy's father in *Peter Pan*. She looked pretty, and rather excited, and made perfectly good sense.

After the movie we went to a French restaurant. Mama said, really, she would have preferred the California Kitchens because she was homesick for California, and I appreciated her saying this, because California Kitchens is just a hamburger place, and it was clear to me that she was trying to save Ford money. Ford was masterful about the French restaurant, and I liked him, too.

Midway through dinner, Mama said, "You know, I think I sort of understand why you have taken me out to dinner."

Ford said, "Why Selma, my dear, one would think I had never taken you to dinner, hmmm?"

Mama said, "I know perfectly well you've taken me out to dinner lots, but anybody can tell there's a special reason

this time." She ate a little of her dish, which was chicken
in wine sauce, and said, "The funny thing about being
drunk is that in a way you know perfectly well what's
going on.

"Anyway," she said, when no one answered this, "I wasn't
drunk the other day, Helen, not really; I mean, I'd had
quite a few drinks but I wasn't drunk, if you get the distinc-
tion? Anyway, what I'm talking about is my saying Ford
was going to marry me. I know perfectly well he isn't; it
was just that back when I thought he would marry me I
imagined your coming to see me and I rehearsed telling
you about it and I still wanted to."

Ford said, "Selma, my dear."

I said, "That's all right, Mama, I thought it was something like that."

Mama giggled and put down her fork. "Poor Ford was
so bothered, weren't you, Ford?"

"Well, really, my dear . . . "

"He's been trying to reform me. But it's been terribly
difficult. I guess when he started out he thought it would
be easy, or fun, or maybe both."

"Really my dear . . . "

"Never mind. It was a good try. What is it they say,
Helen?"

"The good old school try."

"That's it. And what was that thing about angels that
your grandmother used always to be spouting, Helen?"

"I've done my best, an angel could do no better."

"Exactly."

I liked Mama's hair with the braids arranged in a way
that made me think of *Kristin Lavransdatter.*

I thought that I had not seen her like this since I had

been in Washington, and also not for some time before she had left Berkeley. She was just a little bit hectic; otherwise she seemed like her old self.

"Never mind, Ford. It probably was worth it."

"I'm sure it was, Selma."

"Think of all the fun you've had. Even if it didn't work. It certainly must have been more fun than painting in oils."

Ford looked interested, but rather puzzled.

"When you're painting in oils you're never sure how it's going to come out," Mama said. "At least, I never was. I would start a picture that I wanted to be a migrant worker and it would come out looking like one of the girls. Isn't that right, Helen?"

"Yes, I remember that one, Mama."

"So it's that way with a lot of things. Now, Helen here . . . " She stopped eating again and put down her fork and rested her head on her hand.

"What is it, Mama?"

"Everyone tries to make me over, and I would say that it's too late and I'm too old except that I *do* seem to be changing. What did you want to make me over into, Helen, when you told me to leave home?"

"I didn't tell you . . . "

"Never mind, dear, it doesn't matter. It has all come out all right, I'm certain; so what difference does it make?

"Don't worry about it," Mama said. "Anyway, I can see perfectly well you had to do it."

"Selma, my dear," said Ford, "I remembered I will not be here for your birthday, and while I could of course send you something, I wanted to give you a gift connected with Washington, something we had looked at here together."

He produced a little antique pin, the kind in which the initial letters of the jewels spell a word. This one was *respect*: ruby, emerald, sapphire, pearl, emerald, cat's-eye, topaz. I thought that Ford must have had to look far and wide to find a pin with just the right degree of affection in its initials, but it seemed they actually had admired it together in a store window.

The idea of being bought off, or at least of being appeased by a gift, seemed oppressive to me, but Mama acted very pleased. She attached the pin to the front of her dress, and laughed, and lost a little of the feverishness that had been glossing her manner before. She said, "Well, you really have tried with me, Ford."

Ford offered to get wine to go with the meal. "You know, of course, Selma, that I do not take wine; I don't feel it's safe for me to have it. But I'd be glad to order some for you."

Mama said, "No, thanks, Ford; I'm really not a complete fool," and we finished the meal very amicably. Mama was needling Ford about the way he held his coffee cup, but he didn't seem to mind.

That night, even though it was late when I got back, I stayed up long enough to write a card to Clara describing our meal and saying that Mama was better. The next morning I had a letter from O'Connell:

Well, Butchie,

You made it as clear as a bell that you didn't think I was ever going to write to you, and that my dear put me on my metal and I decided it was one of my duties in life so here goes.

Darling I have only gotten through the eighth grade so

the letter may not be so hot from the standpoint of the little things.

Dear old Butchie, that room looked so flicken empty after you went I went back and paid the rest of the bill not having enough cash when we were there earlier and I went up and looked at the room and it was as if it had never been. And then I opened a drawer and you had left me a suvenir in a drawer babe namely one postage stamp and one bobby pin.

Never mind darling you were with me today. I walked down State Street and I saw this girl, looking like you with lots of hair and a swell figure and she was hanging on to this guys arm and looking up at him and laughing in a way that was making people turn around. Well, dear I thought of you both ways, she looked like you and she sounded like you.

And so I went to sleep thinking of you Butch and I'm sending you all my love.

I am sick to death of this damn trucking outfit but what I do when I am not signing my name to some list of things that the Sgt. has made a list of is to think about you and the way you always want to know the words of the song and also that last time up in the room and what you told me that you did not make it before you were with me. And there is your colored laugh dear and if I am really lonely for you I can always remember about my sore shoulder.

Well dear much love from me that last was a joke and now much love from

John O'Connell

Chapter XI

𝒯 THE NEXT DAY it was bright and cold and I went to see the Washington Monument. I felt pretty good all day and after dinner I walked over to see Mama.

Ford met me at the door of Mama's gray-shadowed subterranean dugout and pulled me energetically inside. It was dark, but even so I could see that his little soft face was twisted with anxiety.

"Oh, *heavens,* I am so glad you came. I didn't want to *call* you, you have so much on your shoulders, but this is the first time since *P Street* that I have not been able to . . . sometimes I really wonder if you should . . . "

Mama was sitting in the middle of the brown dog-hair rug. She wore her ever-open, drooping bathrobe; everything about her appeared to droop except for the long, bright evenly spaced waves of red, messy hair. She leaned over a glass which sat unsteadily on the floor in front of her.

"I can't think of anything else to *do*." Ford looked at Mama and tensed and untensed his hands.

"Fairy," Mama said, softly and venomously. "That's what he is, Helen. A little fairy. A fairy, Helen, is a lover of boys."

"Mama, do up the front of your bathrobe."

"I wouldn't have minded so much," Mama said, "except that he did once ask me to . . . " She took a deep swallow from the glass. "Damn him to Hell. Damn him to Hell.

"Everyone thought I was crazy of course. Why would anyone want a little fairy for a boyfriend unless they were crazy. Of course I am terribly terribly drunk, Helen, I don't know whether or not you realize that."

"You've had enough to drink, Mama, give the glass to me."

Mama downed the rest of the drink and threw the glass at Ford. It bounced against the wall beside the door and fell to the floor in pieces. "Nobody minds these days; after all, everyone knows about pressures, childhood influences, and things, if it weren't for making up to you rubbing up against you hoping some of it will come off . . . "

My mother had bent her mad head and was crying; her hair in front of her face mostly hid the crying, but not entirely. "Because all the while they are thinking, you smell, you flop, you're saggy, your breasts bag, you're not neat and pretty like a little boy . . . You menstruate," Mama said. "I want to be dead."

Ford stood with his face fallen in and his hands hanging helpless. I walked over and said, "Do up your bathrobe, Mama."

"Helen, listen to me, nobody really minds these days,

just if they want to come and fatten off you and then when
they find it won't work going away and all the time looking
at you as if to say you drink like a fish you sag and . . . oh,
God . . . " She lowered her head, looking, I think, for the
drink she had thrown. "I tried to get things onto another
pla . . . another plane . . . more understanding . . . because
of course I knew, but of course what does it matter because
of course we are all subject to the same press . . . pressures . . . " Something happened and she fastened her bathrobe and tried to tie the cord.

"Because oh my dear God," said Mama trying to struggle
to her feet.

"Better stay sitting down, Mama."

"I have to go to the bathroom."

I helped her down the hall to the bathroom, she leaning on me limply, smelling strongly of bourbon and perfume. I was in agonies that we wouldn't make it in time;
in my mind's eye I could see that great spreading puddle
of pee sending out little trailers into all corners of the
uneven cement floor. Oh, glory, hallelujah, here we are;
we've arrived. Plop her down on the wobbly old toilet seat,
which squeaks in protest. My God, a good thing we made it.

She tried to go to sleep on the toilet, but I hoisted her
up and we started on our wavering way back.

Forgot to flush the toilet. Well, hard lines for the next
poor soul.

I was out of my mind to come to Washington. Clara
and I were out of our minds to think I could help. If I just
go away the State will come and collect her.

On our way back into the room I stopped to open the
grocery cupboard door and felt into the back of it. There
was no gun. I tried again. Still, no gun.

Oh, hell.

"Now, Mama, how about tucking you into bed?"

The sight of Ford had reminded her of her grievances. "I'm not going to go into the bed that that little fruit has been having his little sleep in. Sleeping and tucking his little knees up into my back and hoping that . . . " She was crying again. "I wish I were dead. I wish I were dead." In the stress of this I led her to the bed, where she sat, but she wouldn't lie down.

Ford was not much good, although who could blame him, really. He gave the impression of sitting on the edge of the red chair with his knees together and his hands in his pockets. Poor man still looked sad, dignified, genteel.

My goodness, I hope you don't take to the drink again, too, as a result, Ford. Some pretty mean things being said here.

Sitting beside Mama, with my arm around her, I was trying to make lipreading movements to him. "Doctor?"

No answer.

"Doc-tor?"

Eyes rolling wildly. Poor Ford's neat helpless eyes. My God in heaven, that woman has said some pretty awful things about him tonight. Still, as he says, there is her vitality. Nuts to her, and nuts to her vitality.

More lipreading movements. Gun?

The second time round this got a response. My God, he's been bitten by a bee. Eek. Headline: BITTEN BY BEE.

I have got to be serious about this. I think what Ford is indicating by leaping around that way is that he doesn't know where the gun is and hasn't thought about it so far tonight. Too busy soaking up those juicy insults. All right, we have no doctor and we have no gun.

I said, "Mama, wouldn't you like to lie down now?"

She had been half asleep, but this popped her up into consciousness again.

"Fairy," struggling into a sitting-upright position. "Oh-dearlord. A hopeless gooey little fairy." She began to laugh very hysterically.

I mouthed "Doc-tor," at Ford again. I thought, if he doesn't get out of here and get some kind of a doctor I am going to strangle him. I am not going to spend the rest of the night sitting here holding up this drunken mad sad old bag. I am going to walk out and slam the door behind me and leave him with this mess; it's his mess as much as mine. I'll leave him holding the bag. Joke, haha. I must have gotten some of this conviction into the look I gave Ford, because he nodded and smoothed his hair back and sloped quietly off while Mama was still laughing. His narrow shoulders as he squeezed through the door had a protesting, defeated look.

After Ford was gone I poked around among Mama's shoes and behind the cushions of the chairs for the gun. No luck. Mama sagged, still sitting up, on the bed; every time she realized that I had left her side she would pull herself together and yell for Ford: "Where's he gone? Has he left already? God . . . thought things . . . going to be different; knew fairy of course, how can you not, but . . . where are you? Helen, darling? Oh, God I wish I were dead."

I almost came out and said, Mama, where did you put the gun, but decided that might give her specific ideas she didn't yet have.

Between going back and holding her and looking for the gun, I began to worry that the doctor would want to put her into the nearest institution. That's what any sensible person would have done. That's what Grandmother would have done. But it wasn't what Clara and I had decided to do. I planned to tell the doctor that she was seeing a psychiatrist, and thought up a name for him.

It beats me how anybody, especially anybody with only half her wits, can be that good at hiding things.

"Helen, Helen."

Ford finally, lightyears later, returned with a small, tired doctor. Really not a very interested doctor; maybe Ford knew where to go for a specialist in noisy drunks. He gave Mother a shot and said that she would sleep now. And collected five dollars.

It took a while for the doctor's prediction about Mother to be realized. She finally subsided slowly, like a balloon with the air going out of it, and Ford and I stood looking down at her. When she was still I put on my coat, and Ford came to the door and stood massaging his hands and munching on his lip. "*Really*, you know. I hate to say it, of course."

"Yes, of course; you have to get out of here."

"Well, yes, yes."

"Why don't you just go? She'd get used to it. I think."

"We'll give it a few days," he said, handwashing.

"You've really been very decent about the whole thing."

I almost added, "You poor old sod," but of course I didn't.

Dear Butchie:

Your postcard with a picture of the Washington Monument was not the most exciting communication I ever had in my life, but at least it was something. I was much glader to hear from you than I ought to have been dear, I think something is the matter with me.

Well dear I hope your poor old Mama is not giving you

too much of a hard time. If I remember the lady right she was capable of it.

Butch I dont know what to think really. I think about you a lot of the time Butch.

It is cold as English justice in Chicago today dear, that wind comes whipping off the lake and goes right up your pants legs and I thought of you and your little fur coat dear, maybe every poor boy has wanted to be in love with a girl with a fur coat. But no kidding dear, something about that wind made me think of you too, because I thought of the way you suddenly go cold and pull back into yourself sometimes. I don't know what you got exactly, what the attraction is, it's hard to put it in words, it's as if you are always thinking. Well everybody is always thinking you'll say but with you a person can look at your face and hear that little chilly russle inside the skull. Well enough of that.

This trucking job is as boring as a mother-in-law's love, the Sgt. has run out of lists of things to sign and nothing seems to be the matter with the truck motors and dear I am really bored with thinking of you too if you must know.

The only thing is that this cold weather is making my shoulder hurt and a good thing too.

Much love dear from

John O'Connell

P.S.   I am making a big speech Wednesday night in the union hall of Ridgeley, W. Va.

Love

J. O'C.

O'Connell's letter reached me on Tuesday. The next morning I got up early and walked up Connecticut Avenue and turned right on Fifteenth Street toward Ford's apartment. I wore my cat skin coat and marched with my hands in my pockets. In my purse I had our most recent dividend check. Clara had sent it to me at the Y, and Mama had signed it this morning. I had waked her up, put the pen in her hand; she was asleep again before I laid her back on the bed.

It was a bright crisp day, smelling of leaves.

Ford came to his door wearing a striped silk robe, half of a mask of shaving cream on his face. The silk robe seemed right for my concept of Ford, but somehow I hadn't thought of him shaving. The soap made a firm casing for one side of his face, the other side was bare and shiny. He held a razor in one hand.

"Well, dear, *en déshabille.*" Those words, at least, were what I would have expected from Ford. A look of alarm crossed his eyes and eyebrows. "Selma?"

"She's all right. Can you get this cashed for me?" I waved the check under his nose.

Ford and I walked to the bank. He talked about the power of prayer. He wasn't absolutely sure that prayer had any power at all, but he thought it might. He owned a rosary made of sandalwood which had been blessed by the pope. He had been saying Hail Mary's on it, and he thought they were efficacious.

The dividend check was for $212. I divided it into 50 for me, 50 for Clara, and 112 for Mama, with cashier's checks for Clara and Mama. Then I told Ford that I wanted to walk and think, and Ford took off on the streetcar for his job at the library. I waited until the next streetcar came along and got on it. I was going to Union Station.

Ridgeley, West Virginia was a hard place to remember the name of because it was so ordinary. The station clerk told me I should get off in Cumberland, Maryland, which was the town contiguous to Ridgeley. They shared a common metropolitan area, he said. I looked at him to see if he was joking, and I couldn't be sure. He wore a visor and a pencil over one ear, like a railway clerk in a comic strip. He seemed pleased that I wanted to know about Ridgeley, West Virginia, probably because most of the people in the long line passing in front of his window were asking where platform twelve was and where to check a suitcase.

I bought a newspaper and looked for a place to sit down with it. There was no place to sit down. The high ceilinged station echoed and rocked with noise, like an enormous bucket that someone had turned upside down and was banging on the bottom of. The "Loose Lips" banner had slipped, and hung crookedly, quivering occasionally. I went outside and sat on the edge of an empty ornamental fountain. I had three hours to kill until my train to Cumberland. First I read the paper from first page to last. Then, chilled, I went inside and stood in line for doughnuts and coffee. Then I went back out and walked in the direction of the Capitol. This walk took me through an area that had been described in an article I had just read in the *Washington Post* as a *depressed colored area.* The sidewalks were dusty, they got the toes of my suede pumps dirty; there was a lot of litter in the gutter. I didn't care. I walked along, kicking scraps of bread wrapper and streetcar transfer out of my way, and thinking about O'Connell, imagining how he would look, making his speech at the Workers' Hall in Ridgeley, West Virginia. I had trouble forming this mental picture. I could outline O'Connell all right, O'Connell sitting in a chair, leaning forward, hands on knees, elbows bent out, full of some story, or I could imagine O'Connell eating and talking, resting one arm on the table, but when I tried to put him on the platform of the Workers' Hall, making a speech to his boys, and his girls' union combo, then I lost him. Well, it didn't matter. I'd be there myself that evening.

The train left at two o'clock. It was old and crowded, and was going all the way to Chicago, but with twenty-five or thirty stops along the way. I got a dark green carriage, chipped and dented, the seats in mostly hairless blue plush. I found a seat by the window. I liked trains, I said to myself. Maybe after the war I would ride on a new, freshly painted, clean train that smelled of new machine oil instead of hot oil and dust and had abraded, squeaking, square wheels.

It was hard to imagine life after the war. None of us seemed to fit into that life very well. Clara and Mama and I seemed stuck at this particular point, atoms moving around in an agitated container; what would happen when it stopped revolving? And now here was O'Connell, crossing the field of our agitation like a wild particle. Perhaps after the war none of us would have any existence; we lived only now, just to be chaotic and creating energy, now.

The train was due into Cumberland at a quarter past six. For the last hour of our trip we climbed slowly, the scenery broken into clumps of woods, gradually getting darker as night fell, trees that had lost most of their leaves but still had a scattering of red ones. I began to feel quite excited.

I had half expected O'Connell to be at the station to greet me, but of course he wasn't there. Part of the Cumberland Station was an old hotel that had high windows with carved, grooved moldings over them. I went into the Cumberland Hotel and had a slice of apple pie and a cup of coffee and then I went outside and took a cab to the Ridgeley Workers' Hall.

The taxi was an ordinary black Plymouth with Taxi painted on both doors; the driver said the Ridgeley Workers' Hall used to be the Socialist Workers' Hall until a Republican state senator organized a change of name. "But this is still a big socialist area," he said. "And a while back, all in here, they voted for Debs, Eugene V. Debs, that is."

The hall had the same kind of high Victorian windows as the hotel, and a set of double doors opening directly from the street into the hall, where about one hundred and fifty wooden chairs had been set up in rows. All the chairs were filled; people were standing across the back of the room. At the far end, on a raised platform, against a backdrop of an American flag, a CIO banner, and a wartime industry poster of factories and their smokestacks, O'Connell stood, talking.

I squeezed into a spot against the wall. I couldn't tell whether O'Connell noticed me or not. His audience was listening attentively, the hall silent except for a few creaks and shuffles and O'Connell's baritone voice with its underlying edge of enthusiasm. Perhaps it made me a little jealous to hear that interested tone in his voice; I knew it well. Maybe I had thought it was just for me.

"And do you know how the union started here in the Cumberland mill? Everybody here heard that story?" He began a description of a meeting at someone's house. Apparently this person was here tonight; additions to the story came from the audience, laughter, shouts back and forth.

It was hard for me to put a name to why I loved O'Connell. It had sneaked up on me like any habit, like smoking.

He sat down, to a lot of applause. His speech was followed by another from a middle-aged woman with gray hair who was introduced as Thelma, our sister from Pittsburgh. Then there was a question-and-answer period, mainly tributes, people who got up and said: "Now I know we all know we would be nowhere here in Ridgeley and Cumberland and Lonaconing if we didn't have the union to help us." I had never been to a union meeting before, but I had been with Mama to plenty of political meetings, so I was used to the enthusiasm that accompanied immersion in a cause. I watched O'Connell, who sat on a folding chair to the right of the podium. I thought he had seen me by now. I was noticeable, standing in the back, tall and reddish-blonde and dressed differently from everybody else.

The meeting ended with applause and the singing of "Solidarity Forever." The audience stood to sing this song, which was to the tune of "The Battle Hymn of the Republic." Then people began to walk out slowly. I stayed in my same spot, letting the crowd go by me, watching O'Connell, who moved down the aisle, shaking hands, being greeted.

I had been watching him for a couple of minutes before I realized that he wasn't alone; he had a woman with him. At first she was a little bit behind him, then she moved up and took his arm.

" . . . working the twelve to eight shift . . . " a voice beside me was saying. I began to push and shove very determinedly toward the door. Except for a few exclamations of "Hey, take it easy, will ya?" people made way for me.

Outside, the light from the meeting hall spread across the rutted pebbled road in a wide fan. People lingered, talking. I pushed through them and started to walk toward Cumberland, which showed up as a smear at the bottom of a hill. It had been about five miles, I thought, from the station to here. I hadn't been expecting to walk five miles in my black suede pumps which I had worn especially because O'Connell admired them. There wasn't a hope in hell of getting a taxi back to Cumberland. You could tell simply by looking at this street that taxis didn't cruise along it.

"Butchie," said a voice behind me. I slowed down, only a little bit. I was still near enough to the meeting hall that I thought maybe I had manufactured O'Connell's voice out of my own imagination and out of some of the stray sounds from the meeting. "Butchie." A hand touched my shoulder.

"This is my sister Kat," O'Connell was saying. "Kat, this is Miss Reynolds. Miss Reynolds is a good friend of mine."

A good friend of mine, I thought. My God. I looked at O'Connell and then at Kat, a tall spare woman in a crepe dress and her good coat. She had glossy black hair, and I knew now that she didn't fit at all with my concept of O'Connell's wife, not even with the one piece of information he had given me about his wife's appearance: my wife has gray hair, but it used to be brown. Kat was tall and energetic looking. She seemed to be staring at me intently, but it was hard to be sure in the uneven light that came from the meeting hall door.

"Kat lives here in Ridgeley," O'Connell said. "I'm going back to her house and you're invited. I guess you haven't had dinner." He put a hand in the middle of my back and started me down the street. On his other side, I could see, he was holding on to his sister. Now that I thought of it, of course, she looked just the way O'Connell's sister ought to.

We reached a car, which apparently was Kat's because she walked around to the driver's side of it.

"You're crazy," I said to O'Connell while his sister was opening her car door. "You're stark raving crazy."

"Yeah, I guess I am." I sat in the front, beside O'Connell's sister, and O'Connell sat in the back. "Hey, how did you like my speech, Butchie? Did I sound the way you thought I would?"

At O'Connell's sister's house I asked for the bathroom and locked myself into it. The bathroom had a linoleum floor and a tub with claw feet and soap in the shape of a rose. The rose was in honor of O'Connell, I could tell; you hadn't been able to get soap like that for years now. Kat had been saving it since before the war, waiting for O'Connell to come visit her. I sat on the edge of the tub and cried.

"Miss Reynolds, are you all right?" It was Kat knocking on the door.

"I'm okay. Please call me Helen." It would be nice to have someone in O'Connell's family calling me by my true name.

O'Connell's sister's house was built up the side of the hill with one or two small rooms at each level. The house was very clean and had a lot of blue and red Catholic pictures on the walls. We ate soup and fried chicken at an oil-cloth-covered table in the kitchen, which had a linoleum floor and a picture of the Sacred Heart, Jesus pointing with two fingers at his heart resting outside his chest. The kitchen furniture was the table with its checked cover, four green chairs, a shiny black stove with a white enameled oven, a new green refrigerator.

"That's the only green refrigerator in Ridgeley," Kat said. "Everybody likes that green refrigerator.

"Johnny got it for me," she added. "Johnny can get

things like that." She was proud of him, you could see that easily.

She wasn't very talkative, but she wasn't unfriendly either. Perhaps she had decided not to speculate about me. She worked in the Celanese mill, she told me. Her husband was dead. She had four children, but only one of them was still at home, a girl named Kathleen who was working tonight. "I named her after myself. Doesn't show much imagination, does it? In our family, we're not much on imagination. Johnny is the only one of us has any imagination."

O'Connell and I did the dishes. Several times, when I put a dish in the rinse water and he took it out, our hands touched. This wasn't intentional at first, and then it was. I looked at him. I had expected his expression to be amused, or daring; maybe I expected him to wink at me in his skillful way, contracting only one side of his face and leaving the other side clear. But what I saw on O'Connell's face was what I felt on my own: tension, fear, a muscle in the cheek twitching. He touched the back of my hand with his forefinger and dried a cup carefully.

After we had finished the dishes and I had hung the aluminum dishpan on its hook under the sink, I said, "I guess I should be getting back to the station." I announced this into the air under the sink. It seemed presumptuous somehow to address O'Connell as "O'Connell" in front of his sister, and I couldn't speak to him any other way; he certainly wasn't "Johnny" to me. Probably the sister would have hated that worse, if I had called him Johnny. "Maybe there's a midnight train," I said, still speaking to the back of the dishpan and the wrung-out dishcloth.

"Well, dear," O'Connell said, "there isn't any midnight train to Washington. There isn't any train until 9 o'clock tomorrow morning. You could go to Pittsburgh if you wanted to. But you can't go to Washington."

"You could also go to Chicago," he added. Jesus Christ, I thought. Go to Chicago, indeed. Let's hope Kat hasn't registered that. I stood up and faced him and Kat. There was about a minute's silence.

Finally Kat said, "Well, Helen, I guess you stay here." Her voice was noncommittal.

She led me up the creaking, narrow, wooden stairs, like a catwalk, to show me my room—a tiny one at the top of the house, where she and I made the bed together. After the bed-making we returned to the kitchen, and we all sat down around the kitchen table, Kat resting her arms, white and well-muscled, just a bit saggy above the elbows, on the edge of the table. She stared at her hands, clasping and unclasping them and talking to O'Connell about her work in the Celanese mill, the union there, her position as shop steward. She sounded excited, telling things to her brother. I had the idea, though, that some part of this conversation was aimed at me, sort of a showing-off in front of company. Her conversation was sensible and practical; I could see what she had meant by saying she had no imagination.

"You never get anything that way," she was saying. "Never. Just decide what you're going to do and do it. Don't jump around." She reminded me of someone. Finally I remembered who it was: Clara.

How would Clara feel about O'Connell and me, if she were O'Connell's sister? Well, she certainly wouldn't leave us alone in her kitchen, nor anywhere else in her house, that was for sure. Clara would know that wasn't fitting.

"Hey, Kat," O'Connell said, "How about a game of poker? Butchie here plays a great game of poker."

Kat played poker much better than I did. After three

games I felt reckless and suggested we bet real money or
real objects: Mama's fur jacket, I said, my ticket back to
Washington. O'Connell wouldn't agree.

"Anything to get your sister out of here." I didn't say
this aloud, of course. I was becoming hysterical, with some
part of my mind not attached to the rest of me, not visible. I
started making bargains in my head: what I would give to
be alone with O'Connell for half an hour, not so much for
the sex, just to be alone with him. I got tricky with these
bargains. I'd give one year after I was fifty for each minute
now. That could hardly be said to count as a promise; I
didn't believe in the possibility of being fifty.

Kat's cold water faucet dripped. It was audible while we
talked and even when someone was shuffling cards. In the
spells of silence it became obtrusive: drip, drippety.

"I have a friend in Chicago who just bought a hotel," said
O'Connell. "It's south of the Loop. He named it the Roseleen."

"That's not a good part of town," said Kat.

"No, it sure isn't." O'Connell put a winning combination
down and raked in the pot. We were betting pennies, each
of us had a wobbly pile of them, with Kat ahead—she had
three stacks of coins. "Why would he do a thing like that?"
Kat asked. "Buy a hotel in a cheap part of town?"

"Recklessness," said O'Connell. "Imagination. No, aspiration. Why do people do things?"

Kat looked suspicious, or maybe just wary, feeling the
air full of O'Connell's and my thoughts. Twice I had said
I was going to bed; each time O'Connell urged: "Have another round, Butch. Please. I feel sociable."

"Sociable. Listen to him. Does he ever *not* feel sociable?"
That was Kat.

A train whistle sounded, and was followed by the prolonged echo of the train circling the valley and receding. I thought about the last time O'Connell and I had been together in the Hotel Roseleen; finally I managed to stop thinking about that.

"This is it," I said, aloud. "Bedtime." I disregarded O'Connell's protests and went creaking up the two flights of ladder-like stairs. Probably Kat's husband had built most of this house, adding on to a cabin that began as the kitchen and one other room.

I stripped to my slip and climbed into Kat's creaking bed; then I lay there, bolt awake. The ceiling of Kat's room was not one of those on which you could watch the reflections of passing cars' headlights, because there were hardly any cars in Ridgeley and, in any case, the room was probably too high to catch the reflections. There was no moon tonight. The curtains hung limply, white smears. I had left all the windows closed; it was too cold tonight to open them. I tried to stretch myself out and relax. Fat chance. Another train went by. That took up about twenty minutes.

I thought a little bit about Mama, which of course was not a subject conducive to sleep, and then I tried to find a safe topic, one that would make me drowsy. Riding on trains was not safe. Nor scenery, nor eating, nor anything that might have any remote connection with travel. Not my writing, which I had not been doing any of lately. Not Will—I had dreamed about Will one night, dreamed he was dead. Clara was almost a safe topic, but Clara, if I imagined her, brought her into being in this room, would not approve of me now. I tried imagining a vast, clear, white light. That was more like it. That might almost work . . . a great movie screen, the ultimate clarity, all that would be left at the end of the world. The stairs creaked. I thought about the movie screen some more. The stairs creaked again.

"She'll hear you," I said. O'Connell was dimly outlined in the half-open door of the room, then he moved across the floor, his feet slapping; he was barefoot. He sat on the edge of the bed, pulled off his pajama bottoms. When he slid into bed beside me his legs were warm and damp and he smelled of Kat's soap. He must have just had a shower.

He said, "Darling. Darling Butchie." He leaned his weight against me. "I don't care about anything," he said. "The hell with it. The hell with everybody." And he made a chorus, a whisper in my ear. "The hell with it. The hell with it."

I said, "Oh, my God." Everything about him that I had been having trouble remembering came back full force: the shoulders, square on top, round in the parts that faced me. The jut of a rib just above where my hand was resting. "I shouldn't have come here," I said.

"Yes."

"I just got on a train and did it."

"Don't talk."

"All the while the train was coming here I was saying to myself 'Don't.' "

"Butchie. My Jesus."

After we had made love we lay side by side, our faces pointing up at the ceiling. We whispered at each other in a tinny chorus:

How are you?

Not too bad.

How's your mum?

Crazy.

That bad, huh? Dear, you look skinny.

(*Darling, you look sad.*) (I didn't say this aloud.)

I thought about you lots, Butch.

You said that in your letters. Thanks for the letters. They were good letters.

Oh, God, darling.

Me too.

And finally we simply lay in bed, holding hands. It was getting light when O'Connell got up and creaked out the door. He stood for a minute in the door and looked back at me. I couldn't make out the expression on his face. The last thing he said was "Safe journey back, dear," which seemed a peculiar admonition; after all, I was going only a hundred and fifty miles away, on a train.

I didn't see O'Connell again in Ridgeley. He had left by the time I came downstairs.

Kat called a taxi for me. "I hope you slept okay," she said as the cab pulled up in front of the house. She looked me straight in the eyes, her voice was even. While I was climbing into the cab I asked myself if it mattered, and decided that it did. Everything seemed to matter some, these days.

Chapter XII

I CAME BACK FROM RIDGELEY to find Will waiting for me in the lobby of the YWCA.

When I first saw him I couldn't believe it. I thought that he was a soldier who looked like Will. I had already noticed that people in public places could remind you very heart-stoppingly of people you knew well.

But he began to walk toward me, looking well-pressed, and contained, like Will, and I didn't know what to do.

I wanted to walk rapidly in the other direction, out the door of the Y, down the avenue, on and on, past L Street, K Street, H Street, and so on, finally into Union Station, on-to a train. I also had an idiot desire to fix my hair, which was flopping disheveled around my ears. I wanted to say, "Will, why in the Hell are you showing up now of all times? Whatever possessed you?"

I said, "Hello, Will, how are you?" and walked forward and gave him my hand. We stood that way for a minute, Will holding my hand in both of his; finally he leaned forward and kissed me on the cheek. Then we went into the sitting room and sat down side by side on two fake antique chairs with imitation leather seats. Will let go of my hand just as we sat down; he rested his fist on the mahogany arm of his chair, clenched it and said, "Helen, I'm going overseas."

"Will! I'm so sorry."

"In a couple of weeks."

"I'm sorry, Will."

Well, say something else, for creeps' sake. There sits Will, thinking about going overseas, and trying to decide how he feels about it, and how he feels about you and what the world is made of. Say something like, Will, you've been right all the time about Mother, who is a horrible schizy drunk Will, your uniform fits nicely, and you look well put together. You are very handsome, with your crisp brown hair, your brown eyes with their alert stare, the lashes long, curling.

Will, I have been sleeping with a married Army Transport Corps lieutenant. I've been sleeping with him a lot. That's the first thing you should know about me.

Around us the YWCA was asserting itself. A buzzer sounded five times. That meant that someone on the fifth floor was wanted on the phone. You were supposed to pick it up and find out who. Really a stupid system. There was a sign about a talk on "Bullet Proof Bibles?" Cute title. Also a sign about a typing class and one saying that the Girl's Friendly Society would meet Thursday at eight. A friendly girl was playing the piano. Someone's voice rose above the clatter: "It isn't the starting that's so hard, it's the stopping, if you know what I mean."

Probably discussing knitting a sweater. Or riding a bob-sled.

Will said, "Helen, will you marry me?"

He said, "I've thought about your mother. I've thought about her a great deal.

"Of course I do not like her, as you know.

"I don't think you stand a chance of improving her. I know that what you're trying to do won't work.

"But I can understand that you have to do it. I really have understood that all along."

The girl playing the piano switched to "Black Magic." She started to sing it.

"Anyway, Helen," said Will, looking determined and angry, "I love you. I want to marry you."

Will has absolutely clean shoes. His socks stay up—they don't wrinkle over the ankles the way most men's socks do. His pants have a good, brittle crease in them.

I said, "Mother's been worse again, Will."

He made a movement with his shoulders. "We talk too much about your mother." Will is not stupid. The opposite; he is very intelligent. He is crazy about Renoir, and that is an intelligent and interesting thing to be.

I opened my mouth to say, "There's really nothing I can do about it. It's all over with us. There's nothing left. I wasn't ever in love with you anyway," and then I didn't say anything even remotely like that. What kept me from saying it was more than just simple cowardice, although that figured in it, too. Will looked vulnerable tonight, younger than I had been remembering him, extremely clean, almost shy in his starched tan uniform, knotted cotton tie, curly hair mashed wetly back. I didn't want to hurt

Will. That's what I said to myself, anyway, adding in a criticizing voice, a harpy's voice, halfway between Grandmother's and my own: and in addition you're a coward, Helen. A lousy little coward.

"A lot has been happening to me lately, Will," I said. "I need to wait some." When I looked at Will I saw that he was hurt even by this. The set of his firm shoulders told me so.

That girl couldn't carry a tune in a bucket.

"It's been frantic this last month, Will. I haven't had a chance to catch my breath."

"That's what your mother does to you. I knew it would be like that." But he put his hand back down over mine.

My goodness, that girl has finished up with her "Black Magic" and has gone on to "Deep Purple." Will doesn't remember it, but "Deep Purple" is *our song.*

"Let's take it easy." I looked again at Will's crisply curling hair and handsome quiet face and air of general honesty and dependability. That dependable atmosphere was inside him; it really didn't all come from that neat fit of things. Now what have you gotten yourself into? the harpy inside of me asked. What are you starting now?

Nothing, I told her. "Let's go for a walk, Will," I suggested.

And I will not tell you about O'Connell and I also will not tell you about my troubles and I also will not think about them. I stood up and shook out my skirt.

"You look tired," Will said.

"I *am* tired."

"I'm sorry. I wish you weren't."

It was too damn much. I had to go into the Y's ladies' room and cry and rub my eyes with rough paper towels to erase the ghost of Ridgeley, West Virginia. "Come back and see me if you're ever in Ridgeley again," O'Connell's sister had said, as the cab honked for the second time. Had she meant it? Was she being sarcastic? "That's probably the last time I'll ever see him," I told myself as I crumpled the paper towel back and forth to soften it so I could blow my nose on it. Obviously, O'Connell and I had to stop. And now seemed a better time than most. To stop. Quit while you're winning, so to speak.

Mother was sober again. I went into the basement on M Street, where the balls of dust had collected in mouse-like wads on the dog-hair rug.

Mama was in bed. She looked the worse for wear, laid fragilely against the pillow with purple and green pouches under her eyes. The doctor had not been too gentle with the needle, and it had left an irregular bruise on her luminous quaking arm. She was sitting limply, from time to time leaning forward and writing her memoirs in green ink, her red hair piled messily on top of her head and held there with bobby pins and a black grosgrain bow. She wore an old blue sleeveless nightgown, torn and low-bosomed. Nothing could make her look really awful; she looked like a great beauty who had been in a bad accident.

My mother wrote a sentence and put a hollow green dot over it. I think that what she actually was writing was a letter to Clara. She laid down the pen and sighed with a hand up to her head. "Helen, what on earth did I say last night?"

"It wasn't last night, Mama, it was the night before that."

"Did I say anything awful to you?"

"You didn't say much of anything at all to me, Mama, but you were filthy unspeakable to Ford."

"Was I?" She sighed again and after a minute I heard

another noise, a peculiar one. When I looked at her closely I saw that she was laughing, leaning tiredly back against the pillow and holding the sheet against her mouth.

I said, "Mama, as far as I know there is no law that says just because you're my mother I have to put up with a lot of stuff from you and I just want you to know that you were atrocious; you weren't cute and you weren't funny and it isn't funny now just as it wasn't funny then. You were filthy drunk and it was filthy and I hated it."

Mama had stopped laughing; she wedged herself further into the pillows, or at least gave the impression that she was doing this, and said, "Of course I know that, Helen."

I felt that I had just gotten started on my subject. "I don't care what Ford has done to you. I think he's been trying to be helpful, but maybe he's been presumptuous and superior; that doesn't make any difference. You can't say the things to people that you said to Ford. You don't really think anybody else is out there. You go through life feeling your way like a sleepwalker and not believing other people are real at all. Well, Ford's a real man and you hurt him a lot, and I'm real, and it frightens and upsets me when you get drunk like that."

"I know I've been a lousy mother to you, Helen."

"And there you go, more of the same damn thing. If it's not one extreme it's the other."

"No, it's true; I think it was seeing you again that made me drink."

"Then maybe I should have stayed away."

"Maybe you should. I've never done you any good. I've never helped you."

This was not the time, I thought, to say oh, yes you have, and so I didn't say it.

"What you said before I left Berkeley was true: you and

Clara could have a good, regular, stable life if it weren't for me."

"That's not really what I said."

"Yes, it is; and it's true. I thought when I saw you again . . . oh, God, you can't imagine how glad I was . . . but that morning then I thought, what am I going to do to her? And I got scared, and thought of all the things I'd done wrong, and then I thought, well, it doesn't matter; she's not going to stay long of course, and the important thing is to know that she does come to see me sometimes." She turned her head and began to cry into the pillow, and the nightgown fell off one shoulder.

"Look, Mama, you always manage to get off the hook this way . . . " I paused a minute and said, "I'm sorry, Mama, really I am." Then after a while I continued, "The point is we were talking about Ford and what I'm trying to say is Ford is an all-right person, I guess, and you can't treat people like that."

My mother sighed and turned and wiped her eyes. "I don't want to talk about Ford; I want to talk about you."

"Mama, don't you ever feel a little sorry for him?"

"I don't know, dear. I really don't know. I'm sorry I upset you, though.

"Oh, Helen," my mother went on, "I'm so glad you came and I'm so sorry I made such an awful mess of it. Oh, God, honey." She sat up and reached for her pen, but then lay back to cry without having touched it.

I said, "Look, Mama, I'm going to make some coffee," in order to give us both something to do.

While I was making the coffee I had an imaginary conversation with Clara. "Claire," I said, "do you realize that at the age we are now most people's parents would be taking care of them instead of the other way around? Do you realize that I am only nineteen?" Clara asked where in hell it got you thinking up questions like that.

Clara then wanted to know what we were going to do about Mama, and I repeated my question, "Do you realize, Clara, that at the age we are now . . . " Clara said, "That doesn't answer anything at all, Helen; you are old enough to be involved with two different men at once," and at that point the water began to bubble and I threw the coffee grounds in too suddenly and the coffee came up out from under the lid and overflowed all over Mama's two-burner gasplate.

When we were sitting down with our coffee (I did not make Mama get up and go to the glass-ringed table with it but instead brought it to her in her bed, and I myself sat on the edge, balancing the Willow cup and a bran muffin which she had made before she went on her binge), I said, "Mama, Will is here; he's come to Washington to see me."

"Will," said my mother. I heard her take a sip of coffee. When I looked at her she was holding the cup away from herself and the tears were running down her cheeks. I didn't ask what was the matter; I waited for her to tell me.

"I'm a little hysterical today."

I thought, not as hysterical as you were night before last.

"I'm so glad Will has come to see you. I always hoped it would work out for you and Will." When I didn't say anything she went on, "I know, of course, that Will doesn't like me, and it used to bother me, because I felt so . . . Will seemed so right for you, and so steady. I felt as if Will were the man you would have married if nothing had ever happened to us and we hadn't had any problems."

"I suppose he's steady," I said cautiously.

She handed me her coffee cup and used the sheet to dry her eyes with. "I had that daydream, you know? That you and Will were married and that all the mistakes I had done didn't make any difference, and your life was going to be—not quiet, exactly—but balanced, even . . . "

I didn't want to think about this picture. "Well, Mama, he's here and he's going overseas. I'll be spending some time with him."

My mother said, "I wish Will liked me."

"Will likes you all right," I said, not wanting to say it, because (a) it was a lie, and (b) I didn't think I should say anything to encourage her.

"No, no, he doesn't, and who can blame him anyway."

I said, "Who, indeed," suddenly feeling very tired. I wanted Clara and started making up a letter to her in my head. It was not going to be a letter with anything in it about Mama, or Will or O'Connell or Ford, or what to do with Mama; it would be simple descriptions of Washington and Baltimore and of the little Washington office girls running back to work after lunch with their hair all full of bobby pins.

Will and I went to the movies and sat and held hands like any old well-adjusted bushy-tailed couple. It did not feel like being unfaithful to O'Connell to hold hands with Will, because Will's hand holding was very controlled, as if Will were as afraid as I of getting in too deep. Anyway I was never going to see O'Connell again. And with Will going overseas (fairly soon, I gathered from the way he talked about it), the whole relationship seemed safe, perhaps even desirable. I couldn't make myself think about it. Mother was sober again, she hadn't had a drink for six whole days; the bruise on her arm had almost disappeared. I was tired. I had written that to Clara: Clara, I am just so tired. Nothing seems to matter. And then I had tried to fish the postcard out of the Y's mailbox with a coat hanger. Well, the hell with it. The trouble with writing that way to Clara was not that it upset her, but that she sent me back lecturing messages.

Around Will and me the movie house was as full of soldiers and their girls as a squirrel is of fleas. As the YWCA is of secretaries. As Washington is of ordinary, well-adjusted couples. Not much different from us, either. Most of them could read and write; some of them wrote poetry, some—many—of the men were going overseas. And that's why they were sitting in the movies, holding hands in the dark, watching Fred Astaire do a tap dance on the deck of an aircraft carrier, with a girlfriend who could also dance but who was being sent into another theater of war because her patriotism had made her volunteer for a different entertainment group. It all came out happily in the end; they were both great successes and nobody got killed.

Will was being very good. He walked all over Washington with me and read poetry aloud and made nasty remarks about Fred Astaire and General Arnold and stood with me by the Washington Monument reflecting pool while the wind shook the thin leaves of the trees and the pool water jumped up and down and tossed the reflection about. He didn't pester me to sleep with him and he didn't try to get an answer to his proposal of marriage. He seemed relieved that I went off to see Mother by myself and wouldn't let him come with me.

Will and I walked home from the movies.

Our route took us past the White House. We stood and gawked at it like any pair of ordinary tourists, holding on to the iron fence and staring up at the upper story. There were several lights on up there.

Will said, "Listen, when we are married I think you should go back to college."

I didn't answer. I had been squelching ideas like that every time they came up.

Will said, "This war isn't going to last forever. Things won't always be like this." He gestured at peaceful, sleeping Washington around us. "Sometimes I think the whole world has always been gray and crazy. Do you remember it any other way?"

"Yes," I said, "I do."

"We'll come out of this all right," Will put his arm around me. "Is there such a thing, do you think, as a Renoir world?"

A Renoir world? Oh, poor Will.

"I think of it," he said seriously, "especially in relation to you. You don't know it, but the first time I saw you—I'd just arrived at your house from the East—I was upstairs on the balcony with your mother, the door opened, you came dashing in below . . . A world of colors. Orange and gold and blue, in little dots. That's the way I saw you then."

Will. Please don't.

"Don't feel bad," he said. "The war will be over and it will all be different."

No it won't.

"And, listen. About your mother. I hate her; you know that. But I understand how you feel about her. You're right, really. I know."

Will had slipped into talking of our engagement as if he almost believed in it. And I had slipped into listening to him as if I believed in it too.

I stared up at the White House, shining out like a symbol of something or other on a Christmas card.

* * *

"Ford, I certainly hope everything comes out all right for you."

Another day, another train. This time poor old Ford was leaving, going to his friend in New York.

Mother had refused to have anything more to do with him, so I was representing the family, you might say, in seeing him off.

My goodness, Ford, I hope your friend is nicer to you than my mother was.

Poor Ford didn't look the way I would be looking if I had let somebody say those things to me. He looked chipper, and sweet, and a little sad, and glad to be off. Maybe it made him feel he was real, and not just a hole in space, to have had a frantic redhead yelling *fairy* at him.

"I'm sorry I couldn't have helped Selma more." Yes, that's the line to take.

"You did, I know. When she gets over this bit now you'll see."

Sigh. Well. She feels too much, perhaps. One has a sense of futility.

Oh, we all do.

Thank you so much, Ford. Write to me sometimes.

Yes my dear, of course.

The sign across the top of the station still said LOOSE LIPS SINK SHIPS. It wasn't hanging crookedly anymore. Hey, I didn't notice that one before, poster of ship going down, just the prow sticking out of the waves, flag still bravely flying with almost every star in place. Caption: SOMEONE TALKED.

Ford had only one suitcase and his overcoat and a cardboard box of books. Have you traveled all through life that way, Ford, or do you have stuff in storage somewhere? He wanted to leave like a gentleman, with the porter pushing the cardboard box on a trolley, but no porter could be seen anywhere, so I carried the suitcase and he carried the box, which required going stiff-legged and holding the string with two hands, very undignified. Never mind, Ford. You came out of this melee pretty well, if you ask me.

Four hundred and ninety-two servicemen were lined up to get onto Ford's train to New York.

Yes, I will write. Not very often, you know, but once in a while.

Really, Ford, you did lots for Mother. She knows it really. She'll come out of this fit and then she'll realize it.

Ford put both hands on the shoulders of my cat skin coat and looked down at me, smiling genteelly and sadly.

"Goodbye, me dear. I shall think of you. So bright and pretty . . . you know, like her, only not . . . "

Only not drunk and crazy.

"Goodbye, Ford. Thanks."

And luck, Ford. Keep smiling. And I will keep smiling, too. I stood and waved at Ford while he disappeared into the crowd. He couldn't wave back at me, because he was now carrying both the box and the suitcase; he probably couldn't even turn around to see me waving at him (it was too crowded to be sure), but I stood and did it anyhow, *pro forma*, a gesture aimed against various kinds of human hurt. Well, I said to myself, if I do it for Ford today, maybe somebody will do it for me tomorrow.

It had started to snow. I walked along Fifteenth Street, which was suddenly very silent, and then along M Street. Mama's little dugout of an entryway already had a pile of snow in it.

She was sitting at the table, still writing away at her letter. She wrote with flourishes and splashes, the writing slanting optimistically uphill, with big tails on the ends of words and hollow dots floating like balloons above. Clara or I used sometimes to follow after her as she wrote and color the inside of the dot in a contrasting color.

She said, "I didn't write to Clara, darling, because I wrote to Clara yesterday; don't you remember that?

"So I thought since I do not need to write to Clara and I do not want to write to your grandmother, who is the other logical person I know well enough to write to, perhaps I would write to God." And she curled away industriously and put a hollow dot over something. I sat down in the reddish-brown gutless chair and watched the snow melt off the side of my shoe and form a puddle on the brown rug.

My mother said, "Of course I do not believe in God and I do not believe in any force greater than man; man is the maker of his own destiny, but for literary purposes one may assume a God, don't you think?"

"What are you telling God?"

"It's a little like a letter to Santa Claus." She sat up straight and picked up the letter and ripped it into a number of strips the long way. Then she put these on the table and put her head on them.

I said, "Mama. Things are not bad at all."

"Helen, I hope you're going to marry Will."

I didn't answer.

"Is it Will's hating me so much that's stopping you?"

"That's got nothing to do with it."

"I can just go away somewhere," she said.

"Listen, Mama, the snow outside is weird; let's go for a walk."

Mother had lifted her head up off the pile of torn-up

letter and was now resting it on her hand. "I understand why Will hates me but I wish he didn't."

"Come on, Mama, I have to get back soon, I'm supposed to meet him. Where's your coat?" Mama's coat was in the closet, a black coat with a light-colored wolf collar; I had her into it and buttoned before I realized she was still wearing her bunny-fur slippers.

"Thank you, darling," she said, obediently slipping her feet into shoes. She had no overshoes and she had no gloves. I gave her one of my gloves, and we went out like Meg and Jo in *Little Women*, each of us with one glove.

I had read *Little Women* aloud to Clara the year I was twelve. At twelve, I considered myself much too old for *Little Women*; I had already graduated to Charlotte Brontë and Steinbeck, but I thought Meg and Jo were an experience Clara should have. She didn't read books on her own, and Mama no longer read to us since Daddy went to Spain.

What we both liked about the book was that the father was away fighting, like ours. But the lives of those girls were different from our lives in some way that I found it hard to think about. I asked Clara about this, and she was no help. "They lived a zillion years ago; how could they not be different?" She was cross at Louisa May Alcott. "I wish Jo would marry Laurie."

Mama and I scraped along holding hands on the ungloved side. Mama put up her face to the swirling cloud of snow; flakes settled on her eyelashes, each eyelash becoming a frosty spike clustered with white stars, an effect I had seen only on a sprayed Christmas tree. "You look like the enchanted princess. The prince should come and kiss your eyes clear."

She liked the idea. "Then what?"

I got enthusiastic. "That would melt your snowbound heart. You would open your beautiful eyes and he would take one look and fall in love. With your beauty."

I was trying to make her laugh, but she sighed and wiped her nose on her glove. "I *was* very pretty. Your father used to say he felt guilty about it."

"Why on earth, guilty?"

"He thought he shouldn't love me for being pretty. He didn't say that very often. But sometimes he seemed to think it was . . . well, they don't have those kinds of sins in socialism, do they?"

"I don't know." I tried not to get involved in such speculations. They made me uncomfortable.

My father, I suspected, had had almost no sense of humor. What I remembered about him was his appearance —tall, gentle, with a craggy face something like Abraham Lincoln's, and blue eyes. But how could he be Grandmother's child and have a sense of humor? Grandmother would have leached a sense of humor out of any baby before it was two. In the vague way that children know things, I understood that Daddy had become a socialist in order to irritate his mother, but that he had still retained her uncomfortable puritan principles. And he married Mama because she was the opposite of those principles. They had made a handsome couple, as far as I could remember.

"You're still pretty," I said. "Very."

Mama scooped her glove along the top of a mailbox and blew at the crust of snow on the glove. "I'm going to tell Will I won't live anywhere near you. If you get married."

"Quit thinking about it."

"You should. Marry him."

"Tell me about Grandma's Youth Dance." I was asking her about her own mother, the dancer, not about our rigid grandmother Reynolds. Mama loved to talk about Grandma Darcy.

We headed in the direction of Dupont Circle. I don't know what had gotten into me; I was already late for meeting Will, and I was purposely keeping us away from the apartment and asking Mama questions to take her mind off her cold feet.

" . . . And she did the dance for him again," Mama said. "He gave her an opal pendant set in gold filigree. Made by the finest goldsmith in India. But we had to sell it when your father went to Spain."

Grandma Darcy had danced for the Maharajah of Mysore. "A small man," said Mama, "in an ordinary blue suit. Not what you would have expected. But she *did* say he had a turban." I reflected on Mama's narrative gift and the fact that she had never really used it. I loved to hear her tell stories.

Dupont Circle was smooth under an unmarked layer of white. Looking at its orderly outlines, I suddenly became panicky about Will. "What time was your appointment?" said Mama. She had the gift of prescience. I turned us around and started toward M Street.

To take my mind off of Will, I began to tell jokes. "Knock, knock. Who's there?"

All Renoir ladies like a nice joke. Their needs are simple: happy people around them, sunshine, love, food. It's a dirty, dirty trick.

We arrived at Mama's little dugout to find Will camped under the overhang at her front door. He was leaning against the door with his hands in his pockets and his coat collar turned up.

"Will," said Mama. This was the first time they had met since he arrived in Washington. All the jollity drained out of her; she sagged her shoulders and extended the hand with the glove on it. "My goodness, what a surprise." She became smaller.

Then she apparently decided the glove wasn't right, pulled it off, presented the hand again. Will shook it non-committally.

Mama scraped her feet on the snow, leaving scratch marks. A chunk of snow fell off the overhang. I took her pocketbook and searched in it for the key.

In the apartment we were greeted by darkness and a chair left catty-corner across the doorway so that Will tripped over it and swore, and a strong, sweet, burned smell. Mama said, "Oh, God, my cake," in a replay of my first visit with her in this room, and rushed with the gray pillow to the oven, where she extracted a cake, this time quite burned. I turned on the lights and Will pulled the chair out of the way and put his coat on it.

Mama said, "Oh, it's just absolutely hopeless; oh heavens, I feel so silly. No, I don't think any of it can be saved." And poked at the cake with the wrong end of the fountain pen from the letter to God. She said, "Oh, what a shame. It would have been so nice to have had a cake for Will. Of course I didn't know Will was coming, but just the same, it's almost as if I had known, now, Will, isn't it?"

Will said, "Except that you burned the cake." He stamped his shoes and made splatters on the rug.

"Oh, so I did. Foolish Selma." Mama laughed gaily and got no response from Will. She opened the door and set the cake in the hall. "Maybe the elves will come and take it away."

I picked up the coffeepot and went to fill it. The bathtub still had its same gray ring, or another one exactly like it.

When I came back Will was sitting in the red chair and

Mama was perched uncertainly on the edge of one of the brown ones. Will said in a flat voice, looking at his shoes, "You were gone an awfully long time this afternoon, Helen. And we don't have much time left."

Mama said, "Oh, Will, you have no idea, the time went so very quickly, it was so strange." She said, "Will, I was really glad when I heard you'd come to Washington to see Helen . . . "

Some people are able to sit perfectly still while someone else gushes. Will had always been able to do this with my mother.

"It's hard to explain. Why I should like it. It pleased me so much."

I said, "We went for a walk, Will."

"We went for quite a long walk," Mama said. "It's amazing how you can forget about time."

Will looked at the tips of his shoes. I had the surprising conviction, because I usually thought of him as being mature, that he was sulking.

After I got the water on for coffee I went to the table and captured the pieces of Mama's letter and put them in the wastebasket. Will, of course, would not have looked at them; that was not Will's style at all, trying to figure out what was in other people's letters. But I felt safer when I had gotten the shredded pieces thrown away.

Then I sat down in the brown gutless chair and stared at him. He must have been standing a long while in the snow; the toes of his shoes were stained wet and there were damp patches on the cuffs of his pants. A piece of hair toward the front was wet and hung over his forehead. He sat with his hands on the arms of the chair; he looked extremely uncomfortable. It was curious, because Will was older than

I, that I kept finding the adjective *young* to describe him.

Mama hunched with her knees together and fluttered sporadically. My. Dreadful snow. Will, your feet are all wet.

The aroma of burned cake was strong. Will shifted and looked past a spot to the right of Mama's ear. Eventually he said, "Why not open a window, Helen?"

Window? Good God, what a horrible few minutes, crawling slowly like one's worst dreams. I don't really want to open a window or do anything else anybody here suggests. Will, I know my mother looks stupid, like a little hen that has been mesmerized by a line scratched in the dirt. But, Will, do you know that you're making her be that way? Do you understand that?

The water boiled and rattled against the top of the pot. As I stood at the stove performing sleight-of-hand with the coffee I could hear Mama saying, "Truly, when one lives in California one never dreams . . . "

There was no coffee cup for Will or for any other third person, and so I elected myself the third person and poured coffee into a cereal dish. And Mama exclaimed about customs in France, Quebec, and Louisiana.

When we were seated at the table there was a moment of blessed relief while each of us blew into our coffee. I said, "Poor Mama. I'm so sorry about your cake."

"Oh, it doesn't matter in the least little bit."

"If I'd known I would have been reminding you."

"It was a raisin and nut cake, dear."

Will cleared his throat. I knew he was going to say something important. At the age of twenty-three Will already had a special throat-clear for significant moments. "Helen. I'm going away. On Thursday."

Thursday? No wonder Will looked like that. "I'm awfully sorry." Now I felt truly guilty. I wished I had been nicer to him. "When did you find out?"

"I didn't find out; I knew all along. I didn't want to rush you. I could have told you, and I didn't."

He's mad at me; I don't blame him. Will is going overseas. I said this to myself; nothing happened. Behind me Mama made abstract noises.

"I wish you'd told me."

"No point to it. I wouldn't have told you now, except I don't like spending the afternoon alone."

It is possible to feel several contradictory emotions, none of them rational and none of them dominant, and all of them concurrent. I did this now. Will is going overseas. He is behaving badly to my mother. In a minute he is going to pressure me to marry him. I wish he wouldn't.

Mother said, "Will, Helen and I have been talking, and I have just been telling her . . ." She subsided for a minute because I kicked her hard under the table. Will ignored her. "Helen, please try to decide one way or the other. About us. Shouldn't I get an answer now?"

Mama, this time unstoppable, intervened in a bright, shaky voice. "I don't plan to live in Berkeley, Will; I've been telling Helen, Berkeley is too confining."

Will finally turned to her. He looked sad and very polite. "Where would you live, then, Selma?"

"I am going to live here in Washington." Mama smiled fervently. "I have good prospects for another job in Washington. It will be a much better place for me than Berkeley."

He examined her. He didn't seem pleased nor even particularly surprised. It was hard for me to read his face, but, if anything, I thought he looked more pained than before.

"But maybe you won't want to live in Berkeley," Mama said. "Here I am running away with an idea. Of course you might want to live in Chicago. Anyway, you needn't fear I'll be living with you, Will; of course I know we don't get on."

Will cleared his throat. Mama said, "That's just a small factor. About me. But I thought it might make a difference. Because, of course, everything counts." She looked into her lap, where she had clenched her hands tightly.

Will said, "For God's sake, Selma, don't gush." He looked at his wristwatch, as if the time might make a difference, and then looked at his fingernails. He's nervous, I thought. And young. Younger than I am.

"I'm sorry," said Mama. "It just happens. It shows enthusiasm."

Will got up and began to scuff back and forth on the dog-hair rug. "Helen, you haven't answered me."

"I didn't know I was gushing," Mama said.

"I can't answer you."

Mama said, "It just comes out."

Will told me, "You really want to. We had a good time this week."

Mama said, "I'm sorry I irritate you. It's not on purpose. I don't mean to."

Will finally turned to her. "Selma. Shut up."

I said, "Will. Watch it. Stop it."

Mama said, "Really? Is it that bad?"

"If you could just manage to shut up, Selma. And sit still."

"Well, I *did* offer. To take myself out of your life. Forever."

"Christ," said Will. "Christ crucified."

Mama got up. "Never mind. It was a mistake."

"Mistake?" He stopped chewing and pacing. "The hell with it."

Mama wove her way to the bed, where she lay down the wrong way, with her feet on the pillow. She said, "Helen?"

"Well?"

"Did Ford give you a sentimental line about how beautiful I was?"

"Yes, Mama."

"What did he say? How did he put it?"

I didn't answer. I wasn't going to side with either of them. Let them fight it out even-steven.

"I'll bet he said I had mutable loveliness. That's what he used to tell me. Mutable loveliness. It sounds icky."

I was silent.

"Like a mashed flower."

My mother raised her leg and pulled off her shoe. Will, had he been interested, could have seen the top of a stocking, a stripe of blue-white thigh, an edge of ruffled grayish-pink panty. She held her foot out and admired the flex of the toes. She said, "In any case, Will here seems not to care. About my mutable loveliness. And my . . . what was that? Strange vitality?"

"Mama, what are you trying to do? Start a fight?"

"Somebody had better. Here, Helen, here's the gun." She reached under the bed, where the bourbon bottle had been, and pulled something out and threw it at me.

"For Christ's sake," Will said.

"It was never loaded, you know," Mama remarked. "It gave me a charge to have it and let Ford see it sometimes . . . Guns are sex symbols, you know," she added in a pleased voice. "But I never had any bullets for it. It was just for letting Ford find."

Will said, "Selma, you have the brains and conscience of a child."

"Quit talking about being a child." I put the gun in the middle of the glass-marked table. It was a nasty little black snub-nosed monster. "Mama, really, you're the limit."

"Well, I'm sorry I upset you, and that night you were looking for it I sort of understood somehow, but I couldn't do anything about it. If I'd been able to think I would have told you where it was."

I said, "The hell with it." Then I said, "Will, this isn't going to work."

Will stopped marching and stood silently with his hands in his pockets.

"We fight too much," I said.

"You mean I fight with your mother."

"It's the same thing. Almost."

Will took a deep breath. "Look, Helen, I'm sorry. As your mother says about being drunk, I knew it was happening and I couldn't do anything about it." He waited for a minute. "You're right, I guess. I guess you're right. It would always be like this."

I said, "I'm sorry it all came out now, to have let it wait so long; I feel like a heel . . . "

I said, "Will, is it too awful to say . . . ? Yes, I guess it is. Listen, Will, it wouldn't have been any good, though, would it? We would have fought, wouldn't we? We always did fight."

Will picked up his topcoat, which had been thrown across the back of the red chair, and I came around and held it for him. The movement of picking up the coat created a draft in the room and wafted the smell of burned cake toward us.

I said in surprise, looking at the coat collar and the neat back, the well-fitting seam along the middle of the shoulder, "Will, I'm really sorry."

Will turned around, put a hand under my chin and looked, first at my eyes, then at my mouth. "Helen."

He started toward the door. "I apologize to Selma; I'd be pretty much of a heel if I didn't."

As he went by the table he picked up the gun.

I said, "For God's sake, be careful."

Mama said, "There's no need to be careful, I keep telling you. There aren't any bullets in it. Not unless Fag put some in."

Will said, "I know how to handle a gun."

He examined it, looked underneath it—I suppose at its registry number—blew on it and started to set it back on the table. I said, "For Heaven's sake, does everybody have to play with it?" Mama said, "I keep telling you there aren't any bullets in it."

The gun went off and blew out the top panel of Mama's basement window.

Chapter XIII

"I'M NOT EXACTLY SURE why it is, Helen," my mother said, "but I feel this encounter with Will may result in a new breakthrough."

I sat on Mother's flowered, mangy, Indian-patterned bed with one of her defeated pillows behind my head, eating a doughnut. Mama had made doughnuts on the two-burner gas plate. The room smelled like a refreshment stand at the beach. Droplets of grease hung from the ends of the windowshade pulls. The broken window had been boarded up; the landlady said it would take a week to get a glazier.

"Do you remember the theory of dialectical materialism?" Mama asked.

I remembered the theory of dialectical materialism all right, because Mama had had so much difficulty understanding it, and Clara and I, who wanted her Spanish Committee to love her, had tried to drive it home.

"When two opposing forces come together, Mama," Clara had said. "It happens in chemistry all the time."

We finally got Mama to understand, and dialectical materialism became one of her formulas. She made it into a hopeful and sentimental concept. Everything always came out for the best. Any kind of collision would result in something good. We are moving steadily upward. All change is progress.

"The dialectically materialistic result of that confrontation with Will the other night . . . " My mother paused to lug the doughnut vat out into the hall. Her voice continued from there with cheerful phrases like " . . . new start . . . new view . . . "

"Understanding of *you*, darling," she said as she came back into the room. "Because I see again how much you really love me. Although I had known that all along anyway, of course. And then I knew of course, too, that coming out here was entirely for my own good. But still, darling. In that discussion with Will I really *felt* . . . "

"Where did you put that gun, Mama?"

"Gun, darling? I have absolutely no idea."

Well, *I* feel permanently tired. Surely there is no such thing as permanent tiredness, but that's how I think I feel. It will be no good saying: Mama, you've got everything ass-backwards, as usual. I broke up with Will because I wanted to. Quit thinking you are the center of the universe. I was actually very angry with her. A question to no one in particular: what's the point of two dozen doughnuts? Who would ever want to eat two dozen doughnuts?

"Darling! I have a job." My mother had come to the Y to tell me this. She looked disheveled and fashionable and pretty, a pancake-shaped hat over her right eyebrow. We sat in the lobby, my mother on the edge of her imitation leather chair, one leg balanced in front of the other, the way they had taught us to sit for high-school graduation so our skirts would fall gracefully.

"Your research job, Mama?" I was not going to invest much emotion in Mama's research job. That one had not sounded like a good bet to me.

"No, darling." Mama's ears got pink. "This one is with the phone company."

"The phone company?" The phone company is the last place on earth where I would expect you to find work, Mama. I have heard, and I believe it, that the phone company won't hire anyone who is too bright, too emotive, too quick, too moody, or too interesting. I stared at her.

"In the central building. Downtown. You know, there is this big square building with all those offices. And when you come in, right away there is a woman at a desk. She directs you. She tells you where to go."

Slowly, my whole view of the phone company shifted. The lady at the desk. Sort of a seated statue of liberty, a Renoir earth goddess. Maybe, after all these years, Mama, you have finally hit it. Greeting people and telling them where to go. You would be lovely at that. Ineffably lovely, to quote Ford. Maybe the fact that this is Washington will help. In Washington, the phone company must want to have elegance and tone. People, bureaucrats, diplomats, will come in to complain about their bills or the wartime shortage of phones or the wartime curtailment of service or the fact that they can't get an unlisted phone, and there they will be met by my beautiful, gracious mother, clearly a refugee from another and better world, not too efficient, so they won't feel they have been turned over to a mindless, unthinking, uncaring representative of wartime regulations —there my mother will be to greet them and soothe them, and sympathize. Perfect.

"Why, Mama!" I hugged her. I told her she looked lovely. I said I would be around tomorrow night to see how it was going. I didn't say: and to make sure you don't wreck this one by getting drunk first thing. I had a feeling that maybe this time—it was partly optimism and partly something else—something might be different. "Imagine your going out and getting that job all by yourself."

I moved in with Mama during the second week of her phone company job. It was her idea. In a way she pleaded with me to do it, and in a way she didn't; she just assumed that I would, a part of the natural course of events.

She persuaded the landlady to move another bed into the apartment, and we pushed it against the far wall of the room. "My little girl," Mama said. "Back with me at last."

I wrote to Clara that everything seemed to be very good. Maybe it would last. Ford had said Mama could quit drinking if she wanted to. Or that was almost what he had said.

Mama and I settled quickly into a routine that involved my getting up and making breakfast for the two of us. My mother seemed to enjoy those breakfasts. She told me that the oatmeal was lumpy and the coffee weak.

"Your talents are different, yours and Clara's," she said. "Chloe always said to me, 'Selma, they are such sensitive children.' Auras." Mother buttered a piece of toast. "Did I ever tell you, darling, Chloe did your auras and yours is purple? That's so unusual, darling; and so was mine. It seems something about sensitivity . . . I think whole wheat bread today, dear, if he has it, and some little lamb chops if he has those, and if not, well, I guess eggs maybe; I could make a vegetable soufflé. How are the meat stamps?"

O'Connell had sent me a whole page of meat stamps; one of his union members had died and the union got the unused ration book.

"And tomatoes, darling. Goodbye, dear." Mama had a new hat with an iridescent green feather. She put this on, looking at herself in the crazed dresser mirror. Her reflection separated and reassembled in the cracked glass, evocative and romantic, like Will's Renoir.

I kissed her goodbye and locked the apartment door from the inside and sat down at the glass-bottom marked table with my grocery list.

Mama's grubby apartment had the impermanent quality that I associated with children's clubhouses. Clara and I had built one the year I was nine, down at the bottom of the garden, hidden by a bank of juniper. We went there every day that summer, I to write a secret diary, Clara for her zoo of salamanders and caterpillars. In the winter we forgot the clubhouse and the rain washed it down the hill into the fence.

I added breakfast food and margarine to my list. I thought that I was like my imaginary picture of a wife; I tried to imagine O'Connell's wife and wondered if she was at this moment making out her grocery list for O'Connell's dinner. It was an hour earlier in Chicago, but Mrs. O'Connell was a real housewife with a real housewife's schedule. She would get all these things done early in the day, maybe she was by now all finished with her list and halfway done with her marketing, shoving a cart around the A & P; picking up heads of lettuce and carrots. She is wearing a tan wool coat and has a paisley print scarf over her hair. On second

thought, the paisley print scarf sounds drab. I will give
Mary Frances O'Connell a red and gray silk scarf, the kind
we used to get from India before the war. Mary Frances
refused, in my dream, to have a face, but I thought perhaps
she was stoutish and I remembered that she had gray hair.
She must certainly have been glad when I left Chicago. I
don't suppose O'Connell told her about me, but how could
she have helped knowing something. I put my head on the
table. I sometimes thought about O'Connell just as I was
waking up. The window with people's feet in it was in the
same relationship to my bed as the Hotel Roseleen's light-
well window had been. One morning I awakened with a
perfect physical hallucination; O'Connell was next to me. I
even heard him snore; he did that occasionally on an expelled breath.

"How long can it last?" Clara asked on the inside of a
fold-out postcard of California Bay Area scenes. She wrote
this under the picture of the Golden Gate Bridge, to make
it less obvious, but I knew that she really meant Mama's
reformation.

I had written Clara a long letter in which I said that
Mama, after all, might have been reacting, during the last
six years, to our father's death. Anybody should be allowed
six years to get over a shock like that. And while she had
been eccentric and different before he went to Spain, she had
not started drinking until then, I reminded Clara.

The grocery store man wanted to know about me and
Mama. "So nice to live with you mama." (He had asked:
Were we visiting? Living here? Did my mother like broc-
coli?) "To take care of you mama. So good for her."

You haven't the faintest idea what you are talking about,

I thought at him. You think I live on the second floor in one of those nice white-painted Washington apartments: bay windows and a view of a wide, clean street, and in this apartment is my handsome, motherly, ladylike mother. And I go to college. Or I am learning something special at a special school. Maybe I'm an art student. I like that one.

The next day when I went out to do the shopping I walked over to Connecticut Avenue. Connecticut Avenue was elegant that day, with wide streets, gray buildings with large windows cut up into small panes, trees in tubs, neatly contained snow, an occasional doorman, striped awnings. In front of a dress shop on Connecticut Avenue there was a sidewalk revivalist. He had no arms and he had a sign: *World War Veteran,* on a tripod in front of him. He meant that he was a veteran of the last world war, not of the current one. Underneath the notice about war was the question: Are you saved for Jesus? The man played a harmonica attached around his neck on a metal frame. After he played his harmonica he leaned forward and picked up a leaflet with his teeth and extended it toward me. I gave him a quarter. He had dark hair and straight eyebrows and a square face and he looked like O'Connell.

"Jesus is coming again. Armageddon is coming," the leaflet said. Then it quoted some poetry: "Your lovers were all untrue/ Your chase had a beast in view." I went home and tried to look the poem up in Louis Untermeyer, but without much hope; it didn't sound like modern poetry to me. I quoted it to Mama that night: "Your lovers were all untrue . . . "

I was thinking of myself, of course, but Mama thought I meant her. "Your father was a very fine man. He never had an uncertain moment. He was a rock. He was always there. I could rely on him absolutely."

For the first time in my life I asked myself about my father. What about him, then? What do you say about a man who goes off to Spain, leaving his wife and his little girls to wait for him and to live off of what's left of his warehouse after he has sold half of it to pay for his year in Spain and his guns and his uniform and some extra to give away to the loyalists? My family was weird. "I just meant everybody's life was like that," I told my mother.

"I don't know where you get it from," she said. "Certainly not from me. You're a defeatist, Helen. There's a wry, tense quality about you. I can't imagine how it happened."

"It was easy."

"I know what it is," she said. "You're implying *I* did it." We were sitting over the remains of dinner. Mama had used all the meat stamps and prepared something with veal chops and sour cream, chocolate mousse for dessert. "Give me a cigarette," she said.

"You're smoking too much." She had always smoked a little, but she also made speeches about how it smelled, how it dried up the moist tissues. She told me and Clara that drinking was *good* for the moist tissues. Now she said, "Well, if I can't drink."

"What do you mean, Mama, for God's sake, you can't drink? It's *your* decision."

Mama lit the cigarette and drew in on it and giggled. She had her hair up in a roll around the crown of her head, like a lady in the court of Louis the fourteenth. "Don't be silly, Helen. You bossed me out of that drinking."

"I never bossed you."

"Though I must say, it was lovely of you to give up Will for me. I knew you were doing it for me and I knew I ought to stop you and I kept saying to myself: all right, now, stop her. And I simply couldn't do it at all. And it went on and on and got worse and worse and now you don't have Will any more."

"It wasn't like that."

"And I appreciate it ever so much more now that I have my job." She stubbed her cigarette out in the remains of her chocolate mousse.

"Mama, you are absolutely hopeless. You are so self-centered you're perfectly impossible. I stopped seeing Will because I wanted to. Quit thinking the world revolves around you." I stood up and began to collect the plates. Now I would have to take these plates down the hall to the bathroom to wash them. "My God, when are you going to move to a decent apartment?"

"I should think," said my mother, "you would be happier. Do you know, Helen, you sound like your grandmother?"

"That's my line. I've been thinking that about you. Why should I be happier?"

"Why? For Heaven's sake, Helen. I don't understand you. You have everything you want." Mama had been playing with the remains of her chocolate mousse, pushing it around with her cigarette. Now she looked at me; something she saw in my face must have alerted her. "You do, don't you? Everything you've been saying you wanted? I'm not drinking at all and I have a job. And I'll bet that surprised you." She lowered her eyes. "And I think you didn't believe I could go without drinking and it has been a month and I don't really miss it at all. But, you see, I did it for you." She stirred the mousse. "Because you gave up Will for me and I said to myself, well, the least I can do is give up drinking for her. And I must say," she smiled, "I think I have done well and I am astonished how much I don't miss it, but I simply don't understand you, Helen. The more I try the less good it does."

I put my stack of dishes down on the table. "Mama. For God's sake."

"Perhaps I'm nicer when I drink," my mother said reflectively. She stretched out one hand in front of her, fingers extended. "But it was giving me arthritis . . . Maybe I was easier to love when I drank? You seemed to love me more then."

"I love you perfectly fine now." I took the dishes off to the bathroom.

On the way down the hall I dropped one and kicked the pieces into a corner.

It had become impossible recently to find the usual brands of products. Ivory Flakes, for instance, had gone to war. The name of these soap flakes was *Perfect.* They came in a blue package. On the front of the package was a housewife in a blue striped apron who was doing her wash in an old three-legged washtub.

I ran the water hard and looked into the crown of bubbles that rose up under the green brassy faucet and thought about my newest problem.

There was no way I could dodge it any longer; I had to admit it was there. It was almost a month since I had seen O'Connell in Ridgeley and it was almost two weeks since I should have gotten my period, and I hadn't had a period.

It seemed very likely that I was pregnant.

I got up the next morning and made pancakes for Mama and listened to her complaints about how wry and ironic I was. Then I squeezed her into her hat and her coat with the wolf collar. ("Thank you, darling. You always were a beautiful, sensitive child. You're helpful. You're like me.") I did the dishes in the gray stained tub. And finally I sat down in the middle of the broken-spined bed with the Indian coverlet and tried to think about myself.

I tried to remember back into high school and the gossip there about abortions.

Eleanor, my normal friend from school, had gone off to college; she was at Wellesley. Eleanor might know about abortionists. I tended to like women who were sensible and straightforward and had useful helpful impulses, qualities that were otherwise lacking in my life. Eleanor was like that.

I wrote down her name on a note pad. I followed that with abbreviated notes for what I could remember of the ways to abort yourself:

ex: exercise. Any kind might work, but the one that I remembered was jumping off the stove. That wouldn't be possible here. I certainly couldn't climb on Mama's rickety little two-burner stove; it wouldn't hold me. Nor could I climb on her dresser. On the other hand, if I could get up on the windowsill, I could jump from there onto the floor with only a moderate amount of noise. The floor was cement; it wouldn't reverberate.

h.b.:   this hot bath was supposed to be extremely hot, and that wasn't possible here at Mama's apartment, where the landlady kept the hot water down to lukewarm. And anyway, the idea of sitting in the horrible gray tub, steaming, hoping . . . blood spiraling out in the water, changing the gray ring around the tub to a pink one . . .

Is it possible that with some part of you, Helen, you aren't entirely sorry this has happened?

Of course it's possible.

That is very childish, very foolish. How could you be so careless?

Dear Clara:

I don't know how I could possibly have been so careless and foolish. I went to see O'Connell without letting him know I was coming, and . . .

Well, I am not going to send that letter to Clara. I am going to pull myself together and think about this in an organized way.

The home abortion methods that I remembered next were more repulsive than the ones I had already been through. Castor oil. Coat hangers.

I stared at ct. hngers. for a while and put the notebook down. Then I picked it up again and began a list of people: Eleanor (Yes), Grandmother (no), Clara (yes—maybe). I was uncertain whether I was trying to spare Clara or to protect Clara's image of me. Ford. (Yes. Well, maybe. What would Ford know about such things?) Will. (No) Aunt Blonde. (???)

Signally missing from my list is my mother. Doesn't a girl usually consult her mother when she is in trouble?

I shoved the notebook under my mattress. Then I put on my cat skin coat and went downtown to the library. First I read the article on pregnancy in the *Encyclopaedia Britannica* and then I got out a stack of medical textbooks. There was nothing specific in any of them that would help me. Apparently it was possible to seem to be writing frankly and factually and to say nothing at all.

The rumors around high school had said that it was not easy to abort yourself. Around high school the rumor was that you went to the Salvation Army and had the baby in the Florence Crittenden Home, and then someone in Walnut Creek adopted the baby, and you were never the same, ever after.

There was another obvious name missing from that list of people who might help me. O'Connell's name wasn't there. I hadn't thought about telling O'Connell. I returned the stack of medical textbooks to the librarian. She smiled at me, showing yellow horse teeth. She knows. All the women in Washington, D.C. come here, and get the same books out of the library and they never find anything in them; they go ahead and have their babies and that's why the population of Washington is rising.

Dearest Clara:

All this seems so unreal that it's hard for me to write to you about it. I really don't know what I am going to do.

I tore this letter up and put the pieces down the toilet. Then I dug the notebook out from under the bedspring and wrote in it: The end of the world is coming. It is going to be a white light in the sky. I wrote this way for about two hours. The more I wrote, the more it seemed that I had started on an actual story, a story about the end of the world, the sun getting larger, the people at first active and anxious, then more frantic as the days continued: dry, drier, no rain, clouds of pink and gray dust settling on all exposed surfaces, water becoming more valuable than champagne, than liquid mercury. I wrote through the eyes of a central figure, a young woman, who walked through the collapsing city carrying a gun. My story was good. I felt cheerful when I stopped writing.

"Can you give me change for a dollar, please?" I asked the librarian. It was the next day. I was still reading articles in medical textbooks.

"No." She smiled, showing horse teeth. She understood all right. She was enjoying herself. "Even though I happen to have it today. Because you see, don't you, that if I did it for one I would have to do it for all?"

"No. I don't see." I went outside. The nearest shop was three blocks away. I walked, examining the shrunken yellow snow, the cracks in the pavement, the feet of my fellow passengers on Washington's Capitol Hill. At the Capitol Smoke Shoppe I bought a pack of cigarettes and got change. Then I walked back to the library; that was where the phones were, and waited in a line. There was an old woman with her coat on backwards who, it turned out, didn't want to make a phone call, but was simply standing there, and a soldier with his forage cap stuck under his shoulder tabs, who did make a call, but was quick about it. Then I was in the phone booth and had closed the door and had to face the problem of whom I was trying to reach.

Ford in New York. I didn't really think Ford would know what to do about an abortion or a baby or Mama or me, but he would be sympathetic. Ford knew what it was like to be on the outside looking in, feeling different from everybody else in his world. Ford would listen, and he would say, oh, my dear. He would be concerned. He would make me feel better.

"I am sor-ry," the operator said, "all of our circuits are bus-y; please try again in an hou-r." Like the lady in the library, she sounded as if she were enjoying herself.

To my surprise, my California call was accepted and put through immediately. But that was no good, either; the phone rang, no one answered. I stood holding the receiver, listening to the b-ring, b-ring, imagining the scene at the other end, the big living room, curtains open on the view, the phone shrilling by itself on the unsteady mahogany table. Clara must be very lonely sometimes now that I was gone. She never complained.

After a while the operator returned: "Your part-y does not ans-wer." I hung up and collected my money out of the return coin well and put it back in my purse.

"My, my, moody tonight, aren't we?" my mother said at dinner time. She tapped me across the knuckles with the handle of her fork. She had been telling me about a man at the telephone company named Tod Larrimore. "He has a humble job, but that doesn't matter to me at all. He tells me I am *ex*-quisite. He knows how to pronounce it."

I felt better the next day, for no particular reason. I wrote five pages of my story about the end of the world and I went for a walk, avoiding the street that had the armless man on it. I thought about my future. I ought to go home to California. When I got there I ought to look for a job. If my mother could get a job in Washington certainly I could get a job in California. Anybody could get a job anywhere; all it took was trying. I decided not to think about myself for at least a week and a half. Something would come up. Maybe I wasn't pregnant at all. It hadn't been very long, really. I stopped myself from counting on my fingers.

"That's my darling girl," my mother said that night. "A sunny, lovely face. It gladdens life, dear. Surely you know that, dear. And the community in our shelter—our little hideaway from the rest of the world—is so much more har*mon*ious."

My mother was still not drinking. Sometimes I thought, just as she had suggested, that I liked her better when she drank. At least when she drank she was direct and straightforward. She didn't talk elegantly. I remembered the article that said relatives of alcoholics were as much responsible for alcoholism as was the drinker. Relatives of alcoholics liked the victim drunk. He or she was nicer that way.

I wrote some more on my end-of-the-world story. It was getting longer; it was threatening to become a novel.

When the end of the world came, the department stores would be left open and unguarded; people would come in and simply help themselves. It wouldn't be stealing. I imagined the situation: I, with a shopping basket. What would I want? Jewels, art, kimonos for Mama, books? No. Nothing. If everything were free and laid out for the taking. Nothing. What a pity.

"My little girl is back with me again," my mother said. "So lovely, darling, to have you to talk to." This talking was done mostly by Mama. She told me about Tod Larrimore. He was the telephone building's installer and repairman. The phone company building needed its own resident telephone installer because of all the phones in the main building and the public and demonstration phones on the first floor. Mama told me Tod had gray hair, and "the most beautiful blue eyes." He collected model trains.

"Help!" That was in my sleep. I got up quickly; Mama's alarm was sounding. The wave of nausea hit me as my bare feet slapped the thinly covered cement floor.

"Why, darling. My baby." Mama had struggled after me into the bathroom.

I told her that it was probably the flu. Everyone in Washington had the flu. My mother never read the papers, so it was safe to tell her this.

When she had left for work I climbed out of bed and got dressed and went out to the telephone booth in front of the grocery store. The grocery man waved at me and gestured toward the Christmas tree he was trimming all the time I was trying to get my calls through.

Ford. No answer. Clara. "Our ly-ons are all bus-y." Eleanor? Eleanor is in California now, too. It's Christmas vacation. That's what normal young women, who are in college, are doing now, Helen. They're home for Christmas vacation.

O'Connell. O'Connell's sergeant answered. O'Connell was at the Repo Depot (Repple Depple, the sergeant called it). He would be there all day today. Maybe all day tomorrow. The sergeant thought I was calling from some Washington office, and I let him think that.

"Mama," I said that night. I had been rehearsing all afternoon, and felt that I had finally got it right. "Mama, I have to go back to California. Briefly, for about a week and a half. I hate to be away over Christmas, Mama; I know that's bad. I'm so sorry. But Clara is having problems. Maybe I'll get back earlier than that. . . . " I had thought this through carefully, and had a list of crises that would repel and distress my mother: A lawsuit. Roots in the sewer. The neighbors have complained. Grandmother insists.

My mother sat on the couch, her feet tucked under her. She leaned back against the cement wall, two pillows in the small of her back, her red hair spread in disarray against the wall, strands of it snagged against the cement in a contrast of textures and colors. In her lap a tangle of stockings which she was sorting, "This is a really big hole, I must fix that," putting the mess of silk to one side. Her sewing would be a series of loops, a bunched place where the hole was gathered up. Still, she looked so sweet, so domestic, that I had to repress an impulse to tell her everything.

"Just for a little while, Mama; I'll be back by New Year's. And, of course, I would never dream of it," I said, "if you were not doing so marvelously well. We're so pleased, Clara and I, both of us. So proud. And your job! So marvelous, Mama, really."

She looked beautiful, sitting against the uneven gray wall, in the bad light from the broken-spined bridge lamp which was pulled cockeyed towards her so she could see the holes in her stockings. And what was Renoir's earth goddess supposed to know about the gritty practicalities of life? Renoir's earth goddess simply *was*. She existed. That was enough. "Of course, my darling." Tears. "I'll be brave. You certainly wouldn't do it if you didn't have to. Not at Christmas time. Not leave me alone."

Frankly, Mama, I don't really have to do this right now, over Christmas vacation. It's just that I can't stand another single minute of this waiting.

"I'll be brave. Even though I'm alone at Christmas. I *will* be."

Well, so will I, Mama.

"I'm glad you're over your flu, darling."

Chapter XIV

BY THE NEXT EVENING I was almost ready to start back to California. I had packed most of my suitcase, washed my hair. I went out to call Clara; the operator told me that the ly-ons were busy. I walked back, thinking about *hold the ly-on*. That one had a good mental picture to go with it; it was better than most of the things they said to you on long distance.

When I rounded the corner I spotted the Western Union messenger. He was just going down the steps into Mama's apartment. "Hey, wait," I yelled. I sprinted and caught him before he had reached the door. "That's for me," I said, so firmly that he didn't argue.

It had been sent over from the Y. It was from O'Connell.

ARRIVING 8 P.M., GREYHOUND BUS STATION.
KILL THE FATTED CALF. JOHN J. O'CONNELL.

I thought: he didn't have any idea I was trying to reach him. He did this all on his own. "Thank you." I tipped the messenger a quarter.

I asked myself, what in hell is "J" for?

Down in the apartment I told my mother that I was starting for California tonight. Clara might be meeting me halfway, in Chicago, I said. I told her this to cover all possible fluctuations in schedule. In many ways, it was helpful to have a mother as innocent of life's realities as mine was. She asked me no practical questions at all.

I understand, I do understand. Maybe Tod Larrimore . . . dearest, you *will* come back?

Of course I will.

Soon?

Of course I will.

I feel so . . . uncertain sometimes.

Mama. Dear.

Maybe Tod Larrimore will come to see me.

Yes, Mama.

Would you like, dearest, to borrow my new hat?

Leaving, I kissed her. "Mama, where did you put the gun?"

"I have no idea, darling. My, that becomes you. I'm going to be brave."

It helps to have several things to worry about at the same time. It's like the Indian remedy for pain—stick your hand in the fire, forget your toothache.

The Greyhound Bus Station was a low-ceilinged, rectangular cement room with a set of small square windows up under the roof, a bank of jukeboxes against one wall, and two sandwich stands against the other. From someplace in the neighborhood of the windows a woman's voice was insistently announcing: bus for Norfolk, bus for Philadelphia, local bus for Bethesda, Maryland, platform twelve, platform nine ... A lot of people, most of them soldiers, pushed each other in different directions. By the door of the platform entrance a small blond soldier lay on the ground, squirming. I thought he was having an alcoholic fit, but I couldn't be sure.

O'Connell's bus was late. I stood against a wall waiting for it, and stayed leaning against the wall to watch him disembark. He did this slowly, as if he were stiff, holding a tan zipper bag in one hand.

"Butchie." When he saw me he put the bag down and stepped on it and held out his arms. After I was close to him, though, he simply put a hand on either shoulder and kissed me on the cheek. People bumped into us from all sides. He said, "You got my telegram. I like that hat."

The loudspeaker made squawking noises. The delirious soldier seemed to be cursing.

In the taxi, O'Connell held my hand and stared out at Washington. "Feels funny, doesn't it? At first?"

But at the hotel he seemed more like his old extroverted self. The hotel was a good one with a red carpet and mahogany walls. O'Connell unwrapped a small bottle of tequila. "They make this stuff out of cactus and old gym shorts; anyway, it was all I could get and I thought we should drink a toast to each other." And he went into the bathroom and got the two toothbrush glasses.

In the middle of unscrewing the cap he set the bottle down and put his arms around me and kissed me gently. "We been apart thirty-seven days, Butch. I been counting."

I had on a blouse which fastened down the front; he

swore at the fastenings. He said, "I can't believe it myself, how much I thought of you. It's funny, sometimes one thing and sometimes another, like a view of the back of your neck, comes across my mind like a still on a movie screen, damnedest thing I ever heard of, or I think about your ears; now, that's pretty bad, isn't it, thinking about a girl's ears?" He had the blouse open now and put his hand inside it.

There was that story I read aloud to Clara, the story where the woman's husband goes off to jail and she says to him, good-bye, if I don't see you again in this life I'll see you in glory.

At the height of our lovemaking I heard myself saying, "Oh, God, I missed you so much." I hadn't intended to tell O'Connell that. Not this time. I wasn't even sure it was true.

Then I wanted to cry. I stifled this and got hiccups instead.

O'Connell pulled me upright against the pillows "Good God, babe. Well, this tequila will cure anything; if you can't stop after this I'll give you another one.

"Has your mom been giving you a hard time?" he asked, after a minute. "I know the little lady is nutty as a fruitcake, but there's not really any harm in her. Being that she's your mom, you might have some trouble realizing that."

O'Connell's question pushed a button in my psyche and I fought tears again. "Kee-reepers, honey." He put a bare, warm arm around me. "Listen, what do you say we go out and investigate the dives of Washington?

"Or listen," after a minute, "on second thought, we haven't really talked, you know, talked, at all, not in Ridgeley, and damn little in Chicago. Maybe we need to sit up in bed and balance a tray of coffee on our stomachs and talk. I have this thing, you know, about having breakfast with you, only got to do it a couple of times in Chicago, seems like the best thing in the world you can imagine. Well, dear, I've had hardly any meals today, let's celebrate breakfast. Let's send down and get some; is that all right with you?"

I said, sure. I sat up and fixed the pillows so we could lean against them. Then I climbed out of bed and got O'Connell's bathrobe out of his suitcase and put it on. I said, "I worry about the bellboy; I don't suppose you do."

"Bellboy?" In a tone of astonishment. "Ah, God, Butchie. Well, in honor of the bellboy I'll drape a towel around my Irish middle."

He ordered orange juice, eggs, toast, and coffee, and settled in beside me and took my hand. "I guess you've been having a tough time of it, Butch. It's hard for me to think of your life; I guess I'm like those ancient nabobs that would snap their fingers and say, bring out that gorgeous dancing girl, the one that was so pretty and bright last week. They didn't sweat much wondering where the little lady had been since then.

"I'm being too mean to myself; it's not like that, but you exist for me in the times we're together and the rest is a blur. And then, I'm a little scared of you; I don't really understand you." He reached out and fooled with the hair at the nape of my neck.

The bellboy arrived with our evening breakfast. It looked very nice, set up on two folding tables at the side of the bed, with three times the necessary number of pots and plates and metal covers to keep the hot dishes warm. O'Connell, who was closest to the supplies, handed me orange juice and buttered the toast.

"Has your mom been a pain in the neck?"

"Yes," I said vaguely.

"Butch, we've got to think about what it is all about."

I didn't say, oh, my God; I've been avoiding that, for sure.

"What all this is doing is making a scared old satyr of me and I must say . . . well, you put up such a good front usually, a guy tends to forget.

"Listen, this is so stupid when I've got so many things I want to tell you. All last week in Chicago, I been saving up these things, salting them away to tell you when we were together again. Like the fact that somebody dropped a pot full of geraniums out of a fourth story window and it missed me by one eighth of an inch. Fact, dear. Made a breeze as it went by. And I stood there and looked at it, broken pot hunks from here to West Hell, and thought, Butchie would have been a widow. Surprised me some. And then I went to a Polish party, some political hassle for the ninety-second ward. They wanted a union organizer to flash in the eyes of the faithful. Well, dear, it was a good party, reminded me of the early days, lots to eat and lots of beer, a wrestling match, everyone pleased with themselves. And then I thought, Butchie would like that; she would warm up and even go out there and drink and eat meatballs and laugh at their corny Polish jokes and dance those dances that we are too old and tired to do, because, for all you pretend that Queen Victoria bit, you loosen up sometimes, and when you do you're my Butchie that I miss so much . . . "

I said, "O'Connell, who's we?"

"What we, dear?"

"The we that is too old to do the dances?"

"Well, that we is me and Mary Frances. She was with me."

"O'Connell," I said, "I'm having a baby."

It was rather like the time I had attacked him with the scissors. This time, too, I was surprised by what I had done. I was even surprised by the way I had said it: I am having a baby. I imagined a picture of this baby, not a standard baby at all, not looking like either of us, but long and thin and pale, like a Dutch Jesus, with a crown of red-gold hair and a solemn intelligent face.

Beside me, O'Connell made a slight movement, as if he had drawn in his breath or pulled his knees up suddenly. I turned to look at him. He was holding a plate of buttered toast in one hand, and he had put his other arm, tender side up, across his eyes. He looked as if he had been hit. He looked like a news photograph of a soldier who had been shot.

"Honey," he said. "Butchie. My God."

O'Connell and I checked out of the red-carpeted hotel and rented a car and went to Cacapon State Park in West Virginia. I didn't ask him how he knew about this place smelling of rain and pine on the crest of a small mountain. The ranger gave us a cabin made of logs chinked with plaster; it had a fire in the fireplace, austere hard, twin beds smelling of evergreens and straw and damp. Outside it was raining, although I thought, judging from the calendar, that it should have been snowing. It was almost Christmas. Christmas would be in four days.

We lay on the floor facing the fire, he on one elbow, I with my head against his shoulder.

O'Connell wore a green and white bath towel with the words WEST VIRGINIA STATE PARKS woven into a stripe down the middle of it. I wore nothing at all, except that on my right hip bone, the one that was uppermost as I lay

partly on the floor and partly against O'Connell's bare
shoulder and belly, there rested my mother's new hat with
the peacock feather. I had been walking around the cabin
wearing it, looking at myself in the mirror on the back of
the closet door and in the glass over the two sepia-toned
landscape photographs. Now I asked O'Connell if I looked
like my mother.

"Yeah, you look like her."

"Am I prettier?"

"*Now* what am I supposed to say?"

"Just tell me. Prettier? Uglier?"

"Je-sus. You sure like to live dangerously."

"It runs in the family. O'Connell?"

"Yeah?"

"You knew Mama really well, didn't you?"

"*No.*"

I stood on the hearth, used the glass on *The Cumberland
Gap by Moonlight* as a mirror, tipped the hat over one eye,
pulled my hair behind my ears. "Yes, you did. Know her
well. O'Connell?"

"Yeah?"

"Did you ever get her pregnant?"

"*Christ* almighty crucified!" Reflected in the glass of
The Cumberland Gap his face seemed, actually, to go pale.
He rose and grabbed me by the shoulders from behind, so
tightly that I was forced to acknowledge, look down, see the
twin crests of fingernails digging into flesh. "Stop. You're
hurting."

"God damn it to bloody hell, Butch; what . . . what's
wrong with you?"

"Nothing. Everything." I pitched the hat onto the floor.

"Don't you *ever,* damn it all, not *ever,* do that . . . "

"You like it," I said. "You know you do." I put my hands behind me and touched him. In *The Cumberland Gap* I could see two bodies, pale blue, pink where the firelight highlighted them, O'Connell behind me, his hands beginning slowly at first, to move down my breasts, across my belly.

I climbed into one of the twin beds. It had thick white blankets. The mattress was filled with something strange that felt like pine needles, some substance which grated and shifted when I moved. The sheets smelled of the Berkeley Springs Laundry Service, whose indentifying stamp was on the corner of the sheet under my chin. "Come to bed," I said to O'Connell.

"Okay." He stopped to stir the fire.

The ranger had left us a Christmas tree with pale new tassels on the ends of its branches. The fire flared up and illumined the tree, shone on the front of O'Connell's kneeling figure, burnished his black hair. "Come on."

"Hey," he said, as he climbed into bed. "For God's sake, darling. Hey, for God's sake."

"Are men afraid of women who do that?" I asked, after we had made love. I felt I was getting proficient, knew some tender things, some practical ones: where the joins in the clothing were. I listed them: "button at the waistband of the pants, two buttons at the top of the shorts . . . "

"Yeah," O'Connell was answering my question about men's fears. "Maybe a little bit." He shifted, put an arm under my head. "You'll be in trouble. I shouldn't say it . . . "

"If I meet somebody with different underwear?"

"Butch, you sure aren't afraid to call a spade a shovel."

"It's being pregnant makes me like that."

"You were that way before.

"Did I ever tell you," he asked, "how I imagined us having an apartment together? Living together, waking up together? This was last month—I used to look through the *Chicago Sun*; I knew I was just daydreaming, playing with the idea—and I'd pick out apartments I could afford—one bedroom, one bath, view of the lake. And then I'd think of what kind of curtains there would be in the kitchen, those white ones with flowerpots around the bottoms, maybe. And then I'd put you in the kitchen, we'd be eating at a table by the window. I'd think what we'd be eating, even figure out what we'd be talking about."

"What were we talking about?"

"Pretty much what we are now, I guess." He laughed. "Like the Dutch Cleanser can. There's a picture on it of a girl holding a Dutch Cleanser can. And on that there's a picture of a girl with a Dutch Cleanser can. And so on, forever."

The enthusiasm, I said to myself, yes; that's what I like about O'Connell. Even here, lying in a dark cabin, no light except for the moving firelight, you can see it, it's around in the air like electricity.

"You've been avoiding me," he said, breaking into my thoughts.

"A-*void*ing you!"

"You know what I mean. Every time I try to ask you a question. What in hell are you doing with that hat?"

"The hat trick. What's a hat trick?"

"Something or other in English football. I'll explain it sometime. Darling, we got to . . . "

"Talk," I said. "Yes, I know. What good is it? Je-*sus*."

"I don't like . . . "

"You don't like to hear a lady swear."

"Well, I don't. Now, lie still, just long enough. You got to answer me some questions."

How long are you pregnant?

Why didn't you tell me?

You didn't talk to anybody? Not anyone? Poor Butchie.

The curious thing is that ever since we've been up here in these mountains, O'Connell, my dear, I've felt as if I had a mesh of electric wires pulled tight against my skin. Sensory perceptors, alerted all the time. I can hear them crackle. No one ever told me that about pregnancy. The world's greatest sexual stimulant. No wonder they keep it a secret. All the girls in Washington, D.C., would be getting pregnant, going to the library, taking out those books under the watchful eye of the horse-toothed librarian.

And I haven't had any more morning sickness. Just that one time with Mama.

O'Connell had to get back to Chicago. Back to his Repo Depo. He was supposed to be gone just for a long weekend.

He and I shared an interest in people. "What would your Mama say about this, Butchie?"

"She wouldn't believe it. She's say it was something else. Lots of things can act like that, she'd say."

My mother was most irritating when she acted grown-up. "She'd tell me my aura was wrong. People with purple auras don't have babies young. Or something. She'd say she dreamed about me last night. In her dream I wasn't having a baby; I was climbing a mountain. Or growing wings."

O'Connell stroked my hair, the callouses on his palm scratching, snagging. "What are we going to do, dear?"

"I don't want to talk about it."

"Poor Butchie."

"Don't feel sorry for me. I hate it."

* * *

We went into Baxter to buy Christmas tree ornaments. It was still raining, very fine rain, hardly cold at all. The branches of the trees hung down, each one spangled; they scraped the top of the automobile. We drove under them in a shower of spray, water cascading away from the car in both directions. In the ditches on either side of the car there was a tracing of yellow snow, quickly melting. "Maybe the world ends at the end of this road," I said.

"It doesn't."

"I've been writing a story about the end of the world. There's nothing beyond here. Just space. Or time—a different kind of time. We'll drive through it and come out the other end and discover the war is over. Peace has been declared. Everybody can go back . . . "

"What difference would that make, dear?"

"Not much." I put my fingernail on the shoulder of his jacket and ran it along the seam of the sleeve, down to the cuff. A branch of wet pine hit the windshield of the car and slid along the roof.

I had tried to imagine O'Connell's relationship with Mary Frances and not succeeded. O'Connell comes home at night. He says, "Hello, Mary Frances." (*Not*, "Hi, dear.") She says, "We have a pork roast tonight." Mary Frances is small, dumpy, gray-haired. They don't touch. The house around them refuses to materialize. It doesn't have a living room suite in any color at all, nor walls, nor curtains. Blank, the same kind of nothing is in O'Connell's house as I want there to be at the end of this road.

The general store in Baxter smelled of kerosene and had canned goods in brands of which I had only vaguely heard: Bonnie Lady tomatoes, Clabber Girl baking powder. One had known they existed, and here was where they had been all along, in the Baxter store, hidden from the war.

Christmas tree ornaments came in two kinds, ones made of cut-up and twisted pieces of tin can, and woolen ones, balls and squares, knitted by the local Ladies' Aid. "You choose." I leaned over O'Connell's shoulder while he picked up knitted objects and put them in a flat box. How domestic we look. No one would guess. We look as if we go together. He's a little old for me, but not markedly so.

One of the ornaments had arms and legs and resembled a bear or possibly a snowman. All the rest were just geometric shapes. Probably the Ladies' Aid member who made the snow bears had made lots of them; they sold out quickly because they were more interesting than the other ornaments. She had earned lots of money for the Ladies' Aid.

While O'Connell was paying for the ornaments I bought presents for him: a knife with six different kinds of blades. A pair of workman's gloves.

We climbed back into the car. I had arranged it all in my imagination: the tree set up in one corner of our log house. Woolen decorations on the tree. Presents for O'Connell below. My imagination extended this picture beyond this afternoon, out to Christmas Day, both of us wedged into one twin bed that O'Connell's weight had pushed low so that, for me, it was like sleeping on a steep bank. Get up, O'Connell. It's Christmas. The first one for us.

O'Connell, however, has to get back to his truck depot before Christmas, or he'll be AWOL. I've known this all along.

My grasp of reality is almost as tenuous as my mother's. About halfway back to the cabin I said, "O'Connell?"
"Yes."

"Pull up here. Where we can see through the trees."

Below us the valley spread out, wet, mostly bare, a few shreds and tags of green where grasses had begun to spring up with the unseasonable rain, a few slices of green tree. The light to the west was faintly oyster-colored; somewhere behind the clouds the sun was setting. O'Connell set the brake and leaned forward with his hands on the steering wheel. He had been driving with the box of knitted toys on his lap. He picked one up now and began to pull at it. "Where does Mary Frances think you are?" I asked.

"I didn't tell her anything."

"My mother, either. I didn't tell her . . . " Well, that wasn't strictly true. My mother thought she knew where I was. "We have to decide something, don't we?"

He pulled industriously at the red woolen square. Hunks of thread came out, were dropped onto the floor. "I've been saying that to you, Butch. For two days now."

"So," I said, "since we've got to . . . We ought to find a doctor for me."

O'Connell had finished with the red cube. I put out my hand to keep him from picking up a new one. "There must be doctors in the Army. Somebody you know. That could help us."

"Yeah."

"Maybe someone in Washington."

"Baltimore, it would be. Aberdeen Proving Ground. Outside of Baltimore."

"That's what we'll do, then."

The sky lightened for a minute; a ray of sun crossed the car roof, invaded the interior of the car, illumined O'Connell's hair, the beige upholstery. "How far along are you, Butch?" he asked. "About a month?"

"About."

He rested his forehead against the windshield. The box of Ladies' Aid ornaments in his lap tilted forward. "You couldn't really tell," he said, "at this point, could you, whether it was a boy or a girl?"

Chapter XV

MY MOTHER WAS SOBER when I came home from Cacapon, although the bottle was out, visible, obtrusive, positioned as obviously as possible on the edge of the grocery shelf. Unopened. Label facing out. Like the bottle in *Alice in Wonderland* that said, "Drink Me."

"I knew you couldn't," she said to me, as I entered the apartment. "I just knew you couldn't. Not my baby, my Helen." She held up her beautiful bluish-pink cheek to be kissed.

"Couldn't what, Mama?" I slapped my suitcase down on the thinly-covered cement floor.

"Couldn't desert your Mama at Christmas. Not my dearest girl. How was Clara?"

"Okay." Oh, hell. "You what?" Clara had asked when I finally got her on the phone. "And where am *I* supposed to have been?" Amazingly, my mother didn't ask me how I had managed to get back to Washington so quickly.

Sometimes I thought she was much brighter than I usually credited her with being, and screened out everything she didn't want to know. Sometimes I thought she was really gullible, and never reasoned anything through.

"My lovely girl," she said. "The grocer is saving us a tree. I *knew*. I just knew."

The bottle sat on the edge of the shelf all during Christmas and into New Year's. When I went off to meet O'Connell on the morning of January third for our trip to Aberdeen Proving Ground, I didn't tell my mother anything at all. She was at work at the phone company; I would be home by suppertime. I might not be feeling too good when I came in, but on the other hand, you never knew; I might be feeling perfectly all right. At the last minute I relented and left her a note: *"May stay in town late for shopping. Love, H."*

"This Aberdeen Proving Ground is out in the middle of a duck pond," O'Connell said. "About forty thousand miles of it. And before that twenty miles of Army Chemical Base. They're making stuff to melt the paint off Japanese airplanes and give the whole world plague. It's super-secret. You're my wife."

Oh, Christ.

"Al's clinic is on the periphery. They wouldn't let either of us in the real part. Are you scared?"

"Uh-uh."

Truly, I didn't seem to be. In all the books, in all the stories they told in high school, the girl was always scared. Sometimes she fainted. Sometimes a cold sweat stood out on her forehead. That morning I'd looked at my horoscope in *The Washington Post* and it said today was an important day for investments. I was having a little trouble with that one.

A gate across the road; on either side of it, out to infinity in both directions, barbed wire fence on a swathe of cleared tan ground. A soldier conferred with O'Connell. Something was stamped and signed.

O'Connell and I were visiting Lt. Col. A. C. Weeks, just as friends.

Lt. Col. Weeks's clinic was in a temporary building made of bolted metal. It sat on a streetful of such buildings, flat against the ground, its door guarded by one scuffed gray step. The street was dusty and had scabs of snow.

Around, above, behind the gray packing-case buildings the air was filled with a diffuse thumping, like an enormous hammer smashing. I looked at O'Connell. "Proving," he said. "Testing firearms. At the proving ground."

Dr. Weeks's clinic waiting room was full. It was very noisy. It had not occurred to me in my attempts to imagine Dr. Weeks that he would have a big waiting room full of soldiers. I'd been thinking of our encounter entirely differently: the doctor's deserted office, a secret arrival, whispers, a back entrance.

O'Connell and I sat down on two tin chairs. There were no magazines.

The atmosphere was a peculiar one; it ought to have been sordid, but for some reason wasn't. Dr. Weeks's waiting room had a battered, reassuring, institutional quality. It was warm and smelled of people; the people were talking loudly and seemed cheerful; they were interested in their own illnesses and in those of their neighbors. "Hey, for

God sake." The soldier two chairs down from me was speaking to the corporal beside me. "That is some *han* you got there."

The corporal was starched and fat. He sat with his legs apart and the hand resting on one knee. He had cut it; it bled down his pants' leg, into his shoe, from there made a puddle on the floor. He surveyed himself appreciatively. "Yeh," he said. "Sure is. Got me a real good one."

The soldier continued, analytically, "A mean, jagged cut. Bleedin a lot."

"Bleedin like a son uv a bitch." The corporal's face was pensive. "I shut my fucking hand in the fucking truck hoist."

O'Connell was listening to this conversation, although he was holding the newspaper and pretending he wasn't listening. I had learned to read his postures; there was a head angle which showed he was eavesdropping. He sat forward on his tin chair, held the *Washington Post*, folded into a square, in one hand. His other hand was in his pocket. I put my hand there, too. Beneath my fingers I felt a bodily pulse; something inside of O'Connell was going *thump, thump,* in echo of the proving ground. I squeezed. He said. "Hey, there." I put my mouth to his ear. I said, "He certainly is relaxed about it. That corporal." He shrugged. "What else can he do?"

"Hurts?" the soldier asked the corporal.

"Hurts like hell." Acceptance, amusement, a little pride. The perfect battle attitude.

"Jesus, darling, stop squeezing," O'Connell said. "You scared?"

I shook my head. "I thought they didn't allow women. In a clinic like this."

"Well, they got lots of women. WACs, typists. Where they supposed to go? . . . Hey, *stop* that. You *must* be scared."

It would alarm O'Connell too much if I started to giggle. Maybe I *am* scared, but that isn't how it feels. What it feels like is the tension before you do something really daring, or really foolish.

I watched my one fellow woman in this waiting room, a small WAC with skinny legs. She was knitting. Her dark brown Oxfords, aligned side by side on the gray floor, were too big for her.

Beyond her was a cluster of six soldiers sitting together, their tin chairs pulled into a kind of circle. They were very drunk, so drunk that I wondered if something else wasn't wrong with them too. Three of them were asleep, one bent over with his head on his knees. One of the others was awake and singing, some tune that became almost loud enough for me to recognize it, then subsided. One more soldier leaned into a brown metal wastebasket. The remaining one got up, circled his group unsteadily, sat down, threw his hat on the floor, picked it up. He said, "God damn it to hell, it's the processing, the processing." He said this again, out to the waiting room. O'Connell handed me a section of the *Washington Post*.

O'Connell thinks I'm upset by all this. "I'm not upset," I told him. "It's interesting." I loved to stare at people. You learned something by staring at people.

From behind the screened entry to the doctors office someone started to scream. It was a man's voice, a bass voice, I thought; hard to tell, completely distorted. No words.

"Je-sus," said the corporal. "Heart. Heart case."

"How you know?" asked the soldier.

"*He* told me," gesturing at the doctor's office. "A major. With a heart attack."

The word began to go around the waiting room. A major was having a heart attack. In the medic's office. They're operating on him. Right there.

People leaned forward, passing the word on: "major . . . heart attack." Someone even tried to communicate with the drunken soldiers. "Jeez Christ, man," their leader said earnestly, "what're you tellin me?" He threw his hat down. "I want to under*stan*."

"Ah, fuck off," said his informant.

The WAC quit knitting. She folded up whatever it was (green wool, perhaps Marine Corps socks), and pushed it into a paper lunch bag. Then she sat back and stared at the wall. She had thin, blond eyelashes.

"Jeez Christ," said the soldier. "What a pisser. Hey, what they got to do. To that major?"

The corporal was fully informed. "They cut him open. And when he's open, they massage. His heart. And if that works, well, it works."

"Jee-sus." The waiting room was silent now. I took my hand out of O'Connell's pocket and put it on his knee. I could sense it—we were collectively straining to hear what was happening on the other side of the curtain. No more cries. "Can they give him a shot? For pain?" Nobody answered. Breathing. An occasional chink as of a spoon laid on a dish. The thump from the proving ground. "Jee-sus," said the soldier. "Well, say something *else*," the WAC demanded.

An emotion began to stir visibly in the brain of the drunken soldier with the hat. He scowled, sighed, put the hat on, took it off. Finally he hoisted himself to his feet, tucked the hat into his shoulder tab, and approached the person closest to him, the WAC. "Ma'am," he said, "um very sorry. Beg to apologize. Apologize most heartily." He smiled. He had a sweet smile. "Surely hope you can un-nerstan, ma'am. Feel I mus apologize. To every single person in this room." He tried to make a kind of bow. He appeared to be from the South.

The WAC stared directly past the apologizer's shoulder. But she, like me, may have been slightly touched by the surreal delicacy of his gesture; there was an upward curve to her lips.

"You can't tell," the corporal said. "Might do some good." He watched as the drunk proceeded to the next person in the waiting room circle, a small, dark soldier with a pointed face, who stared hostilely and said, "Nuts."

"Nah," objected the corporal. "It's like prayer, see. You don't ever know, not really. Might do some good."

When the drunk came to us I looked him full in the face, trying to get a clue to something: what he thought he was doing, what he represented. He had light blue eyes with flat, black irises. He said the same thing: "Apologize most heartily." "Okay," I told him. He seemed astonished. His eyes almost focused.

"You can't tell," the corporal repeated. But when the drunk approached him, all he said was, "Watch it, buddy. Don't step in the blood."

"Sure makes you think." Sure does. And gradually the noise level in the room rose again. The apologizer sat down and fell asleep, head thrown back. "Think you're gonna bleed to death?" the soldier asked the corporal. "Na-a-ah." The WAC got out her knitting. I asked O'Connell, "Will they save him?"

"Might. Prob'ly not."

For a minute there had been a unanimity of feeling in this waiting room: everyone concentrating and hoping.

"O'Connell," I said, "it's not that I'm scared."

My reaction was diffuse and would be hard to explain in the future, but it was clear to me now. It had to do with the chaotic but not uncheerful atmosphere of Dr. Weeks's clinic, the man who was bleeding, the one who was fighting for his life, even with the goofily apologetic drunk. The way I understood them must have been in me, not in them. They all seemed hopeful to me. They were making a lot of noise. It was almost enough noise to drown out the thump from the proving ground.

"O'Connell, I'm not going to do it."

O'Connell laid down his newspaper. He had been chewing on our rolled-up admission pass; it projected like a cigarette from the corner of his mouth.

"Not because I'm scared. I just don't want to. I'd rather . . . " I hadn't imagined the other alternative, what happened if I had this baby. You can't imagine something you have no experience of. They claim you can't imagine Heaven. Nor the Beatific Vision. Nor your own death. I gathered up my pocketbook, slung it over my shoulder, stepped politely around the knees of the bleeding corporal, out the door, down the step, onto the street.

Outside, the thump from the proving ground was very loud, it seemed to shake the street. I told myself it was an interesting noise, not really an unpleasant one, one of those sounds that you get used to; when it's removed something essential has disappeared; you miss it.

Footsteps behind me. "Where are you going?"

I slowed down. "I hadn't really thought about it."

O'Connell put his arm around me. "Hey," he said. "You know what? We're never going to find out whether that major made it, or he didn't."

Ridgeley, West Virginia. "Kat," O'Connell said, "you always stood by me."

"Is that the way you see it?" said Kat. We were sitting around her oilcloth-covered kitchen table. Cut-glass vase (new) in the middle of the table. Straw flowers (real flowers that dry to look like imitation ones) in the vase. Kat's Christmas tree, a beauty, was still up in the corner of the kitchen. It was weighted with a pre-war assortment of ornaments: glass balls, tinsel, swag, lights. Under the tree there was a red and white village. There were people inside the largest house. (I had looked to see.) Kat sat with her full freckled arms on the checked tablecloth. She looked like the figure of justice—she was justice; she knew it. "Why'd you come here, Johnny?"

"We were tired of hotels. I wanted you to know."

"So I'm not just a truck stop. With a bed."

"No, Kat."

"You're leaving Mary Frances?"

O'Connell looked down at his hands, her hands. "Yes."

"She'll never give you a divorce."

"This isn't the thirteenth century. It'll come through eventually."

"You'll hurt her, Johnny. You'll hurt her really bad." Kat's sympathies were with Mary Frances, at least for now. And why not? Who am I? A young thing. Pretty, pert. Who got herself knocked up. A clever way of getting a man.

O'Connell reached over and took my hand. A squeeze. Translation: hold on, darling.

"I don't know, Johnny," Kat said. She was trying to

cut a hole in the oiled tablecloth with her fingernail. From this angle she looked like her brother: same planes to the face, dark brows, dark hair. "Everybody wants to, sometimes, I guess. Throw it over. And then we think about it, realize that's no good. We can't leave all that old stuff. It'll follow us around. Wake us up at night. Oh, we all imagine doing something like this. I did, once, imagine I'd do it. And then, knew I couldn't. And, after a while, forgot. You will too, after a while. You'll forget."

"Kat," O'Connell said, "remember the first year I was in the movement?"

"Yes."

"It was the only thing in the world for me, day, night. It made life worth living. A new world. Like taking the old life by its coat collar, shaking it, everything was changed. Suddenly, I was someone. I'd been nobody. Now, I had a meaning."

"What's your point?" said Kat.

"I don't mean Helen is all those things . . . not those same things . . . She's something different from that. But there are times in your life when you know what you should do. You don't have any question about it. It was like that then. And now."

"I don't know," Kat shifted the bowl of dried flowers. "It's not that I don't understand. I do. I just think it's wrong."

She looked us over; maybe she saw something in our faces. More likely she was affected by her brother, whom she loved, by his expression, the jaw determined, eyes apprehensive. "Well, you can stay here," she said. "Go ahead. Stay here. It's okay."

She was abandoning responsibility. She rose from her chair, made brusque arm movements, not unkind—not cordial or welcoming, but not unkind, either. She absolved herself of complicity. She wasn't going upstairs with us; she wouldn't know what happened there. "Go on up, take one of the rooms at the top." She moved around the kitchen, rattled pots, faucets, ran the water hard in the sink. "Lemme know if you need anything."

Upstairs, we lay on the bed, not for passion—just because it was the only resting place big enough for both of us in the room. I propped the two skinny pillows and rolled-up blanket against the tin headboard; O'Connell knelt down to light the kerosene stove. The room had wallpaper—stripes of pink flowers separated by silver bands. From my spot on the bed the view through the pine-framed window was of sky. If I had stood up and gone to the window, the view would have been down the hill, a procession of tin-covered house roofs stepping irregularly down the snow-covered street; the roofs were corrugated, there was a stripe of snow in each parallel roof indentation.

The sky that I could see from my position on the bed was blue. I was still not used to eastern winters: that the sky could be so blue while the temperature outside was so cold.

O'Connell had gotten the stove lit. It glowed yellow. The top was cut into an attractive rose pattern that projected itself onto the ceiling. I pulled the bedspread up under my chin. O'Connell climbed into the bed with me. His feet made two oval bumps at the foot of the bed.

"Tell me about how you joined the IWW," I said.

I didn't want to talk about our present situation. Downstairs, Kat made a metallic clatter. The enclosed, safe room reminded me of the bedroom in Carmel where Clara and I had listened to the ocean.

O'Connell talked. I imagined the scene: O'Connell signing his first IWW card. The hot boxcar smells of straw and cattle; a fifteen-year-old O'Connell wears dungarees, a plaid shirt. Two men hold him with his face against the boxcar floor, his cheek is scraped. But O'Connell is excited and pleased; he's heard of the Wobblies. He signs his name on a red card.

"Was it really red?"

"No. Blue and white, with scrolls and a wheel in the center. And around the wheel the motto: All for one. One for all."

"What if you didn't sign?"

"Oh, they were just play-acting. Wobblies were peaceful. Peaceful anarchists. They believed the working man was basically good. If you left the working man to himself, they thought, he'd come up with a perfect government. No structure. Just people living together, not interfering."

"And you don't think that."

"Of course not. But I wish I could. Everyone does, I guess."

When O'Connell talked, the anarchists and their friends became clear. Meetings in railroad yards, in hobos' camps. Dust, heat. An old man, tanned, frayed, a teacher, his only possession a pocketful of pamphlets. "Jake, his name was. Lectured in the park. Didn't care if he had only two people in his audience.

"That was part of it," he continued, "not having a following. You weren't supposed to get famous. Or rich."

"No women, though."

He was made uncomfortable by this question. "We got women in the *movement*. Now tell me . . . "

Yes, dear, I'll talk about myself now. O'Connell was a

good listener, unlike Will. Will had to stop you halfway in your sentence and give you a better version of what you were trying to say.

"So why'd you go out with him, dear?"

"I liked him."

O'Connell didn't want to believe that I liked Will. "No, I did," I said. "And then, he was *there*. He lived in the house, he was like a brother. It was hard for us to make friends, because our lives were so funny. I hated to bring people home."

"Yeah, but, dear . . . " O'Connell also didn't want to believe that I would have slept with just anybody who occupied our spare bedroom. "There must have been something more."

"He was so clean. So organized. Well cared-for. He seemed like the opposite of us." I tried to tell O'Connell about Will's brown and tan saddle shoes.

"Where does that leave me?" He meant, if you liked Will because he was clean and organized, what do you want me for?

I had thought about this, and was able to answer. "All those years that Mama had her enthusiasms, I hated them; they seemed so vague and unfocused. And silly. And still, there was something there. I wanted to like them. And then I met you, and you were what she'd been pretending at, and had never understood enough to do it right."

"So I'm a dream come true." His tone said that he liked this, and didn't.

I didn't tell O'Connell that the world of the workingman's perfect government sounded a little monotonous to me. Some people are basically wry and hard to satisfy, just as my mother said.

The kerosene stove made a small, gentle noise like a coffee percolator. Its rose, much magnified, flowered in sections of light on the ceiling. The inside of the window had steamed up; the blue sky glowed behind it.

Chapter XVI

O'CONNELL AND I stayed with Kat for two days.

O'Connell was a celebrity of sorts in Cumberland. Walking the uneven streets (Cumberland streets were paved only occasionally; most of them were hilly, rocky, uneven, snow-pitted, afloat with a mixture of red mud and snow), pausing in the entrance to the hardware store or the A & P, he was constantly approached: "Hey, aren't you the guy who . . . " Everybody in Cumberland belonged to the union and had been at that meeting where O'Connell, backed by the American flag and the CIO banner, was the principal speaker. His back was slapped, his hand pumped. Women, literally, reached out to touch him.

"Hey, I recognize you from . . . "

And quick as a wink, she had pinched a bit of his army overcoat between thumb and forefinger—not to tear off a sample—just to feel the real labor leader's arm-protecting sleeve. Eyes alight with joy and . . . There is a lot of sex in that concept of the handsome, capable, outgoing union organizer, as who should know better than I.

There was a brief snowstorm during one of our two days. That made for local interest. Cumberland was higher than Washington; the snow there was professional, serious snow. It got O'Connell, Kat, and me out front shoveling, and it also routed out Kat's daughter, Kathleen. I had been surprised by Kathleen, whom I had pictured as a younger, smaller Kat, or maybe a younger female O'Connell. But, instead, she was short, plump, dark-browed, with straw-colored hair and a lively round face. She seemed to accept me without question. Her voice had the true, slurred Cumberland accent. "Hoo, God," she said, tugging at the buttons of her sweater, "I am *sopping*." She pitched her shovel into a bush, sat down on the step with her plump, red-trousered legs spread wide, and pulled out a mashed cigarette. Kathleen was only sixteen but she looked and sounded older.

"How was it going to school here?" I asked. She seemed not to mind this conversation-making question.

"They sure didn't teach you anything." She drew on the bent cigarette. "And if you were a girl—well, they *sure* didn't teach you anything. But not the boys, either . . . You know what?" she added, after a moment's contemplation. "What was missing . . . what do ya callit . . . *aspiration*. The aspiration to ever get out of *here* . . . " with a gesture she indicated hazy Cumberland's red mud and new white snow, its clusters of leaning houses, the distant railroad tracks. "Grow up, get laid, go to work in the Celanese mill. That's what *we* aspired to." She exhaled smoke through her nose.

* * *

There were three places for recreation in Ridgeley-Cumberland. One was the movies, one was the bars; finally there was the railroad.

The movie houses were two: the Paramount, in downtown Cumberland, between the hardware store and the Sears Roebuck catalogue office, and the Metro, uptown, closer to the Pennsylvania Railroad tracks, with the offices of the *Cumberland-Ridgeley Daily Argo* beside it.

O'Connell told me that everyone in Cumberland and Ridgeley went to the movies on weekend nights. Tonight was a weekend night. "They got two kinds of movies they show in this town. One kind is animal pictures. The other is cowboy pictures. Sometimes a picture is both at once."

No, he hadn't been in Ridgeley a lot. Maybe three or four times before this. But he and Kat had kept in touch; she sent him cards at Christmas time. And in this socialist town the union made him a personage, sort of.

There was a warm feeling in the Paramount Theater, where the movie was a cowboy one. The hero was cheered, his horse was cheered. Advice was offered to the hero's girlfriend: "Loosen up!" There were a few servicemen in the audience who, I supposed, were home on temporary leave, but there were many older men and lots of women.

After the movie everyone went out to a bar. We went to the one with the old-fashioned mirror that had iced designs of flowers across its top.

I was introduced as "Miss Reynolds, my good friend." Nobody seemed to care one way or the other about this. I thought of O'Connell's fantasy about the Polish picnic—that I would loosen up and talk to everybody—be a social success in socialist circles—but tonight there didn't seem to be very much for me to say.

I watched O'Connell laughing and gesturing. He was

separated from me. I observed him; he was a figure in a play, an interesting person sitting near me on a train. And just as I thought this, felt pleased and protected at having thought it, the woman next to him, a Wave with a full bosom, one of those female O'Connell-touchers, leaned forward and rested her hand on his forearm, talking enthusiastically into his face. My response was physical. I thought: oh, hell. I wondered what was going to happen to us.

I'm afraid of you, Butch. That's what O'Connell sometimes said. Last night, staring upward at the yellow rose on the ceiling, he had said it again. Stroked my hair: "I don't understand you. You're my golden girl."

"Is that the way you see me?" I was thinking about my golden girlhood.

"Yeah. You've got all that hair. And you come from California."

"My hair is red."

"And you're rich. No, don't answer. To me, you're rich. Even if you're poor as hell, it's your background I mean. That's the way I see you. Like a photograph with a gold mesh across it."

"And then," he added, "there's your age."

"Cut it out about my age." His mention of age irritated me more than the rest of it.

I thought about that now in the bar. The lady with the bosom was a lot older than I was.

"I have to call my mother," I told O'Connell.

Both he and I were a little drunk, and didn't think that it was late to be calling one's mother.

But my mother was there, all right, and she was awake. The phone was picked up right away. "Mama," I said, "this is Helen."

There was a pause and a sound like a jukebox getting

ready to play a record. Then a smash. The receiver had been slammed down, hard.

I called her back. She picked up the phone on the first ring. "Are you with John O'Connell?"

I didn't say "um" or "hah" or any of those things. "Yes."

"How long have you known John O'Connell?"

"Three months." It was none of her business.

"I must say, Helen, of all the low, underhanded . . . "

"You've been going through my mail."

"I had to find out where you were. I found this telegram . . . " She began to cry. She did that for about half a minute. Then she hung up again.

When I came out of the phone booth O'Connell was leaning against it, talking to the Wave.

"Is *she* a golden girl?" I asked him, as we drove back to Kat's through the silent streets.

"Hey! You're jealous." He squeezed my shoulder.

"My mother was drunk."

"Yeah. Well, your mama always did have a short fuse."

"How about *her*. I bet she was a golden girl. The very first one."

"Give it a rest, darling." O'Connell whistled "Avanti, popolo." I leaned against him. I thought forward, to Kat's room, the narrow bed, the pearled windows with moonlight behind them. "Light the kerosene stove tonight."

"Okay. That's a little dangerous, if we should fall asleep."

"I'll remember." I was tempted to say, I didn't say, something about living dangerously.

I do a lot of wandering in my relationship with O'Connell, I thought, as I walked down Cumberland's main street, and then up and down the cross-streets—the street north of the railroad track, the one that went at an angle up the hill. O'Connell had a meeting of some kind. Walking on the Cumberland streets was different from walking around Chicago. First, there was the lack of sidewalks, second, there was the architecture: special, capricious, individual, the result of each householder's having added to his small dwelling in the springtime, on weekends, with re-used lumber, when the spirit moved him, a room here, a new level there. There was a great deal of reddish-brown paint on these Cumberland houses because that was the color of the B and O freight cars, and that, therefore, was the paint available free for home improvement.

I had persuaded Kathleen to come with me on this walk around Cumberland. She wore a green imitation leather coat and puffed energetically at one of her bent cigarettes; she made them herself, I had discovered, on a machine constructed of rubberized cloth stretched across a tin frame. "That," she said, gesturing with her cigarette, "is where Buz and Etta made their suicide pact."

Buz and Etta, she told me, were Cumberland's most recent romantic scandal, the most dramatic of what, she suggested, had been a long series of such. "Not much else to do. Well, honest. At least screwing is something." Buz had shot Etta, then had gone down to Forester's Bar and Grill and eaten a hamburger and drunk a large coffee, leaving Etta's cooling body stretched in the middle of their tan and pink linoleum rug. "Not that I saw her there," Kathleen explained, "that part is imagination. But I sure had seen that rug enough times. I could certainly picture her on it."

Then Buz had returned to their second-floor apartment in the red-painted Victorian house, climbed out on the window ledge, hooked a rope around a projecting roof support, and hanged himself. "We could see him, turning around. It was seven-thirty on a Saturday night in July, broad daylight, everbody in town out on the street, *but*, by the time they got up there . . . "

"He was dead?"

"Jus completely gone. And a real nasty mess, too. Don't *never* hang yourself."

"Okay."

"Me neither." We had been staring at the spot where Buz's body had been, and now we started to move up the hill. "What else you want to see?" Kathleen asked. "We could go look at the school where I went, but there's nothing outside of it but a empty playground. Or we could look at the railroad. Or, we could see if they got any new dresses down to Gorsuch's."

"Why did Etta and Buz do it?"

"Love." We turned toward the drygoods store. "He was married and she was married . . . I guess it just seemed too much trouble. It just seemed easier to kill yourself. Listen, around here. You'd be surprised. There's a lot of people kill themselves."

Gorsuch's tilted wooden floor and opaque, silver-streaked mirrors were enlivened by a display of unseasonable summer dresses in strange colors—somebody's stock from before the war, I guessed, inspecting the wide seams, full hems, fly-speckled fuchsias and oranges, faded where their folds had been exposed to the light.

"Honest, they think they can sell us anything here." Kathleen, wearing an orange scoop-necked sun dress, surveyed her reflection. "Listen. What do you think? You and Uncle John gonna stay together?"

When I said I didn't know, she moved her shoulders. She looked charming in the old dress, its skirt too long by current fashion standards. "One thing you just better remember," she told me. "You are an *awful* lot better looking than that Mary Frances."

After the bars and the movies, the railroad was the place for recreation and diversion in Cumberland. There were two railroad lines which ran through the town: the B and O crossed it on the south side, the Pennsylvania on the north. In between the two sets of tracks Cumberland sat, five blocks of stores, bars, houses. The Cumberland Hotel straddled the Pennsylvania tracks, the trains actually running under the hotel and shaking the dishes in the dining room.

People in Cumberland stood beside the tracks to watch the trains. These were often dramatic hundred-car freights, with square, shrieking wheels, three engines, several cabooses. "Well, of course they watch them. They got relatives working on them," O'Connell said when I mentioned the train-watching. In spite of all the trains I had ridden I still saw these as romantic.

Sometimes the trains stopped, and forced people to stand and look at them. O'Connell said they stopped sometimes for as long as an hour; they tied up the whole town. When there were trains on both the upper and lower tracks, people crawled between them to get to work. "The kids in the town here, they climb under them. I hate to see that."

"Under them." I was visualizing it.

He shrugged. "Pretty stupid. But I used to do stuff like that plenty, when I was a kid."

O'Connell and I were walking to the Cumberland Hotel

for coffee. The Cumberland Hotel was not at all elegant; it wasn't even clean. Perhaps I was the only person in Cumberland who found it interesting. I liked the thick white blue-bordered pottery in the dining room, with *Cumberland Hotel* along the top of the plate, *Pennsylvania Railroad* around the bottom. "Tell me how you met your wife," I said to O'Connell. I wasn't being jealous, I told him; I was trying to fill in my picture of Mary Frances.

"No."

"Why not?"

"It's not interesting, for God's sake." Almost in the same sentence, he told me: "I was working in the plant. And she was working in the plant; she was a polisher. And she was pretty and nice and her mama worked on the mini-assembly line, and her mother had a car and used to give her rides to work. And she started giving me rides too.

"And that was that," he added. "Surprising, sort of. How things work out."

"What's a mini-assembly line?"

"Butch, I never will get used to the kind of questions you ask."

"I think I'll understand it. If I can imagine it."

"A mini-assembly line is for the little parts of an automobile. Like on the dashboard."

We had arrived at the Cumberland Hotel dining room. I paused by the greasy dark window with its direct view out on to the railroad tracks and into the train station, roofed with iron struts. There was no train on the tracks, but there would be one pretty soon. We had been hearing it during most of our walk into town.

We sat down and ordered coffee. I was silent, thinking about the automobile plant in which O'Connell had worked, the night shift, the day shift, the swing shift, the men . . . resentful? Friendly? Cheerful? The big room, probably looking a lot like this train shed outside. I put O'Connell into this setting, and that worked fine. O'Connell wore striped coveralls and worked fast, with emphatic motions. He was the one in that big, crowded, noisy room that you would want to watch if you had to sit there for a while. Then I tried to imagine Mary Frances. Mary Frances was a polisher. I was vague about what a polisher did. I tried to put her into the room, holding a cloth, to polish with. No, that wouldn't do. Then I gave her a small, hand-held machine. Nothing.

I said to O'Connell: "I keep thinking of all sorts of funny questions about us."

He shifted in his chair and suggested that I drink my coffee. "Listen," he said, "I've always felt if you have to do something you just do it."

"Yes."

"Comes up in the labor movement all the time. Some poor guy has a wife that needs an operation and a senile grandmother and three deaf kids and the boss is going to help him cure all that. And if he joins the union it all goes down the pipes. And so what do I tell him to do? I tell him to join the union. Because that's what he has to do."

"Yes."

"So, do it. Don't talk about it. Do it."

His voice sounded a little defensive to me.

I love O'Connell because he is simpleminded. Loving him just for that seems like too easy a proposition.

"How are you feeling?" And now, maybe his voice has a touch of special pregnancy solicitude. Borrowed from the movies.

"I'm fine. Here's the train." The noise level in the dining room rose suddenly; all the dishes jumped.

It was a curious feeling to sit, holding your coffee cup down, watching the train's amalgam of wheels, pistons, open doors, labeled cars snap by, only a few feet from your face. Steam covered the window, dissolved. Sparks hit the glass. After several minutes there was a prolonged high screeching, a rhythmic shiver, the cars moved slow, slower, finally, with many echos, came to a halt. Our window was blocked by a brown boxcar inscribed: "Feather River—The Route of Hiawatha."

O'Connell suggested that we go outside and watch the train from the crossing.

There were about a dozen people at the crossing. A camaraderie seemed to have developed among them already; as we arrived an older man was taking bets on how long the train would be stalled. Various explanations were offered for its stopping: the engineer went to take a leak. The engineer went to lay his wife. He dropped off for groceries, to go to the movies. "This train always stops here at ten o'clock," a shrill little boy told me. "Because at ten o'clock, once, a long long time ago, the engineer's brother was killed, see, right on this crossing."

The signal bell banged monotonously but not distressingly.

The child with the legend about ten o'clock was a small pale boy with greasy blond hair. I looked at my watch; it was almost eleven. The boy sensed that he had lost me and tried another attention-getter: "Step onna track, break my mother's back." I thought: I've only heard it *crack*, not *track*. Local color, here. The boy stepped on the track, close to the wheel, and looked up at me to see if I was shocked. I was.

The man standing next to O'Connell greeted him. "Hey, I know you from the union. I heard you speak in Ridgeley. Hey, now." He shook hands. The three of us sat down on the green-painted base of the ringing signal.

I found the ringing bell, the train's subliminal snorting and shifting, their conversation, the winter sunlight soporific. I was half asleep when several things happened at once. Air was expelled up ahead someplace, from a set of brakes. The train gave a creak and started to move. The boy, who was again on the track next to the wheel, screamed. He dived under the train.

O'Connell told me afterwards that there is room beneath a freight train for a thin person who will lie absolutely still. Few people can do that because of the sparks and heat and noise.

O'Connell moved fast, and what happened next was simple. He waited until the first set of wheels went by, then he reached under the car, timing himself to avoid the hardware on the undercarriage. He pulled the boy by one arm and one leg, out and over the track. He did it before the next set of wheels arrived.

It looked easy. The bystanders congratulated him, but no one got terribly excited. O'Connell's union friend said he would have given that kid something to remember us by, except the kid looked in pretty bad shape; his face was cut. Someone went to get a doctor. The union friend held the child and made deprecating noises.

"Hell," O'Connell said, as we were walking home, "all the time I rode on freight trains. In my Wobbly days."

I held his hand. I was quite sure he hadn't been in danger during any part of the experience. But maybe he had been. Maybe his rescue of the child at the train crossing was like other feats of agility, and looked much easier than it was.

The whole thing made me very uneasy. Cumberland in general made me uneasy. I squeezed his hand until I felt his ring cut into my palm. "I love you," I said. It just slipped out. I hadn't planned to say it.

"We have to go see my mother," I added quickly. "We should go tonight. Before you go back."

Chapter XVII

O'CONNELL HAD NOT, I thought, been all that anxious to go see my mother.

Well, on the one hand, who could blame him, but on the other hand . . . I slumped in a corner of the car, with my fists in my pockets. O'Connell is certainly right, one should not be reflective; don't think about your actions, just do them. One also should not intercept the future: don't try to invent that unimaginable apartment where you and O'Connell and baby will live in a socialist idyll, don't imagine the end of the world, *do not* permit yourself the picture of Buz hanging out over the late evening Cumberland street. "You certainly have got fast reactions," I said to O'Connell, meaning the scene at the railroad crossing.

"Nah."

"*I* was scared witless." Do not think about the ladies who touch him in bars.

"You don't need to talk to her at all," I said, after a while. It was dark outside and there was a moon rising.

"Yeah. Well."

"*I* don't know what *I'm* going to say." I noted, listening to my own voice, that I was dithering. O'Connell, you haven't ever told me that you love me. You have said that you miss me, that you think about me, are crazy about me, that I am your golden girl . . .

The interior of the car was gray plush, reminiscent of Grandmother's Buick with the bud vases; O'Connell had laid his hand on his own knee, fingers splayed, his driving arm was wedged into the armrest. The plush pull moved above his head. The car swayed rather than bounced, its inside smelled artificial, probably something to do with the upholstery, maybe something the car-hire people had sprayed it with. It was a good car. In spite of the war, O'Connell was able to come up with luxury in cars. After all, that was his union, the Auto Workers. I glanced toward him. A snow-piled something—a road clearer?—slid by outside behind his dimly visible, solemn, handsome face. How does that song go? "Be sure it's true/When you say, 'I love you,' . . . ?" Sappy song with easy, danceable rhythm. Will and I had danced to it by candlelight one night in the living room.

I hummed the tune.

"Well. Feeling pretty good."

"Millions of hearts have awoken," I improvised, "Just because those words were . . ."

"Cut it. Out."

Actually, I realized, it was "Millions of hearts have been broken . . ."

Outside of the car the outskirts of Frederick, Maryland,

began to appear: brick, wide-spaced, gentle. This was the town where Barbara Frietchie said, *Shoot if you must*; someone was selling candy and offering "Story Free"—Barbara Frietchie's story, presumably. Through lighted windows I could see cheerful, domestic-looking wallpaper and lamp bases. I am not going to think about that baby.

"Lots of things rhyme with *broken*," I said. "Token. Hoboken."

"I am gonna drive this damn car. Right into a lamp post."

Good. I have got him to sound like himself. I allowed Frederick to thin out and dissipate, countryside to begin collecting around us. "Let's stop at a roadhouse."

"There are none."

"There have to be."

"Butch, there do *not* have to be. Look at it."

His gesture indicated a brightly moonlit landscape, and, yes, it was different from that around Cumberland. The difference was in things which showed an attention to detail. The edges of the asphalt highway no longer ended in a random sticky puddling of asphalt, but had been neatly cut off and finished. Messages about damnation and Burma-Shave had disappeared. The ragged conifers, crusted snow, bent windswept bushes of the Cumberland area had been replaced by well-fed trees. The mountains, too, had smoothed themselves out. There were miles and miles of clean, painted fence.

"This is really rich country," O'Connell began. Information-sharing lifted the color of his voice. "Listen, Butch, this is the Northern Southland; that's what they call it. Everyone in this part of Maryland has got two things: they have got horses and they have got money. You brag about the first and you don't mention the second. And nobody around here stays up late, they go to bed at ten; they got to get up early and trot their horse around the horse yard."

Passing us now were low flat fields, with the white crystalline sparkle that meant a surface of crisp snow. The fences seemed particularly eastern and expensive to me, their white-painted crossbars attractively geometric. In Berkeley there had been no fences at all, while the surrounding California countryside had usually liked barbed-wire. Beyond the Maryland fences and fields winked an occasional house, a few lights; the rich could afford to be careless. And why would Hitler bomb Montgomery County? Hitler could probably not even imagine Montgomery County. Nor could I, really. "There's got to be a town along here some place."

"I'm almost due," O'Connell said, meaning that he might be late getting back to Chicago. I thought about the phrase, and the way women used it, and how O'Connell had never thought of it that way, and put my hand over his on his knee. We drove along that way for a few miles of clicking fence rails, barred and hardwared gates with carriage lanterns on their gateposts, distant spectra of black trees, houses with corbelled roofs.

"Your hand feels good," I told him.

"Yeah. Yours too."

The car rounded a bend and, without preamble, there was a cluster of building shapes: a gas station (closed), grocery store (closed), antique shop (closed, of course), all white-painted, colonially designed, the local shopping havens of Montgomery County. There was a fourth building, unlabeled, but with lights behind blackout curtains, some kind of restaurant or bar. "Oh, stop," I said, "stop; stop."

Probably Clara and I had gone to too many movies dur-

ing the height of Mother's stress period, or perhaps I remember in images and pictures so that every picture I have
ever seen is inside me waiting to be summoned up; anyway,
the scene that we walked into was one from several movies
Clara and I had seen. It was from the thriller where the
couple have been stumbling around on an English moor.
They open the door of the pub. Inside the pub, silence falls
on the assembled crowd, a few glass objects clink, all eyes
are turned in our couple's direction: suspicion, threat are
palpable and visible to any moviegoer. Our pub now, the
one that O'Connell and I quietly entered, was a very nicely
furnished lounge or living room: oriental rug, leather arm-
chairs, walnut bar across one corner, paneling, capital M
money, and turned toward us were the eyes of four people
seated informally around a coffee table, holding various tall
and short drinks. O'Connell shut the door (blast of cold
air to ruffle ashes in cut glass ashtray), we stood against it;
the movie message in the four pairs of eyes was clear:
intruder.

"Ah. Mmm," said the man seated nearest to the door. He
wore a clerical collar and looked like Ford.

Ford the Second, Aunt Chloe, the Y Secretary, Gertrude
Stein—the drunkenness of events supplied me with names
for all four of these people. Those imaginary names, even
that night, were all I could remember, although real ones
were later offered. (Gertrude Stein was male; I mean no
disrespect for the real Gertrude Stein's beautiful face and
elegant short hair.) "I am so. Sorry," said the Rev. Ford.

O'Connell cleared his throat. I didn't look at him, but I
knew that in moments of trial he pulled over his face a
gentle, hopeful, guileless and particularly Irish mask, and
I was sure he was using it now. For myself, I tried not to

look too haughty; that was my usual cover for insecurity.

"You see," Rev. Ford fiddled with his leather chair binding and fixed hopeful light-blue eyes on O'Connell. "This is a. Private club. Just for . . . us around here." A generalized gesture indicated the air beyond the door.

"Oh, sure. Of course. We really didn't want to. Ah, we're really sorry." With each phrase O'Connell's voice became more ingenuous, Irish, measurably sincere. "We wouldn't have for the world. It's just . . ." In the ensuing friendly pause, the Rev. Ford could be seen retreating further into his leather chair. "It's just that . . . You see, we're . . ."

What now, I wondered. Something is coming.

"You see, we just got married. Just now. About an hour and a half ago. And, well, we wanted a drink, and of course . . ."

And no inn on the road.

And no place to take them in.

The bridegroom and his bride.

Oh, wicked, wicked O'Connell, how much I do love you. How can anything ever be settled. Somewhere, my mother is having a nervous breakdown. I am going to follow suit. Like mother, like daughter. Around us the room ungells, who can resist a newly-married (just this evening, five-thirty, it was) couple, Irish-American Army officer and red-haired, much younger, dazed bride; chairs are pushed up, drinks produced (No, you really cannot pay for them, this is a club, you are our guests, rather fun really, we get bored with each other, see so much of each other, quite nice, really, to have two . . .)

We were taken into the neighborhood bosom. Aunt Chloe proved to be sharp and witty, with a fund of really good stories; the Y Secretary raised horses. We were on the outskirts of Gaithersburg, Maryland. The room smelled of cedar (that was the paneled walls), of perfume, cigarettes, Scotch, of horse, faintly (somebody's shoes?) I wasn't wearing a wedding ring. What should they make of that? But who could doubt the word and guise of so sincere, loving, outgoing, and friendly a young couple? I was wrapped, head to toe, in warmth. It was all going to be all right. Something wonderful, besides this moment and this Scotch, was going to happen. I am overloaded, I told myself, like an electric circuit. Splat. Fireworks. Too many prongs stuck into too many holes.

O'Connell was holding my hand, lacing our fingers back and forth. We had downed two drinks. I leaned against him, somewhat restrainedly, but with my head near his shoulder.

"It has been so nice. So very nice," Rev. Ford said. "A real treat for us." Our party, it seemed, was concluding, our nuptial reception drawing to a close, our hosts ready for bed. The four of them crowded into the doorway to wave at us as we backed our car into the highway. They made, I thought, a reassuring, sweet, archaic picture.

O'Connell and I, with little conversation between us, headed for Washington.

I asked O'Connell to wait in the car outside Mama's apartment; he could come in later, when I had reconnoitered a bit.

"Hey, Butchie," he said as I was climbing out of the car. "Yes?"

"I love you, dear." He said it easily, as if he hadn't needed to think about it.

I used my key to get into the apartment. Mama was sitting in the rumpsprung chair wearing her orange kimono with the green circles. One toe protruded from the front of a bun-ny-fur slipper; she had kicked a hole in it. Her lipstick was smudged. She was clutching a glass. "Well, Hallelujah!" she said. "Look who's here!"

"Hello, Mama."

"Hello, Mama, hell. Who the hell do you think you are, going off, not a word, just *off*. You pack up your tent like an Arab and silently steal . . . what is it they steal? Something important. Have a drink, oh thief."

It was the "oh thief" that did it. "You aren't drunk at all," I said. "Hardly at all. So cut the act."

"Act? Act?" She moved her glass around.

"Listen. When you're really drunk you get less and less elegant. Remember that the next time you want to con somebody. I hate blackmail." I sat down on the bed. "You're trying to make me feel miserable. Because I went off. For a couple of days."

"You went off," my mother looked interestedly into the inside of her glass, "with somebody I know . . . somebody I used to know."

"You used to know a lot of people."

"He was a friend of mine. A good friend."

"Mama, what does that have to do with anything?"

"He dated me when you were fourteen years old."

"I'm not fourteen now."

"Helen." She leaned forward and put her knees apart as if she were doing a setting-up exercise. "He's married. You're nineteen years old. He's forty years old and he's married . . . I need a drink."

"You have a drink."

"It's not so much that he's twice as old as you."

"Twice plus one."

"Yes. Forty. Helen, see if there are any ice cubes."

I went out into the hall and wrenched open the door of the refrigerator. There weren't any ice cubes. My mother's voice followed me. "How could you? Things were going so well. And you gave up Will for me; that was the most marvelous thing that ever happened to me. God damn it, it was going to be so nice."

"You forgot to fill the trays." I came back in and sat down.

"They were so nice, those evenings when I came back and made your dinner. So cozy. So homey."

I stared around the gray, battered apartment, at the window with people's feet, putty smeared around the new window pane. The feet going by at the moment wore rubber galoshes with ladder-type fastenings.

"It felt so settled. Everything so lovely. I loved you so much. God damn it. Helen, why aren't there any ice cubes?"

"I met him on the train," I said.

"On the train? What a story. My God. You crossed the *country* with him? As soon as my back is turned, fooling around with my old—my *old* boyfriends—older than I am, for Christ's sake."

O'Connell wasn't older than she was, but I didn't say this.

She poured herself another drink. "Picking them up, fooling around, and then just when I think things are going really well, when I think we are going to manage, and I'm cooking and working and we have this nice little cozy place and it is all so gentle and pretty and good . . . "

"I lived with him in Chicago," I said.

"In Chicago!" She settled on the place as a major part of her grievance. "I've read about it, that awful city. Such a horrible place. So dark. So dreary . . . I thought you were in Chicago visiting Will?"

Explaining would be much too difficult. "No."

"So I saved you from Will. And all the while I should have been saving you, really saving you, from something really worth saving . . . " She had lost the thread of her sentence. "He's old," she said. "He's married. What in hell is the matter with you. Talk about *my* mistakes. I did better with Fag. Oh, God knows, I haven't been a good mother to you . . . "

She was stopped by the doorbell. That doorbell was a gong over the door that sounded like a school lunch bell. I went to answer it. I knew it would be O'Connell, and it was. He followed me into Mama's apartment and stood behind me so that we were just barely touching.

"Well, speak of the devil," Mama said. "Sit down, John."

O'Connell sat on the end of my bed.

"Long time no see." Mama finished off her whisky and poured another. She swirled it around in her glass and stared at O'Connell with eyes that looked large, flat, and green. O'Connell stared back. His expression was one I could imagine him having for his CIO negotiating sessions— polite and wary. He seemed to be trying not to blink his eyes.

It was a funny moment for me. I set drinks up on the glass-bottom marked table and made noise with the glasses and tried to be very precise about measuring liquor; along with this I watched the two of them.

"So what is it. John?" Mama said. "Something about bearding the lioness in its den?"

"Selma, you look great."

"Let's not start that." My mother seemed to have partly

pulled herself out of the drunkenness that had been increasing so quickly while she was talking to me. Her glass didn't wobble. Her speech sounded pretty good. Maybe something about adrenaline, I thought; it wouldn't last long.

"Well, Sel, I was sitting out there in the car. And I figured it couldn't be any worse in here than it was out there. Go on it, I said to myself. Get it over with.

"Kind of uncomfortable, Sel," he went on. "Still, everybody together."

"Absolutely," said Mama. "A family affair, you might say. A mother-daughter act."

O'Connell turned pink. I had noticed on other occasions that he was embarrassed when women acted ironic or knowing, especially about sex.

"How was your trip east?" my mother asked, genteelly.

"It was okay. Of course, traveling's hard these . . . " O'Connell raised his glass to his mouth. "Sel, what a crock of shit."

"Watch your language."

"Excuse. But, I mean . . . There are things we ought to be talking about."

"So, talk."

My mother gave him no chance. While he was opening his mouth, she intervened, "I guess the thing I need to ask," she said, in a louder voice than the one she had been using, "is what are you going to do about Helen?"

"Do about me?" I said. "What am I? A library book?"

O'Connell said, "Hey, Selma."

"No," said my mother, "that wasn't supposed to be my line, was it? Doesn't sound like my line? Well, anyway, I'm asking. Helen's my daughter. I'm her mother. I saved her from going off with someone wrong for her. I've got a right."

"Sure," O'Connell said. "We want to talk about it."

"You've been sleeping with my *daughter*. She's only nineteen."

"Mama," I said. "There's something you don't know."

"*Do* tell me. Seems to me, there's a lot of things I don't know, just plenty of them." She helped herself to a new splash of drink. "Well, Miss Hoity-toity, what is it that I don't know?" She held her drink up to her mouth. I could hear it rattling against her teeth. I took a close look at her. Yes. She was crying; her whole face was wet. "Tell me what you know that I need to know," she said. "Lots of things like that, these days."

I glanced at O'Connell. He moved his head slightly, *no*.

"You're forty," my mother said to O'Connell, when I was silent. "And you're married, and even if you weren't, it wouldn't be any good."

"Mama," I told her, "shut up. Quit the injured mother act." I stared at her. I seemed to be having very few emotions, except for interest. Interest was high. The scene produced its own novocaine for whatever else I might be feeling. O'Connell sat on the edge of the bed, looking concerned, uncomfortable, but also looking like his old capable CIO self. We'll manage, I thought.

"You're married." Mama had now adopted a prosecuting attorney's voice, fast, rising at the end of each phrase. She was still crying, and she was a prosecuting attorney. "Even if you *weren't*, you're too *old*, you're too old to leave your *wife*. I know you, remember that, if you did leave her you would be too *old* and taking up space in Helen's life; that space ought to have somebody *else* in it."

"If it weren't for the war," Mama said, "you wouldn't ever have gotten her."

This was close to what I had once said; it seemed visibly to disturb O'Connell.

"The war. And her father. That was hard on Helen. That made her sus . . . Darling, what's the word?"

When I didn't answer, she supplied it. "Susceptible . . . Listen, when she's forty . . . "

"When I'm forty he'll be sixty, Mama. Big deal."

"When you're forty he'll be sixty and he'll be dead of a heart attack. Look at the way he lives.

"And there's his wife," my mother went on.

I said, "Mama, you don't know anything about it." O'Connell got up and put his drink down on the table.

"But most of all there's Helen. Helen has the whole world before her. She's young. And beautiful. And per . . . personable . . . "

Suddenly, I grew very tired of this discussion of how young I was and how old O'Connell was. In all our dealings, this had been the argument that seemed to mean the most to him, and meant the least to me. The debate as to whether he would leave his wife, now that seemed more like something. "Mama," I said, "stop talking as if I'm deaf, or I'm not here, or I'm a child. I'm one of the two people involved in this. There are things about both of us you don't know." Again, I was about to tell her that I was pregnant, and didn't. Her raddled, wet face stopped me.

"You," she said. "Throwing yourself away."

"I'm not throwing myself away."

"He's had lots of other girls." She was having trouble with her diction. She tried "other" twice: Udder. Not good. Oth-ther. "Oth-ther one night stands. Want to know the names of some of the others? The other ones that lasted one night?"

I got up and stood beside O'Connell and looked down at my mother. "There were lots of them," she said. "I collected their names. I can say . . . say them for you. Be glad to."

I moved until O'Connell and I were touching. I could feel the warmth of his body through the back of my dress.

For the first time in my life I felt quite removed from my mother. She wasn't an aching version of me anymore. She wasn't someone whose mistakes I was responsible for, whose mistakes I had to search out and redo. She wasn't me without my father's genes to make me stand up straight. She was somebody different from me, saying things that I would never say, drunk or sober. A separate, independent being, Renoir's woman with all her defects, few of her attractions. After the boating party, Renoir's lady went to the bar and got drunk and cried, anybody who looked at that picture could tell you that.

I had tried to help my mother. I *had* helped her some; it hadn't lasted; there was a limit to everything. Some people's mothers had heart attacks when their daughters got interested in men; mine got drunk. I thought about my father and the dry yellow hillside on which he perhaps had died. I moved a little closer still to O'Connell.

And then my mother did an amazing thing. She was sitting on the edge of her chair. She put her glass on the floor, and bent her head, and leaned forward and crossed her arms over her breast. She had no way of knowing it, but she was in exactly the posture of the female collaborator in *Time* magazine, the one who had been captured by the partisans and had been made to kneel down and have her hair clipped, the woman in the picture I had been looking at when I first met O'Connell.

My mother didn't know she was mimicking the woman in that news picture. But as I've said, Mama had the gift of prescience. Perhaps she sensed what to do especially to upset me.

"Selma," O'Connell said. "Selma, dear. Come on. It's not that bad. It'll be all right. You'll see."

He too had been touched by her posture. He didn't know the associations I had with it; still, he was moved.

My mother looked up at us. Maybe it was worse for her to see us standing together, feeling sorry for her, offering comfort, than it had been to perceive us as her enemies, arguing.

I thought: I can't stay with her now, after all this, that would be wrong. I've got to go out; leave her alone. Maybe, after half an hour or so, I'll call a doctor.

I walked over to her and kissed her on the side of the head, on top of her marvelous red hair. I said, "I'll be back, Mama."

She wasn't, as we left, bent over any longer in her huddled posture. She was sitting up, and appeared to be reaching for her glass. Generally, I thought she looked better than she had been looking.

Outside, O'Connell and I stood on the sidewalk. "Well, what do you think?" he said.

"I don't know."

"Maybe you could go back in in about ten minutes."

"I don't think I should."

"Could you call somebody to come stay with her?"

"Maybe." Tod Larrimore? A doctor? There was no doctor interested in us, nobody who'd come do a fatherly act. "O'Connell," I said, "for the first time . . . "

"Yes, Butch. The first time?"

I was trying to find the words to explain that I had seen my mother in a new light. I reached out and touched O'Connell's sleeve.

We were distracted by a small noise. It was hardly anything, a muffled *pop*. Not the sort of sound you react to really. I waited with my hand outstretched, touching O'Connell's arm with one finger, trying to identify. The two of us stood; I bent my head to hear better. The sound circled in the air above us. "Holy God," O'Connell said, and started to run. But I was ahead of him, I was already running, down my mother's steps, wrestling with her front door.

I opened the door on a room full of the firecracker smell of cordite. A blue haze hung in the air, spreading slowly. Mama's slumped figure lay in the middle of the rug, left side down, her hair spread out in a puddle of bourbon and ice. She had found her gun again.

Chapter XVIII

MAMA WAS NOT DEAD. She had shot herself in the left breast and had missed the heart. "Most of them do, most ladies," the doctor said kindly. He was some kind of a Latin, Guatemalan, I think. His name was Dr. Mendoza. "The ladies shoot themselves in the breast." He demonstrated. "They don't want to mess. The hair, the face. Maybe she didn't want to mess you house?"

"Maybe."

"So they shoot the breast. And they miss. Miss the heart. She was sad?"

"She says it was an accident."

"Maybe," he agreed. "Surely. This is quite possible."

"She misses the heart," he went on, after a minute. "But not entirely. A little piece is damage. And some rib. And some lung."

O'Connell spent the night in the hospital with me. There wasn't much he could do. We sat in the waiting room, each of us with a magazine in one hand, Cokes on the table next to us. I'm not sure O'Connell realized it, but I was hysterical, with the kind of hysteria that is quiet and finds it difficult to understand questions.

"You better get some sleep, Butch."

"What?"

"Sleep."

I didn't answer. He said, "I asked him about a specialist."

"What?"

"The doctor. I asked him about calling somebody in."

"O'Connell," I said, "do you think she knew what she was doing? She did, didn't she? She knew everything she was doing. All of it."

In the morning O'Connell had to go back; he was already late returning from his three-day pass. I was hysterical about that too. "What happens to you? Some kind of trial?"

"Prob'ly not."

"They put you in jail?"

"*No*, Butchie." He looked at my face, touched the corner of my mouth. "The Sergeant probably covered. Don't worry. Not about me."

I walked him to the lobby and stood with my hands on his shoulders. "Good-bye," I said.

He said, "Let me know the minute there's something."

I didn't answer. I was trying to memorize his appearance.

"I'll come to see you next weekend," he said.

No, you won't, I thought. *I won't let you.*

"I'll call you tonight."

I won't answer the phone. This is it, O'Connell, darling. End of the road. Nothing over the horizon. "Good-bye," I said. "I'll see you in glory."

When I got back upstairs the nurse grabbed me by my

elbow and made me sit down. She took my blood pressure and then gave me a shot in the arm. "Your pressure is down in your socks," she told me.

The next three days had a rhythm like that of a series of lights you pass in a car—flash, dark, flash, dark. The nurses—there were four of them over a twenty-four-hour period—were very nice to me. They made the official gesture of throwing me out at the end of each regular visiting hour. Then one of them would come into the waiting room and say: you can go in again now, honey.

The phone company sent little bouquets, big bouquets. A bank of flowers sat at the foot of the bed.

"She'll live." I stated it as a fact.

"One can hope," said Dr. Mendoza. "She could. She is not young."

"She's not old, either."

Dr. Mendoza shrugged. He gave me a prescription for sleeping pills for myself. I didn't take them. I wanted to be awake.

I sat by my mother's bed and said, "Mama, please. Try. We'll work it out, somehow. It's Helen here, Mama."

HELEN REYNOLDS
GEORGE WASHINGTON HOSPITAL
WASHINGTON D. C.

UNABLE REACH YOU BY PHONE. ARE YOU O.K.
CALL MY OFFICE COLLECT. JOHN.

HELEN REYNOLDS
GEORGE WASHINGTON HOSPITAL
WASHINGTON D. C.

URGENT. PLEASE CALL ME COLLECT. AM WORRIED.
WANT TO HELP. JOHN

On the third day Mama ran a high temperature. Dr. Mendoza came to see her five times. "She's bad, isn't she?" I said to Laura, the afternoon nurse.

"Yeah, I guess. We're doing everything."

"I know you are, Laura."

"You should get some sleep, Hon."

I didn't tell Laura I couldn't sleep. At all. I hadn't slept last night, nor the night before.

"When does your sister get here?" she asked.

"Tomorrow." I took Mama's hand in mine. It was dry, crumpled, hot, and light. It didn't feel like a hand at all. It felt like a felt potholder, one that had been left on top of the oven too long. She lay on her back, her head thrown back, her eyes half open, rolled back in her head so you couldn't see any pupils, just whites, with little lines—red veins—in them. She was breathing through her mouth, her teeth caught on her lower lip. A dribble of spittle ran down the side of her cheek.

She had a bandage on her chest. Body lacerations, Dr. Mendoza said. Internal injuries. Tearing inside. I started to talk to her. Mama, I said, do you remember the time you made me the clock? You were going out, and you drew a clock and said you would be thinking of me.

Mama's room was green, hospital green. Her bed was an old metal bed with a white head and foot. About four in the afternoon (I was looking at my watch) she arched back against the metal bedstead and made a noise. Her eyes opened wide, but I still couldn't see the pupils, just the bottoms of them, showing under the rim of each eye. I wondered if I should go and get the nurse. All the bones of her face stood out, the eye hollows clear, defined.

I put both arms under her neck. I said, Don't, you mustn't. I thought: where in hell is her god-damned doctor. I pushed the nurses' call button. But what could any of them do? They had been doing it, everything.

Mama, I said. I began to talk fast. I told her all I could think of. Do you remember, I said: talks with Aunt Chloe. Labor Day in San Francisco. Do you remember the time of the earthquake? You were brave then. That was a good time, then. And I loved your dinners. This last month in Washington . . . I held her in my arms. She was hot, dry. You can't, I said. It's selfish. It's not fair. It's not fair to *me*. I got angry. With my arms around her, I shook her. She was so light, so hot, so boneless it was like shaking a blanket that had been left out in the sun all day. You're doing it on purpose, I said.

I felt strength flow across my shoulders, down my arms. We'll go back, Mama. You'll be better. You'll be different. It will be new. You'll understand it all, I know you will.

It seemed to me I could do anything. Certainly I could cure my mother. Mama, wake up.

Laura arrived and used her pressure gauge and her stethoscope and then pulled me away and said, "I think we've lost her, dear." I couldn't believe it. I just couldn't believe it.

"Listen, Hon," said Laura, "you've got to."

"No."

"You're no good to anybody. You'll scare your sister to death. Pills? Come on, honey, just one. Honest, sleep is the best way. Let go for a while."

"No."

They had given me a room in the hospital. I lay on the bed, dressed the way Mama had been at the end, in a green hospital gown that opened up the back. Finally Laura went away. She left the pills beside the bed in a glass cup. I turned on my back and stared up at the ceiling.

My vision seemed unusually precise; I saw the ceiling in special detail, as if with a pair of extraordinary glasses. It was a flat ceiling, painted hospital green like the rest of the room. It had a slightly uneven finish; in one corner was a raised place shaped like San Francisco Bay, in another a mark which made a woman's profile. But every bump and wart on this ceiling was distinct, each with its little shadow; I wondered what that meant? I must breathe deeply, I thought; each completed breath is about a half a minute. When someone dies the world stops and says, what a shame, too bad. That pause in the world's activities lasts about a week and then the surface closes over, heals without even a scar to show where something has been cut away.

I won't let that happen. I'll take a pledge to think about this all the time.

That won't work.

Yes it will. I can do it. Oh, my *God.*

Take your pill.

But I feel so terrible. There's got to be something.

Go to sleep.

I'll never sleep again. I'll stay awake forever.

I lay on my back and watched the ceiling blur and fade, the blot the shape of San Francisco Bay expanding to drown all of California, the one shaped like a woman's profile trying to be my mother's face.

And finally she came to me. I knew that she would. Willpower could do it. I knew it. A voice beside my ear, a picture in the inner eye. Mama. Tell me.

"*Why, what dear?*"

"Why did you do it, with all your life, some of your life, ahead of you?"

No answer.

"Was it an accident? Or did you kill yourself? On purpose?"

"*Not exactly, dear.*"

"But I feel so terrible."

"*Nonsense, darling, cut it out.*" There's a note in her voice that I haven't heard for a long while.

"*You mustn't try to take it away from me,*" she says. "*It's the big thing I've done recently.*"

"What? Killing yourself?"

She is wearing her orange bathrobe. She's parading up and down in it, walking handsomely, like a fashion model. The bathrobe is properly tied, for once. "*I didn't say I killed myself.*"

"It was an accident?"

"*What I was talking about was John O'Connell. I got you to look at him a new way.*"

"Mama, you're impossible. I wanted him. I loved him."

"*Don't be silly, darling. Will they miss me at the phone company?*"

"Moth-*er!*" (I haven't called her *that* for a long time.)

"*That was a nice telephone installer. He liked me, I could tell. A lot of men do that, decide they like me before they even know me, idealize me is what it is . . . I really do think . . .*"

"Mama, you can't dodge the question this way. That's typical of you. All my life . . . "

My mother spreads her arms as if she is going to call the birds from the corners of the sky. She's wearing her green dress now, her face is turned upward, it's shamelessly illuminated by a flattering subdued light that brings out the bone structure. "*What are you trying to do. It's mine, it's all mine. You can't take it away from me.*"

"What, Mama? I wouldn't try to take anything from you."

"*I came through at the end. I was a real mother. I helped you free yourself from an entrammeling passion . . .*"

"You sound like a bad movie."

"*Why, even Will would have been proud of me. And now. That is what you should do. Of course. Marry Will.*"

"The hell with that. Not in a million years."

My mother in her green dress, her red hair a flat sheet of shiny wet because she has just pulled me from the sea at Carmel, bends over me, she is laughing and laughing. The water drips off the glistening edge of her hair and onto the hospital pillow. She kisses me on the forehead, on the cheek. "*I was drunk, darling. Drunk as a skunk, think of that. Now take your pill, like a good, good girl.*"

All the colors of her get lighter and softer; she's fading like a photograph left out in the sun, her large downward-slanting eyes grow paler, their lashes stuck together with water.

My mother really had won, hands down, all down the line, every way there was. That night I got my period, the most racking and painful one I had ever had. "That's the way it always is," Laura said. "Any lady I've ever seen that had a shock like that, she got the worst period of her life. And then, staying awake the way you did, four nights in a row. Now hold still, hon, just a second."

Very gently and professionally, she gave me a shot in the rump. "You'll be amazed," she said. "After that, you'll sleep like a baby. And when you wake up, you'll feel better, honest you will." She raised the sides of the bed. "Why," she said, "sleep is a great cure-all. Listen. Sleep can make almost anything that happens to you seem better."

The next morning I put through a call to O'Connell on the hospital pay phone. I leaned against the window of the mahogany phone booth and listened to the operator tell me to hold the ly-on. I tried hard to picture that ly-on; its tan and brown bulk and anxious tugging personality were going to have to get me through this conversation. The worst part of the conversation would be the beginning of it, then bit by bit O'Connell would listen to me, and then finally, after a while, he would begin to understand. I was pretty sure of that; he would understand in the end, because he had to.

Chapter XIX

THE SETTING IS GREAT SALT LAKE. Clara and I have spent the month since Mama's death in Washington, and now we are on our way back to Berkeley. I have suggested that we get off the train in Ogden. Clara is willing, in fact interested. It dawns on me that she's curious about me and what I've been seeing and doing.

In Ogden I rent a car from the same place where O'Connell got his. The man remembers me and we get the car cheap. He puts chains on the tires and tells me how to drive if I come to some icy bits (slowly, don't step on the brake). And we're off. I haven't driven since I was here before, but I'm doing fine. The scenery is snow-covered, quite magical—long hills and valleys so white they are dark blue, the shadows of bushes dark blue beside them, a clean snap in the air.

In a way the country is not recognizable as that over which O'Connell and I drove several months ago and in a way it is perfectly the same, still astonishingly spare, hard, clean, and Biblical.

Clara, beside me, blows on her mitten. Clara has grown since I saw her last. I do not simply mean that she has gotten taller, although she has, perhaps a half an inch. She has changed in some other way. Her round, firm, gentle face is older, more squared at the jaw. There is a mark at the corner of each of her wide green black-rimmed eyes— their whites so white that they're shiny on the surface—a mark that will some day be a wrinkle. She still wears her hair parted in the middle, fastened in a braid. It is flat, smooth, mouse-blond hair. Clara is so beautiful, with her composure, her grave, awkward movements, her straight, thick legs, her navy-blue coat with the wooden buttons, that I can't stop looking at her.

"Hey, Helen," she says, "steer a bit for a change, huh? We get stuck in one of those snowbanks, we'll never get out."

"Tell me if you see any rabbits."

"Why?"

"I just thought you might. Do you remember . . . "

"The rabbit family? Good grief!" Maybe Aunt Chloe was the only person in the world who couldn't make rabbits breed. "But, Helen, didn't you think, afterwards, that they were both . . . "

"The same sex? Sure." It's funny the number of times Clara and I have been doing this recently—discovering we've been thinking about something in the past, reaching the same conclusion about it.

We pause at the rise where the road goes down to the

water. The highway stretches, blue-gray, shiny, a high white bank on either side, the edge of the lake lacy with snow, the lake itself not frozen. Clara supplies a number from physics. "Everything freezes, but salt has to be awfully cold."

The EATS is boarded up, but a path has been shoveled to the door since the last snow. Clara and I scuffle along it. I am wearing pumps, and my feet are going to get wet, but I decide I don't care. "There's a porch in back," I tell Clara. "It has a gorgeous view. It's really worth it." We climb a fence and scuff around the outside of the building holding on to the piers that raise it up in case of flood. Then we climb these, brushing the snow off as we go, and so up to the porch. The lake stretches out before us, flat and blue-gray and shiny, its surface smooth as cellophane, like a mirage on a western highway. Clara leans on the rail. A small cold breeze picks up some sprigs of hair that have escaped from her braid. Perspiration blooms on her upper lip. "It's gorgeous, Helen. I wish I were like you. You always know to do things like this. You have really good ideas."

Oh, sure, Claire, you bet. Some of the ideas I've had, some of my really famous ones of the past, I don't want to think about, at all.

There is something I want to say to Clara about ideas and Idea. Clara, if there is such a thing as Idea, you are it, the pure thought. But I can't phrase it.

"*She* would have loved this," Clara says. "I wish she could see it."

She would indeed. I try hard to think what she would have said. Sometimes those voices of the dead are very clear, and sometimes not.

We walk down to the far end of the porch. There are two soft drink crates upended there, and we brush the snow off them and sit down. "There's nothing here but us," Clara says. "No sound. Just our voices."

The line of the horizon seems drawn with a ruler. Some trick of light makes it a broad gold mark riding firmly on the far edge of the water.

"I heard about that scholarship," I say. "I think I can probably get it."

It is curious how things work out. Ford wrote to me, right after Mama's death. He pointed out that I would be getting Daddy's social security benefits as long as I was a dependent. I should go to college, he thought. And he found a scholarship that I was eligible for. The hospital where Clara and I were born gave money to educate girls born in that hospital. It would be easy to get. Almost no one applied.

Clara and I turn back to look across the water. The gold bar at the horizon makes a mark on Clara's chin. She says, "Do you ever think that you'll be alive in the twenty-first century?"

"Never."

"Imagine. Writing the year 2000 on a check. What will we be doing, do you think?"

"In 2000 I'll be seventy-five. If I'm still around."

Clara turns to me in astonishment. "But seventy-five isn't old, Helen. Lots and lots of people are seventy-five. You'll be alive, and so will I. And we'll both have accomplished . . . something wonderful!"

There has been too much discussion of age in my life recently, I think.

I feel seventy-five now, Clara.

I'm astonished that, after all the things that have hap-

pened to me in the last few months, I am now about to go
back to living. Just ordinary, simple, day-by-day living.
Other people will be able to tell, though, that I'm different.
They won't dislike me for it; maybe just the opposite, maybe they'll like me, but they'll know. Some of us are different,
and that's the way we stay: different.

O'Connell said it was hard to put into words. What was
special about me. As if I were always thinking.

And it's hard to put into words about you, too, O'Connell.

Maybe we won't ever see each other again in this life.
What Mama did is so powerful that we'd always have her
between us—poor, sobbing, vindictive, loving ghost. But
I think about you a lot, really I do. So what is it that's special
about you?

Once I told myself that you were Life. But when I think
back and remember you, physical, present beside me, perhaps on a train, its wheels making their basic encapsulating
noise, your handsome American-Irish face lighted by the
reflected glow from the desert, talking about your CIO organizing campaign or your girls' union singing combo, then
I think it more likely that you represent some particularly
American brand of hope, something usually forbidden to
people like me, the children of too much experimentation.
Whatever it was you had, it was certainly something I
needed.

While Clara and I are talking, I've been watching the
corner of the deck. On the edge of the planking, under the
rail, is the piece of weatherworn bottle that O'Connell set
down there five months ago. It glows purple, sand-scrubbed.

I bend over and pick it up and put it in my pocket.

Diana O'Hehir is the author of two books of poetry:
Summoned (University of Missouri Press, 1976), and
The Power to Change Geography (Princeton University Press, 1979). Her poems have appeared in *Poetry, Paris Review, Massachusetts Review, Antaeus, Poetry Northwest*, and many other magazines, and she has been the recipient of several poetry awards, including the Devins Award for a first book of poems and the Poetry Society of America's Di Castagnola Award for a work-in-progress.

She teaches English and Creative Writing at Mills College in Oakland, California.

Printed in the United States
19323LVS00002B/210